Über diese Lernhilfe

Liebe Schülerin, lieber Schüler,

Englischkenntnisse werden heute nahezu überall vorausgesetzt. Deshalb ist es wichtig, sich fundiertes Basiswissen anzueignen und dazu gehört auch ein guter Schulabschluss. Unsere Lernhilfe unterstützt dich, dieses Ziel optimal vorbereitet zu erreichen. Mit dem Trainingsteil kannst du noch vorhandene Lücken schließen und dann mithilfe der Originalprüfungen der Jahre 2017 bis 2019, 2021 und 2022 sowie zwei zusätzlichen Höverstehenstests inklusive Lösungen (zum Download) gezielt die Inhalte der Prüfung trainieren. Im Jahr 2020 gab es aufgrund der Corona-Pandemie keine zentralen Abschlussprüfungen. Ausführliche und schülergerechte Lösungswege sind im herausnehmbaren Lösungsheft enthalten.

Farbleitsystem Englisch-Training | Englisch-Prüfung

Training
- Alle wichtigen Themenbereiche der Klasse 10
- Erklärungen
- Typische Aufgabenstellungen mit ausführlichen Musterlösungen
- Übungsaufgaben zu jedem Themenbereich
- Verschiedene Schwierigkeitsgrade

Prüfungen
- Originalprüfungen der Jahre 2017 bis 2019, 2021 und 2022

Audiodateien
- Audiotracks zum Download und per QR-Code abrufbar
- Zusatzaufgaben Hörverstehen zum Download

Lösungen
Alle Lösungen findest du im herausnehmbaren Lösungsteil.

- Sollten sich nach Drucklegung noch Änderungen ergeben, findest du aktuelle Informationen unter www.pauker.de/info-aktuell

Das Themenverzeichnis
Dieses Verzeichnis dient zum schnellen Auffinden bestimmter Englischinhalte. Zudem sind auf einen Blick alle Audiotracks zu den LCT-Texten zusammengestellt.

Prüfungsinfos und nützliche Tipps
Ab Seite 8 sind alle wichtigen Prüfungsinfos für dich zusammengestellt.

Extra „Schule – und dann?“
Das Zusatzkapitel gibt nützliche Tipps und Informationen zum Start in den Beruf, von den wichtigsten Bewerbungsunterlagen bis zu Einstellungstests.

Inhaltsverzeichnis

Allgemein

Training

Prüfungen

Extra

Themenverzeichnis

Mit dem Themenverzeichnis lassen sich einzelne Aufgabentypen schnell und einfach finden.

Reading

Comprehension									
2017		2018		2019		2021		2022	
Seite	Nr.	Seite	Nr.	Seite	Nr.	Seite	Nr.	Seite	Nr.
46	3	54	L	62	L	70	L	79	L

Vocabulary

Vocabulary									
2017		2018		2019		2021		2022	
Seite	Nr.	Seite	Nr.	Seite	Nr.	Seite	Nr.	Seite	Nr.
48	4	56	W	64	W	72	W	81	W

Writing

Various tasks									
2017		2018		2019		2021		2022	
Seite	Nr.	Seite	Nr.	Seite	Nr.	Seite	Nr.	Seite	Nr.
50	5	58	S	65	S	73	S	82	S

L = Leseverstehen, W = Wortschatz, S = Schreiben

Hörverstehen

Jahrgang	Texte	Aufgaben	QR-Code
2017	Seite 88	Seite 43	
2018	Seite 90	Seite 51	
2019	Seite 91	Seite 59	
2021	Seite 93	Seite 67	
2022	Seite 95	Seite 76	

Alle Hördateien auch zum Download unter:
www.pauker.de/msa-nrw-e/audiotracks/

Prüfungsinfos – Englisch

Prüfungsbeginn: 9 Uhr

Bearbeitungszeit

Es stehen neben der normalen Bearbeitungszeit im zweiten Teil noch 10 Minuten Extrazeit zur Orientierung zur Verfügung.

Inhalt

Die Verwendung eines Wörterbuchs ist in der schriftlichen Prüfung nicht erlaubt.

<table>
<tr><td>Prüfungsteil 1</td><td>Hörverstehen</td><td colspan="2">Aufgaben zu gehörten Texten</td><td>20 Minuten</td></tr>
<tr><td rowspan="3">Prüfungsteil 2</td><td>Leseverstehen</td><td colspan="2">Aufgaben zu zentralen Aussagen von Texten</td><td>20 Minuten</td></tr>
<tr><td>Wortschatz</td><td>variierende Aufgabenformate zur Überprüfung von Inhaltswörtern usw.</td><td rowspan="2">kombiniert:
1. Wortschatz
2. Textproduktion</td><td rowspan="2">80 Minuten</td></tr>
<tr><td>Schreiben</td><td>Schreiben zusammenhängender Texte</td></tr>
</table>

Die Bezugskulturen für die Englisch-Prüfung sind Großbritannien und Südafrika, ab 2021 die Republik Irland / Nordirland.

Erster Prüfungsteil

Beim Hörverstehen werden dir von einer CD zweimal hintereinander, im Abstand von jeweils 30 Sekunden, gesprochene Texte vorgespielt. Meist handelt es sich hierbei um Sach- und Gebrauchstexte sowie fiktionale Texte wie z. B. öffentliche Ansagen, Texte auf Anrufbeantwortern, Werbespots, Fernsehnachrichten, Interviews, Alltagsgespräche oder thematisch gebundene Diskussionen, Auszüge aus einem *audiobook, radio play* etc. In diesem Teil gibt es geschlossene und halboffene Formate wie Auswahl-, Zuordnungs-, Einsetz- und Kurzantwort-Aufgaben.
Nach der Bearbeitung wird der erste Prüfungsteil abgegeben. Die Punkte können pro Prüfungsjahr variieren.

Zweiter Prüfungsteil

Der zweite Teil der Prüfung beginnt mit dem Leseverstehen. Dabei wirst du es mit Zeitungsartikeln, Info- und Werbebroschüren, kurzen Lexikonartikeln, Leserbriefen, Briefen allgemein sowie angepassten erzählerischen Kurztexten oder diskontinuierlichen Texten wie Cartoons, Grafiken, Tabellen oder *graphic novels* zu tun haben. Mögliche Aufgabenformate sind Richtig-/Falsch-Aufgaben, Multiple-Choice-Aufgaben, *Matching*, Lückentexte bzw. Einsetzaufgaben sowie Kurzantwort-Aufgaben.
Anschließend werden zum einen deine Wortschatzkenntnisse anhand von Einsetzaufgaben, Multiple-Choice-Aufgaben, Ergänzungsaufgaben usw. abgefragt, wobei die Wortschatzaufgaben thematisch meistens mit einem Lesetext verknüpft sind. Zum anderen sollst du mithilfe unterschiedlicher Aufgabenformate einen eigenen Text schreiben. Dabei handelt es sich beispielsweise um das Verfassen einer E-Mail, eines Briefes, einer Stellungnahme, eines Lebenslaufes, Bewerbungsschreibens, eines Tagebucheintrags, eines Erfahrungsberichts, aber auch um das Fortsetzen einer Erzählung, die Versprachlichung von Bildergeschichten oder das Schreiben szenischer Dialoge. Die Aufgabenstellungen können Stichwörter, Bilder oder inhaltliche Vorgaben enthalten, aber auch Fragen bzw. Arbeitsanweisungen, die sich auf einen Text bzw. einen Textausschnitt beziehen. Häufig ist der Bereich Textproduktion mit einem anderen Teil der Prüfung kombiniert, sodass du es leichter hast, genügend Informationen für deinen Text zu sammeln. Die erforderliche Wortzahl

bewegt sich zwischen 80 und 120 Wörtern. Als Faustregel solltest du immer lieber etwas mehr schreiben, als verlangt ist. Beachte auch, dass Wortschatz, Rechtschreibung sowie Grammatik mit in die Bewertung einfließen.

Hinweise zu den Corona-bedingten Anpassungen (2021)

- Vertiefung von *„describe, summarise, explain, analyse, comment on, write and text type"*.
- Drei statt zwei Teilaufgaben im Prüfungsteil „Schreiben".

QR-Codes im Trainingsteil sowie für alle Hörtexte

Dem QR-Code (Quick Response) sind Informationen, Bilder, Videos oder Hördateien hinterlegt. Alle Inhalte sind lediglich zur Auflockerung des Lernalltags gedacht und verschaffen keinem Schüler und keiner Schülerin einen Vorteil.

In diesem Buch sind alle QR-Codes außer der Audiofiles nummeriert. Für alle, die kein Smartphone besitzen, haben wir im Folgenden hinter jeder QR-Code-Nummer die entsprechende Internetadresse aufgeführt, unter der die jeweiligen Inhalte abrufbar sind.

(1) www.buhv.de/download/Pauker/Body_Art.pdf
(2) www.buhv.de/download/Pauker/Bullying.pdf
(3) www.buhv.de/download/Pauker/Narrow_boat.pdf

Audiofiles: www.buhv.de/Schule/hutt.lernhilfen/Pauker/msa-nrw-e/audiotracks/

Tipps zur Prüfung

Cool bleiben!

1. **Rechtzeitig mit dem Lernen beginnen**
   Eine gute Vorbereitung ist die wichtigste Voraussetzung, um gelassen in eine Prüfung gehen zu können. Dazu gehört vor allem, dass du rechtzeitig mit dem Lernen anfängst. Die Erstellung eines Zeitplans, der feste Lernzeiten vorsieht, ist hilfreich. Denk dabei auch an Wiederholungsphasen.

2. **Motivation ist wichtig**
   Teile deinen Lernstoff ein. Trage in deinen Zeitplan ein, wann du mit einer Lerneinheit fertig sein möchtest. Hast du eine Einheit abgeschlossen, kannst du auf deinem Plan einen Haken hinter diese machen. Die Haken verdeutlichen dir, wie viel du schon geschafft hast. Das motiviert und lässt das Ziel näher rücken.

3. **Keine Angst vor der Angst haben**
   Viele Menschen haben Angst vor einer Prüfung. Das ist ganz normal und halb so schlimm, denn in einem gewissen Maß kann Angst sogar die Leistungsfähigkeit fördern. Bist du allerdings zu aufgeregt, beeinträchtigt dies deine Konzentration. Deshalb gilt: Am Prüfungstag trotz Anspannung cool bleiben und nicht verrückt machen lassen.

4. **Selbstbewusst sein**
   Durch eine positive Herangehensweise lässt sich eine Prüfungssituation in der Regel besser bewältigen. Denn der Prüfungsstress spielt sich eigentlich nur in deinem Kopf ab. Also anstatt zu denken „Ich kann bestimmt die Hälfte der Fragen nicht beantworten" vielmehr „Ich fühle mich sicher, weil ich mich gut vorbereitet habe!"

5. **Aufgabenstellung genau lesen**
   Lies dir zunächst die Aufgabenstellung aufmerksam durch. Mach dir jetzt klar, wonach genau gefragt ist. Dies gilt gleichermaßen für alle Fächer und alle Arten von Aufgabenstellungen oder Bearbeitungshinweisen. Denn nur, wenn du die Aufgabe richtig verstanden hast, kannst du sie auch lösen.

6. **Den eigenen Weg gehen**
   Jeder hat eine andere Herangehensweise an eine Prüfung. Du brauchst dich nicht an die vorgegebene Reihenfolge der Fragestellungen zu halten. Du darfst mit einer Aufgabe beginnen, die dir leicht erscheint. Dadurch hast du gleich am Anfang ein Erfolgserlebnis, das dich motiviert und so sammelst du auch die ersten Bewertungspunkte. Die schwierigeren Teile kannst du dann anschließend angehen.

7. **Wichtige Textstellen markieren**
   Lies einen Text mehrmals durch. Beim ersten Durchgang ist es wichtig, dass du genau erfasst, worum es geht. Markiere anschließend durch Unterstreichen oder farbiges Anstreichen wichtige Stellen im Text. Du kannst auch Hinweise oder Kommentare an den Rand schreiben.

8. **Notizen machen**
   Bei weiteren Textarbeiten ist es sinnvoll, sich auf einem separaten Blatt Notizen zu machen. Dort solltest du Gedanken und Ideen aufschreiben, damit du sie nicht vergisst. Teilweise kann es hilfreich sein, einzelne Argumente stichwortartig festzuhalten und zuzuordnen. Dadurch hast du es beim Schreiben des Textes später einfacher.

9. **Auf Nummer sicher gehen**
   Am Schluss deiner Prüfung solltest du kontrollieren, ob du auch wirklich alle Aufgaben gelöst hast. Wenn noch Zeit übrig ist, empfiehlt es sich, das Geschriebene noch einmal durchzusehen. In Deutsch und Englisch solltest du besonders auf die Rechtschreibung, die Zeichensetzung, den Satzbau und eine logische Argumentation achten. In Mathe lohnt es sich, den Rechenweg noch einmal kurz nachzuvollziehen und das Ergebnis grob zu überschlagen.

10. **Sich selbst belohnen**
    Du hast es geschafft! Nach all den Strapazen der Prüfung kannst du dich jetzt guten Gewissens mit etwas belohnen, das dir Freude macht. Bestimmt bist du erleichtert, dass du die Prüfung hinter dich gebracht hast. Eine solche Erfahrung gibt dir mehr Selbstbewusstsein für kommende Aufgaben.

Die Abschlussprüfung

Die schriftliche Abschlussprüfung in Englisch ist stets ähnlich aufgebaut. Folgende Bereiche sind Bestandteil der Prüfung:

A. Hörverstehen
In diesem Teil sollst du zeigen, dass du den Inhalt eines Hörtextes auf drei verschiedenen Ebenen verstehen kannst. Man nennt diese Ebenen selektives, detailliertes und globales Verstehen. Selektives Verstehen bedeutet, dass du ganz bestimmte Einzelinformationen (z. B. eine Jahreszahl) aus dem Text heraushören sollst. Beim detaillierten Verstehen musst du den Sinn einzelner Sätze oder Abschnitte erkennen. Beim globalen Verstehen schließlich beantwortest du Fragen, die sich auf die allgemeine Aussage des Textes beziehen.

B. Leseverstehen
Beim Leseverstehen hast du es mit unterschiedlichen Textarten zu tun, wie beispielsweise Zeitungsartikeln, Info- und Werbebroschüren, Briefen oder auch adaptierten narrativen Kurztexten. Es werden dir Fragen zu diesen Texten gestellt, die du auf unterschiedliche Weise beantworten musst. Mögliche Aufgabenformate sind z. B. Richtig-/Falsch-Aufgaben, Multiple-Choice-Aufgaben, Lückentexte bzw. Einsetzaufgaben sowie Kurzantworten.
Bei einigen Fragen genügt es, wenn du die allgemeine Aussage des Textes verstanden hast. Für die Beantwortung detaillierter Fragen hingegen musst du dir den Text sehr genau durchlesen und darauf achten, dass du keine Informationen durcheinanderbringst oder vergisst.

C. Schreiben
In der Prüfung werden dir neben Fragen zum Hörverstehen und Leseverstehen auch Aufgaben gestellt, bei denen du selbst einen längeren Text schreiben sollst. Das kann z. B. ein Brief *(letter)* oder eine E-Mail sein, ein Zeitungsartikel *(article)*, ein Dialog *(dialogue)* oder auch ein Kommentar *(comment)*. Auch hier ist das Thema meistens mit einem Lesetext verbunden.
Im vorliegenden Trainingsteil findest du viele Aufgaben, mit denen du das Schreiben üben kannst. Wie in der Prüfung sind diese immer mit einem Lesetext verknüpft.

D. Sprache
Darüber hinaus gibt es in der Prüfung auch immer eine Aufgabe zum Wortschatz. Du brauchst hier eine gute und sichere Grundlage an Vokabeln, damit du die Aufgaben lösen kannst. Um gezielt auf diesen Bereich der Prüfung lernen zu können, findest du hier Wortschatz- und Grammatikübungen.
Denn je sicherer du Vokabeln und Grammatikregeln beherrschst, desto ruhiger kannst du an die Prüfungsaufgaben herangehen und sie lösen.

A. Hörverstehen

Erklärung

Die Vorbereitung
Am besten bereitest du dich auf diesen Teil der Prüfung durch intensives und wiederholtes Hören von englischen Texten vor. Du kannst dir zum Beispiel englische Fernsehprogramme ansehen oder beim Anhören englischer Musik versuchen, die Texte zu verstehen. Sieh dir die nächste DVD doch einfach mal im Originalton auf Englisch an – mithilfe der Untertitel lässt sich das Gehörte einfach nachvollziehen.

In der Prüfung
Die Hörtexte der Prüfung variieren in Länge und Art, meist sind es kurze Gespräche, Interviews oder Durchsagen. Die Fragen darfst du dir vorab schon durchlesen. Hierbei solltest du auch die Fragestellung genau beachten, damit du weißt, auf was du dich konzentrieren musst. Keine Angst, wenn du beim ersten Hören nicht jedes Wort verstehst – es sind nicht alle Details des Hörtextes für die Aufgaben wichtig.
Wenn du sicher bist, dass deine Antworten richtig sind, kannst du sie schon nach dem ersten Hören eintragen. Beim zweiten Hören kannst du dich dann auf die Aufgaben konzentrieren, die du noch nicht gelöst hast. Du kannst dir auch während des Hörens auf einem Extrablatt Notizen machen: Wer? Was? Wann? Wo? Wie? Versuche, auf jeden Fall alle Aufgaben zu lösen, auch wenn du dir nicht ganz sicher bist. Teile dir deine Zeit so ein, dass du am Schluss nochmals alle Antworten in Ruhe durchlesen kannst.

Typische Aufgabenstellung

You are going to hear a story about a terrible experience at a fairground.
Listen to the story and tick the correct box for every task.

Hörtext

Fairground Attraction

Hundreds of different coloured lights, loud music and the typical scent of sugared almonds attract thousands of people to the fairground every year. The variety of attractions ranging from booths to rollercoaster, carousels, fairground rides and of course the beer tents fascinate people young and old. Everywhere there is something to see, to buy or to try out.
Mary and her friends had come here every year since they were kids. But in time, the attraction had shifted from anticipating the rides and sweets to spending the evenings partying and drinking in one of the tents. People danced on the benches and tables to loud music swinging their beer mugs. The party-people understood each other, everybody wanted the same: to drink as much beer and to have as much fun as possible. But this time everything went wrong.
At four o'clock in the afternoon Mary and her friends waited in the long queue in front of one of the tents. They were early. After half an hour of waiting they were let in. They sat down at one of the tables already filled with other young people and ordered their first round of beer.
After a while of partying and drinking Mary heard loud screaming and yelling and before she even knew what had happened someone had pushed her off the bench she was sitting on. A beer mug flew over her head and smashed right into her friend Daniel. Soon David and Julia were getting involved too, everyone was shouting and shoving each other around. Mary had skinned her knee and Daniel was bleeding from a head wound. Security showed up quickly, broke up the fighting crowd and escorted them out of the tent. Mary and Daniel were taken to one of the medical tents where they were treated by paramedics. Julia and David were waiting for them outside.
Afterwards they went straight home, they weren't in the mood to party anymore. They didn't even know exactly what had happened. But for Mary and her friends, one thing was very clear: if it wasn't possible to drink beer and still party peacefully they'd rather not go anywhere near one of those tents again. Fairground attraction had come to an abrupt halt.

1. Thousands of people …

a) ☐ believe that the music which is played at the fairground is too loud.
b) ☐ go to the fairground every year to stay young.
c) ☐ are fascinated by the variety of attractions the fairground offers.

2. In the course of time the fairground …

a) ☐ has come to be seen above all as an opportunity to party and drink lots of beer.
b) ☐ has stopped offering rides and sweets in order to put up beer tents instead.
c) ☐ has lost a lot of its attraction because of the party people in the beer tents.

3. Mary and her friends …

a) ☐ arrived at the beer tent early, found an empty table and ordered some beer.
b) ☐ sat down at one of the tables in the beer tent and watched the other young people at their table ordering their first round of beer.
c) ☐ got into the beer tent after half an hour of waiting, joined some other young people at one of the tables and ordered a round of beer.

4. During the fight in the beer tent …

a) ☐ Mary and Daniel were hit by beer mugs.
b) ☐ Mary was pushed off the bench and injured her knee.
c) ☐ security showed up, but at that moment another fight broke out in the crowd.

5. Where were Mary and Daniel taken right after the fight and what happened there?

____

6. When they went home …

a) ☐ they did not feel like continuing to party.
b) ☐ they were not in a bad mood any more because they could not remember exactly what had happened.
c) ☐ their mood became even worse when they remembered exactly what had happened.

7. After the terrible fight at the fairground …

a) ☐ the fairground attractions were closed immediately.
b) ☐ Mary and her friends decided to stay away from the drinking crowds at the fairground in the future.
c) ☐ beer drinking in the tents was no longer possible because it was forbidden.

Lösung

1. c) **2.** a) **3.** c) **4.** b)
5. They were taken to one of the medical tents where they were treated by paramedics.
6. a) **7.** b)

Übungsaufgaben

1. Four Teenagers Killed in Car Accident

(Audiotrack: QR-Code rechts / Hörtext S. 40)

You are going to hear a report about a terrible car accident.
Listen to the report. Tick the correct box or write down the information needed.

1. In the car crash …

a) ☐ Alana and Mike survived.
b) ☐ Alana and Maggie survived.
c) ☐ Maggie and Mike survived.

2. What did Alana tell the court yesterday?

____

3. The teenagers …

a) ☐ had been forbidden to leave school by their boarding school teachers.
b) ☐ were afraid their teachers might find out that they had left school without asking for permission.
c) ☐ wanted to be back at their boarding school for supper to ask for permission to leave school.

4. The accident happened because …

a) ☐ the car was broken.
b) ☐ Mike drove very dangerously, thus losing control in a bend.
c) ☐ Mike tried to impress his friend Tim by accelerating and braking.

5. How had Mike tried to show off and to impress the girls?

____

6. All the teenagers in the car …

a) ☐ teased Mike, the driver, into driving foolishly.
b) ☐ teased Tim because he was frightened by Mike's dangerous driving.
c) ☐ except Tim, made fun of Mike's driving.

7. What did Alana feel guilty of?

____

8. Maggie B. …

a) ☐ has not yet appeared in court because her injuries are still being treated.
b) ☐ has major injuries she will recover from next week.
c) ☐ feels guilty of having caused the death of her classmates.

2. Hunger in Afghanistan

(Audiotrack: QR-Code S. 14 / Hörtext S. 40)

You are going to hear a report about Afghanistan.
Listen to the report. Tick the correct box or write down the information needed.

1. Afghanistan ...

a) ☐ has been a poor country for over 5000 years.
b) ☐ lies in Central Asia but has only few mountains.
c) ☐ lies in Asia, has a lot of mountains and has a long cultural history.

2. The majority of the Afghans …

a) ☐ are located in Central Asia.
b) ☐ are Muslims.
c) ☐ belong to the groups of Sikhs, Hindus or Jews.

3. The capital of Afghanistan …

a) ☐ has been nearly destroyed by a shattering effect.
b) ☐ has a population of 32 million people.
c) ☐ has experienced a long period of war.

4. Food prices in Afghanistan are high because …

a) ☐ most of the bread that is needed is baked in Pakistan.
b) ☐ its infrastructure has been destroyed and flour has to be imported from Pakistan.
c) ☐ the poor and unemployed are desperate.

5. Why can lots of people in Afghanistan no longer buy enough food?

___

6. The food situation in Afghanistan is so miserable that …

a) ☐ some people steal food or threaten merchants to get food.
b) ☐ the Afghan government has started a World Food Programme.
c) ☐ even the state bakeries cannot supply the whole population with enough bread.

7. The country's food problems will not be solved by …

a) ☐ grain donations.
b) ☐ investment in agriculture.
c) ☐ seed and tools for farmers.

8. What will be the effect of the growing hunger on people in Afghanistan?

___

3. Conversation about the Future

(Audiotrack: QR-Code S. 14 / Hörtext S. 40)

You are going to hear a conversation between the schoolmates Helen, Cathy and Jason about their plans after leaving school. Helen is the girl who wants to go to South Africa. Listen to the conversation. Tick the correct box or write down the information needed.

1. Helen would like to ...

a) ☐ teach at a school in South Africa once she has become a qualified teacher.

b) ☐ go to South Africa to work at a school in order to gain some experience for her plan to become a teacher later in life.

c) ☐ attend school in South Africa to see how teachers help their students there.

2. Helen applied at an agency. Describe the ways in which the agency will help Helen. Name at least two things.

____

3. Who thinks that going to South Africa might be dangerous?

a) ☐ Cathy and Helen's mother

b) ☐ Only Helen's mother

c) ☐ Only Cathy

4. Explain why Jason would like to travel around for a bit after school.

____

5. Jason ...

a) ☐ is going to go to Majorca first. After that he is going to visit Berry and Tyler in Australia.

b) ☐ is first going to go to Majorca to meet Berry and Tyler there. After that he is going to go to Australia.

c) ☐ is going to go to Majorca first and then to Australia. After that he is definitely going to go back home again.

6. Cathy wants to do something with animals. Describe the two suggestions that Jason has for her.

____

7. The suggestion Helen has for Cathy is to ...

a) ☐ do a volunteer's job in a zoo.

b) ☐ tend to and care for animals in her neighbourhood in the future.

c) ☐ work in an animal shelter to try and find out whether caring for animals might be a suitable job for the future.

8. The three schoolmates ...

a) ☐ tried to agree on common interests they all share for their future so that they could stay together after school.

b) ☐ agreed to keep each other informed about what happens to their future plans.

c) ☐ agreed that their interests were so different that they were not interested in what happened to the others' future plans.

4. Interview

(Audiotrack: QR-Code S. 14 / Hörtext S. 41)

You are going to hear an interview between a radio moderator and Patrick Hoji, who is an expert in diet and fitness. Listen to the interview. Tick the correct box or write down the information needed.

1. Describe what happened in the USA between 2003 and 2008.

____

2. To lose weight Patrick recommends young people ...

a) ☐ to stop eating unhealthy food altogether.

b) ☐ to eat healthy food only.

c) ☐ to change the way they eat.

3. What does Patrick say about eating chocolate? Name at least two things.

____

4. Patrick says that when you eat too much fast food like fries and hamburgers, ...

a) ☐ you may get heart problems because they contain a lot of salt.

b) ☐ you may get heart problems because they contain a lot of fat.

c) ☐ you will not get any heart problems as long as you do not put salt on them.

5. Patrick says that ...

a) ☐ fruit, bread and muesli are healthy foods, but carbohydrates are not healthy.

b) ☐ fruit and carbohydrates like bread and muesli are good for your body.

c) ☐ fruit gives us energy for the day ahead, but carbohydrates should be avoided.

6. According to Patrick, ...

a) ☐ the modern world offers so many opportunities for children to do sports.

b) ☐ people had to walk much more 50 years ago because lots of them did not have cars.

c) ☐ children have very little free time because they do too much sport, watch too much TV and play computer games too often.

7. To add more sport into our lives Patrick suggests ...

a) ☐ learning something new.

b) ☐ taking up a hobby you enjoy, like chess.

c) ☐ walking and cycling everywhere as often as possible.

5. A Long Weekend

(Audiotrack: QR-Code S. 14 / Hörtext S. 41)

You are going to hear a story about three teenagers (Bob, Brad and Lisa) spending a long weekend at the lake. Listen to the interview. Bob is the first of the two boys speaking on the tape. Tick the correct box or write down the information needed.

1. Describe what Bob thinks about Brad's suggestion about going hiking this coming weekend.

____

2. When Bob suggests going to the lake, ...

a) ☐ Brad likes the idea, but he thinks that his girlfriend Moira might not want to spend time at the lake.

b) ☐ he thinks of a nice barbecue and some girls to chat up.

c) ☐ Brad is not very happy about the idea.

3. When Brad says that his girlfriend Moira could ask her sister Lisa to come along to the lake so that they could go as a foursome, ...

a) ☐ Bob dislikes the idea that Brad seems to want Moira's sister to become Bob's girlfriend.

b) ☐ Bob does not like the idea because he does not want to watch Brad flirting with both Moira and Lisa the whole time.

c) ☐ Bob is thrilled because he has never had a blind date before.

4. Brad gives Bob some information about Lisa. Name at least two things Bob learns about Lisa.

____

5. On Saturday ...

a) ☐ Bob thought that Lisa was a bit boring, just like her sister Moira.

b) ☐ Bob thought that both Moira and Lisa were both fun to be with.

c) ☐ was really happy that he had agreed to go to the lake with Brad, Moira and Lisa.

6. Lisa ...

a) ☐ would like Bob to help her play a trick on Brad and her sister by turning over their boat.

b) ☐ asks Bob to come swimming with her because she wants to be alone with him for some time.

c) ☐ asks Moira and Brad to come swimming with Bob and herself so that they can all cool down.

7. After Bob and Lisa tipped over the boat ...

a) ☐ they were hungry, but they did not manage to barbecue the steaks, burgers and sausages they had bought because the grill did not work properly.

b) ☐ Brad and Moira were so angry that they had a bad fight in the water with Bob and Lisa.

c) ☐ they still had so much fun at the lake that they finally decided to make a trip like this again.

6. Detention

(Audiotrack: QR-Code S. 14 / Hörtext S. 42)

You are going to hear a conversation between mother and daughter. Listen to the conversation. Tick the correct box or write down the information needed.

1. On this Thursday morning …
- a) ☐ Laura's mother is still a bit sleepy.
- b) ☐ Laura's mother feels really bothered by her daughter's questions.
- c) ☐ Laura's mother is very keen on talking to her daughter.

2. Laura's mother wanted to know where Laura had been the evening before. Describe Laura's answer and her feelings after giving this answer.

____

3. However, according to her brother …
- a) ☐ Laura was at the park with some other young people.
- b) ☐ Laura was lying around in the park on her own doing nothing.
- c) ☐ Laura should not be treated like a little child.

4. Laura …
- a) ☐ did not go to her Maths class because she met with a few friends in the park.
- b) ☐ does not want to tell the truth, which is why she says that she was at detention with Sara.
- c) ☐ tells the truth when she says that she was at detention with Sara.

5. Describe the mother's reaction when she heard about her daughter having been at detention.

____

6. Mr Smith …
- a) ☐ bumped into the shelf where the goldfish bowl was because Sara and Laura had broken his glasses.
- b) ☐ was so helpless without his glasses that he bumped into the shelf with the goldfish bowl.
- c) ☐ fell onto the floor together with the water and the fishes, which is why the whole class was laughing.

7. Laura thinks that …
- a) ☐ she and Sara would probably not have got detention if Mr Smith had shown some sense of humour.
- b) ☐ she and Sara should not have given Mr Smith his glasses back.
- c) ☐ detention is good for people who have a sense of humour.

8. Laura's mother…
- a) ☐ complains about Laura not treating her like an adult.
- b) ☐ complains about Laura behaving like a child but still takes her seriously.
- c) ☐ tells her daughter that she will have to stay at home next week.

B. Leseverstehen

Erklärung

Die Vorbereitung
Um das Lesen englischer Texte zu trainieren, kannst du Zeitschriften wie „Spotlight" oder „Read On" lesen. Diese sind zum Üben gut geeignet, da sie viele Artikel enthalten und für einzelne schwierige Wörter auch gleich die Übersetzung anbieten. Du findest sie am Kiosk oder auch in einer gut sortierten Bücherei.

In der Prüfung
Lies dir den Text zuerst genau durch und unterstreiche dabei Wörter, die du nicht kennst. Meist kannst du deren Bedeutung aus dem Zusammenhang heraus erschließen. Beim zweiten Lesen kannst du dann die Wörter nachschlagen, deren Bedeutung du selbst dann noch nicht kennst.
Achte genau auf die Arbeitsanweisung. Denn hier steht z. B. manchmal, dass du gar nicht in ganzen Sätzen antworten musst (give short answers). Oder, dass mehr Möglichkeiten angegeben sind, als du benötigst. Auf jeden Fall solltest du alle Fragen beantworten, auch wenn dir manche vielleicht erst einmal schwierig erscheinen. Löse erst die für dich leichten Fragen und bearbeite dann in aller Ruhe die schwereren.
Achte vor allem auf deine Rechtschreibung. Fehler können hier zu Punktabzug führen. Berücksichtige auch, dass du in der gleichen Zeitform antwortest, in der die Frage gestellt wurde, z. B. in der Vergangenheit.

Typische Aufgabenstellung

Erläuterung
Du bekommst einen längeren Text und dazugehörige Fragen. Es geht darum, zu zeigen, dass du den Inhalt auch im Detail verstehst. Du bekommst zum Beispiel eine Aufgabenstellung, in der du Fragen zum Text beantworten sollst. Es werden verschiedene Antwortmöglichkeiten vorgegeben, suche die richtige heraus und kreuze sie an.

Body Art

1 Are you a fan of body art? Have you ever thought of getting pierced or tattooed? Among young people in the United States tattoos and piercings are becoming more and more popular. Some people admire this and even call it "body art". Other people don't understand why anyone would want such "ugly things" on their bodies.
Why do so many young Americans like body art? People's motivations for piercing or tattooing could be anything from attracting a romantic partner to just trying to be different from others. A tattoo can be a reminder of an important event in someone's life or it can show their taste in fashion. It can also make people appear "cool" to their social group and so increase their status. Jonathan Daulton, aged 19, has ten piercings on his face. "Honestly, I do it to shock people", says the University of Nebraska student. Another student, 21-year-old Marina Harding from Seattle, Washington, gives her reason as: "This is how I express myself." She likes to wear a T-shirt that says: "I dress this way to shock you!" This statement refers to her bright green hair, and piercings on her tongue, lip, nose and eyebrow, as well as six earrings in each ear. Marina also has eight tattoos and she wants to get more. She says, "I love body art."
On the other hand, doctors point out that certain health risks go along with these forms of self-expression. Possible health problems caused by piercings could be infections and sometimes a long healing time, even up to 12 months. In addition, the American Dental Association has given a serious warning about tongue piercings. The metal in the tongue hits the teeth during eating and speaking. This can cause cracks or broken teeth. The piercing even sometimes damages nerves in the tongue so that some people can no longer speak or swallow properly. Problems with tattoos can include allergic reactions to the ink and also infections. For both piercings and tattoos, the most serious risks are actually life-threatening. If a tattoo salon doesn't take basic health measures such as using new latex gloves and new needles for each customer, Hepatitis B and AIDS infections are a big risk.
Although you may be happy with your tattoos and piercings while you're still young, what about when you get older? If, for example, you have your boyfriend's or girlfriend's name tattooed on your arm and the relationship falls apart, what would you do about the tattoo? Tattoos are painful and expensive to remove. That is why many people prefer temporary tattoos. These last for a few days or even a week. You can remove them easily with oil or lotion. So you can enjoy the fun of "body art" with a new design whenever you like, without any risk.

Adapted from: L. Howard. Read and Reflect 2: Academic Reading Strategies and Cultural Awareness. Oxford University Press, 2004

Read the following tasks carefully. Tick the correct box for every task. Tick only one box for every task.

1. Tattoos and piercings …

a) ☐ are called "body art" only by young people in the USA.
b) ☐ are called "body art" by some people but "ugly things" by others.
c) ☐ could also be called "pop art" because they are becoming more and more popular.
d) ☐ are called "ugly things" by people outside the USA.

2. Body art …

a) ☐ could make it easier for some people to find a girlfriend or a boyfriend.
b) ☐ includes piercings and tattoos but does not include hair colouring.
c) ☐ is often used as a status symbol showing that you belong to a rich social group.
d) ☐ is not used to shock other people but only to show one's taste in fashion.

3. Piercings …

a) ☐ can take a long time to heal.
b) ☐ can be harmful, but they cannot have life-threatening consequences.
c) ☐ always make it impossible to swallow or speak properly.
d) ☐ are never worn by dentists because they know about the risks.

4. Tattoos …

a) ☐ are not dangerous for people infected with AIDS or Hepatitis B.
b) ☐ can cause allergic reactions to the latex gloves used in the salons.
c) ☐ cannot have life-threatening consequences.
d) ☐ should be made by responsible and professional salons taking all necessary health measures.

5. Temporary tattoos …

a) ☐ are not good for older people.
b) ☐ can easily be removed and can quickly be replaced by new ones.
c) ☐ are made with oil or lotion.
d) ☐ should not be used on your boyfriend's or girlfriend's arm.

Lösung

1. b) **2.** a) **3.** a) **4.** d) **5.** b)

(1)

Übungsaufgaben

(2)

Text 1

Boy Who Was Bullied[1] All of His Short Life

A schoolboy bullied from the age of four killed himself because he felt he had failed his family. Karl Peart, 16, overdosed on painkillers after years of suffering at the hands of his bullies. A suicide note to his mother read: "Mum, I'm sorry I have done this, I am not a nice person. I am sorry that I didn't live up to your expectations. I really love you and I will never leave your side. Tell my friends I will always be there for them."

Karl died in May last year after taking an overdose of 25 painkillers washed down with beer. His mother told the court, where an examination into his death is being held, that bullying was a big part of her son's life. "It was horrible and nasty," she said. "I thought he was beginning to deal with it. The older he got the less he spoke about it. Karl planned to get a day-time job and start evening classes to avoid the bullies." Mrs Peart also said, "Bullying is widespread in schools. There should be more care for the victims." Karl was beaten with sticks and a gang would punch and kick him as he walked home. In one incident Karl was held against a wall by the throat and a broken bottle was placed near his face. The gang would wait for him and attack him. He once received a broken finger after he was attacked at an ice rink during a school trip. His mother and her unemployed husband moved him from schools but the bullying continued. His death was recorded as suicide by the court. His mother said, "Karl was a victim. I now intend to help these victims of bullying. I am going to set up a website where the victims can log on to contact someone who knows how to help them."

Annotation:
[1] to bully – mobben, drangsalieren

Adapted from: Mark Lister, Daily Express, January 28, 2004, p. 15 (siehe: https://www.ukpressonline.co.uk/ukpressonline/open/simpleSearch.jsp;jsessionid=7D86CB4D47E77D162D6AE8CD869FBF2D?is=1)

Read the following tasks carefully. Tick the correct box for every task. Tick only one box for every task.

1. Karl Peart …
- a) ☐ killed himself at the age of 16 after years of taking painkillers.
- b) ☐ killed himself because he felt bullied by his family.
- -> c) ☒ took an overdose of painkillers after being bullied for 12 years.
- d) ☐ died because he was given an overdose of painkillers by his bullies.

2. In his suicide note …
- a) ☐ Karl blames his mother for his suicide.
- b) ☐ Karl describes the expectations he had about his life.
- c) ☐ Karl writes he is happy that his friends have always been there for him.
- ->d) ☒ Karl does not mention the bullies.

3. According to his mother, …
- a) ☐ the examination into Karl's death was horrible and nasty.
- ->b) ☒ it seemed that Karl had started to find a solution to the bullying.
- c) ☐ Karl had just started a day-time job and evening classes before he killed himself.
- d) ☐ most of the schools are responsible for the bullying.

4. The bullies …
- a) ☐ cut Karl's face with a broken bottle.
- b) ☐ broke Karl's finger by pushing him against a wall.
- c) ☐ attacked Karl during a school trip while he was eating ice-cream.
- d) ☒ usually waited for Karl before bullying him in different ways.

5. Karl's mother …

a) ☐ wants to set up a website where bullies can find help.
b) ☐ wants to help Karl because he was a victim of bullying.
c) ☐ intends to log on to a website to contact someone who can help her.
d) ☒ intends to set up a website where victims of bullying can find help.

Text 2

A Lost Person in a Lost Place

Every day on my way to school I pass a very old and run-down house. Whenever I pass the house, it makes me feel both sad and scared at the same time. All the window panes are either broken or missing entirely, and in the dark the house looks like a haunted castle. Obviously, the house is uninhabited, and no one seems to care about either doing it up again or pulling it down.

On my way to school yesterday morning I passed the house again; however, something was different this time. It was a cold December morning, and it was still quite dark when I approached the old house. Nevertheless, even before reaching the walls of the house, I made out the silhouette of a figure leaning out of the window right above the main entrance. Due to the darkness, I was not able at first to recognise exactly whether that figure was a child or an adult, a woman or a man. It was indeed a little spooky. When I had reached the main entrance, however, I realised that the figure leaning out of the window was an old woman. Tears were rolling down her cheeks, and she was staring into the distance with a strangely happy expression on her face. She did not seem to have noticed me even though I was walking just a few feet below her on the pavement.

I stopped to talk to her, but something held me back at first. In fact, I simply did not know what to say to the old woman. However, my conscience shouted out to me that I could not just keep on walking as if nothing had happened. Maybe she was lost, was hurt or needed help in any other way, which is why I finally managed to ask her, "Lady, are you okay? Do you need help?" At first she did not respond at all, but a moment later she bowed her head down to the pavement where I was standing. Now that I was able to have a closer look at her face, I was convinced that this was the oldest human being I had ever set eyes on. Her face was covered by quite a few wrinkles, her thin hair was whitish-grey, and her watery eyes were hardly visible within her deep eye sockets. "Please do not take me back there, please," the old woman suddenly shouted in a panicky and shaky tone of voice. "Take you back where?" I asked, taken by surprise. "To this terrible large house with all those old people I have never seen before," she answered. At first I was confused by what the woman had said. Was she disorientated? Was she having hallucinations? Or was she even entirely out of her mind? But then a vague idea of what the old lady might be talking about started to form in my mind. She might not be talking nonsense at all, I thought. "Could it be that you are talking about an old people's home where you were staying before you decided to come here?" I asked her. The old woman laughed in a somewhat sarcastic way and said, "Yes, young boy, I presume that is what they call a house like that: an old people's home." And after a short pause she added, "But that is not the right word for it. It is not a home, or at least it is not a home for me. This is my home." As she finished the last sentence, she began to move her tearful eyes along the front wall of the run-down old house.

The vague idea that had formed in my mind was now becoming clearer, and I was beginning to understand what this was all about. This lady, who looked as old as the hills to me, had run away from an old people's home to return to the house she had probably lived in for a large part of her life. This thought sent cold shivers up and down my spine. I felt such utter pity for the woman. At the same time, however, I knew that I had to do something. I could not simply walk off, leaving the old woman in this cold and dark house all by herself. Then, all of a sudden, I knew what to do. No matter how much I disliked this idea, I was nevertheless sure that I had to follow it and take action accordingly. "Listen. I need to go now because I am on my way to school. But you'll be fine. I promise", I said to the old lady. I must admit that I hated myself for what I had just said and even more for what I was about to do. And yet I walked past the house to turn right just behind it. I made sure the old lady could not see me anymore. Then I took out my mobile to call the police. I did not really have any other options, or did I?

The next day, when I was on my way to school again, I was a bit scared when I reached the old house, because I was not quite sure whether or not I would see the old lady in the house again. In fact, what I saw was the same run-down house which was as empty, lifeless and scary as it had always been before yesterday.

First read the text carefully. Tick the correct box for each task and give one piece of evidence from the text.

1. Obviously, somebody is thinking of either renovating or tearing down the old house.

This statement is

a) ☐ true

b) ☒ false

Evidence from the text:

, and no one seems to car about either doing it up again or pulling it down

2. Yesterday the narrator …

a) ☐ passed a different house on his way to school.

b) ☐ saw an old woman in the main entrance of the run-down house.

c) ☒ at first had difficulty in recognising the person leaning out of the window.

Evidence from the text:

____

3. The old woman …

a) ☐ simply did not know what to say to the narrator.

b) ☐ did not seem to have noticed the narrator at first because she was staring into the distance.

c) ☐ looked as if she was very unhappy.

Evidence from the text:

____

4. The old woman did not show any reaction whatsoever to the narrator's questions about her well-being.

This statement is

a) ☐ true

b) ☐ false

Evidence from the text:

____

5. The narrator …

a) ☐ had a vague idea about how the old lady had come to the old house.

b) ☐ thought that he might be having hallucinations when the old woman spoke to him.

c) ☐ thought that the old lady was talking some vague nonsense about old people in her home.

Evidence from the text:

____

6. With tears in her eyes the old woman said that the run-down old house was not a home for her.

This statement is

a) ☐ true

b) ☐ false

Evidence from the text:

____

7. The narrator …

a) ☐ felt cold shivers running up and down his spine because it was a very cold December morning.

b) ☐ had mixed feelings for the old lady, ranging from utter pity to a deep sense of responsibility.

c) ☐ thought that one of the options he had was simply to walk off and leave the old woman in the cold and dark house.

Evidence from the text:

____

8. For the narrator the decision to lie to the old woman and to call the police was not easy at all.

This statement is

a) ☒ true

b) ☐ false

Evidence from the text:

"I'm must admit that I hated myself for what I had just said and even more for what I was about to do

Text 3

Life in the Slow Lane[1]

I hear the dog before I see it, barking excitedly as it follows us along the riverbank. Small waves form on the surface of the water as our boat, the Golden Valley, moves slowly forward. Then the dog's owners come into view on the path next to the river. We chat for a minute before they continue on their way. I smile and shake my head. This is truly life in the slow lane[1]: we have just been passed by two people walking a dog.

Three hours ago, two friends of mine and I rented the "Golden Valley" from a boat rental company north of Oxford. 'Narrow boat' is the right term for this boat because it is 20 metres long, but only 2.1 metres wide. However, I am surprised to see how much space and comfort the boat offers. It has a large living and dining area, a fully equipped kitchen, a bathroom and two bedrooms, one with a double bed and one with a single bed. The boat also has hot water and heating. It even has a television. But my friends and I agree: "We are not going to switch on the TV during our trip because we are here to switch off."

Britain has more than 6,400 kilometres of inland waterways, including 3,200 kilometres of historic canals. This may explain why the British enjoy boating so much. Every year, 11 million people use the waterways: for hiking, jogging, cycling, fishing, boating and observing animals – or simply for sitting at a waterside pub and watching the world go by. "Water has its own speed and it has its own heartbeat – and when you are in a narrow boat you slow down to that speed and heartbeat," says Lindy Foster Weinreb, who lives near London in a canal-side house where she started her own boat rental company back in 1970.

Before my friends and I got under way in the Golden Valley, we received full instructions by the boss of the boat rental company about how to steer[2] and control the boat safely. Another person working for the rental company even stayed with us on the boat until we reached the first lock[3]. When he handed the controls of the boat over to me and my friends, the boat felt strange and heavy in our hands. However, it only took about another hour or so before my friends and I felt comfortable guiding the narrow boat around the many bends[4] and locks of the Thames.

Boating may seem like a lazy way of spending the day, but it is not. Once you have jumped on and off the boat, opened and closed locks, moved heavy gates, or pulled and lifted bridges (which allow cars to cross the canal), you will find that you sleep extremely well. So as it is now becoming darker and darker on the first day of our trip, we are all looking forward to our beds.

Annotations:

[1] slow lane – Kriechspur (z. B. auf der Autobahn)
[2] to steer – steuern
[3] lock – Schleuse
[4] bend – Kurve

Quelle: nach Spotlight 7/09, www.spotlight-online.de/files/spotlight/Magazine_content/Documents/34-35.pdf, Spotlight Verlag GmbH, Seite 34 – 35

(3)

Read the following tasks carefully. Tick the correct box for every task. Tick only one box for every task.

1. The dog's owners ...

a) [ ] walk just a little bit more slowly than the boat.
b) [ ] walk in front of their dog.
c) [x] show the people on the boat just how slowly their boat is moving.
d) [ ] do not speak to the people on the boat because they need to continue on their way.

2. The boat is called "narrow boat"...

a) [x] because it is only 2.1 metres wide.
b) [ ] although it is 20 metres long.
c) [ ] because it offers a lot of space and comfort.
d) [ ] because there is only space for a single bed in one of its bedrooms.

3. The inland waterways in Britain ...

a) [ ] are 9,600 km long in total.
b) [ ] are very good for people who like being active in their free time, but for people who just want to watch the world go by the waterways are no good.
c) [ ] are quite fast and are therefore no good for people with heart problems.
d) [x] are very popular because they offer lots of different things you can do in your free time.

4. Steering and controlling a narrow boat ...

a) [ ] is very difficult because the boat feels strange and heavy in your hands for a long time.
b) [x] can be learned within a couple of hours if you get proper instructions and a short period of training on the boat by a member of the rental company.
c) [ ] takes a long period of professional training because of the many bends and locks.
d) [ ] is only allowed with a member of the rental company staying on board at all times.

5. Spending the day on a narrow boat ...

a) [ ] means sleeping well for most of the day.
b) [x] means doing a lot of tiring physical work.
c) [ ] means doing a lot of tiring physical work on the boat only.
d) [ ] means doing a lot of tiring physical work, but all those tiring things need to be done only once.

C. Schreiben

Erklärung

Die Vorbereitung
Es ist ein Gerücht, dass man das Schreiben von Texten nicht erlernen kann. Zwar kann man es nicht so einfach üben wie Vokabeln oder Grammatik, aber eine langfristige Vorbereitung ist durchaus sinnvoll. In der Prüfung können verschiedene Textsorten auftauchen, mit denen du dich zuvor vertraut machen solltest. Du musst zum Beispiel deine Meinung oder eine kurze Stellungnahme schreiben oder auch vollständige Texte in Form von E-Mails oder Briefen verfassen. Zusätzlich hilft es, wenn du englische Bücher oder Zeitschriften liest oder dir einen Kinofilm auch einmal auf Englisch ansiehst.

In der Prüfung
Lies zunächst die Arbeitsanweisung durch. Hier wird dir in der Regel genau vorgegeben, was du tun musst und wie viele Wörter du schreiben sollst. Überlege dir, was du schreiben möchtest und mache dir Notizen. Achte beim Verfassen des Textes nicht nur auf den Inhalt, sondern auch auf deine Sprache: Rechtschreibung, Grammatik und Stil sind wichtige Elemente eines Textes. Wenn du ein Wort nicht weißt, umschreibe es oder benutze zur Sicherheit ein anderes, das dir vertraut ist. Bei manchen Textformen gibt es bestimmte Redewendungen, die du dir im Vorfeld einprägen kannst, zum Beispiel Anrede- und Schlussformeln in E-Mails oder Briefen. Plane genug Zeit ein, um deine Texte am Schluss noch einmal in Ruhe durchzulesen.

Typische Aufgabenstellung

Diese Aufgabe bezieht sich auf den Lesetext "Body Art" (siehe Seite 20).

Read the tasks carefully. Write complete sentences and use conjunctions to link your ideas. Make sure to write about all the aspects in the task.

1. **Describe** why body art is very popular among young people in the USA.

2. **Describe and explain** the disadvantages of piercings and tattoos.

3. You have a choice here. Choose **one** of the following tasks:

   a) Imagine you planned to get piercings in your tongue, lip and nose. As you still live with your parents, you talk to them about your plan. **Write the dialogue** between you and your parents.

   b) A lot of young people wear body art because they want to shock other people. Do you think it is acceptable for young people to shock others with their piercings, tattoos or coloured hair?
   Find arguments for and against this view and **state your personal opinion**.

Lösung

1. There are a number of reasons why young Americans like body art so much. First, body art is regarded as helpful in finding a boyfriend or a girlfriend. It may also indicate to others what kind of fashion you are into. Second, body art can represent a kind of reminder of something important that happened in your life. Third, tattoos and piercings may help you to be seen as a "cool" person in the social group you belong to. However, there are also a number of young Americans who want to be different from others, and they believe that body art is one way of showing others that they are indeed different. Last but not least, the most extreme reason for wearing body art is because you want to shock other people.

2. Most of the disadvantages which piercings and tattoos have are linked to possible health problems. To begin with, infections are possible as a result of piercings or tattoos, and the healing time for such infections can be quite long. Tongue piercings, in particular, can harm teeth or nerves, which can make speaking or swallowing difficult or even totally impossible. Tattoos are both painful and expensive to remove, and there is also some risk of allergic reactions to the ink. In fact, both of these types of body art can actually have life-threatening consequences when basic health measures are not taken. Last but not least, piercings and tattoos can have social or emotional disadvantages. If you split up with your boyfriend or girlfriend but have their name tattooed somewhere on your body, this might be quite embarrassing and annoying.

3. a) Y: You M: Mother F: Father

Y: Mum, dad, there is something that I need to talk to you about. You know, a lot of my friends have recently started piercing their faces, and I think it looks really cool. Ronald, the boy who has this great motorbike I told you about last week, even has piercings in his tongue, his lip and his nose. The girls are absolutely crazy about him now, and I like his piercings very much, too.

F: Please, do not tell me that you would also like to look like those horrible homeless teenagers who are always asking me for money on the bus or on the underground. They have tattoos and piercings all over their bodies. I find that very ugly.

Y: But dad, most of my friends have either tattoos or piercings now. And they are not homeless people. You know my friends very well, and you keep telling me that you like them very much because they are nice, friendly and responsible teenagers.

F: Yes, that is true. But why do they want to look like drug addicts or criminals?

Y: Oh, come on, dad, why should people, who have a special taste in fashion, automatically be drug addicts or criminals? Body art is just a way to express yourself, to prove that you have your own individual style and are different from other people.

F: Special taste in fashion? Body art? Individual style? They only want to shock decent, ordinary citizens with their tattoos and piercings. That is all, there is to it. And I do not think, that they have a right to do that.

M: Now you are beginning to be a bit unfair, Archibald. Everyone has a right to have their own individual style and taste. When we were young, Archibald, we had our own dress code, and you certainly remember that our parents did not like the way we dressed. In fact, we were really angry with our parents, because they just did not allow us to dress the way we wanted to. I do not want to make the same mistake now that I am a parent myself. But what I am indeed a little worried about are health problems that piercings and tattoos may cause. I have actually heard about serious infections and dental problems caused by piercings.

Y: Of course, there can be health risks if the piercings are done unprofessionally or without taking the necessary hygienic and health measures. But I would, of course, go to a professional piercing salon, so there is nothing to worry about.

F: I still think that my child should not look like a good-for-nothing thug!

M: Archibald, I would really like you to stop being so unfair and prejudiced! Here is what I think we should do now. Why don't you go to the salon for one nose piercing? As far as I know, this is by far the least dangerous kind of piercing. Moreover, if you start with only one piercing, you can decide after a couple of months whether or not you really like it that much. Then you can either have the one piercing removed or get more.

Y: Thank you, mum. That's a compromise I can really live with, especially because it gives me the freedom to decide after some time what I really want.

F: I am still not very happy about the whole idea, but as a compromise it is fine with me.

b) It is not very easy to decide whether or not it is acceptable for young people to shock others with their piercings, tattoos or coloured hair. On the one hand, shocking other people can be seen as unacceptable because some people, especially elderly ones, even feel threatened by a young person who looks different from them and indeed from most other people, too. From this point of view, shocking people is an unacceptable motivation, because no one has the right to threaten others.
On the other hand, it is often argued that, in a pluralistic, democratic society, everyone is free to do whatever they like, as long as they do not harm anyone else or limit anyone else's freedom. This is a very strong argument because it can be related to a lot of activities and situations in our society.

For example, in most Western societies women are allowed to wear anything from miniskirts and belly-shirts to Islamic burkas in public, depending on their taste in fashion or their religious beliefs. Most certainly, there are some people who find miniskirts and belly shirts 'shocking', while others are 'shocked' by Muslim burkas from a feminist viewpoint. Similarly, men can wear no beard, a moustache or indeed any kind of beard, no matter how long, what shape or even what colour that beard is. In other societies or in other historic periods the existence, the non-existence or a particular shape of a beard is or was regarded as 'shocking' and therefore unacceptable. Obviously, in modern Western societies today any kind of beard is acceptable, even if some people find certain beards "strange" or "ugly".

In conclusion, I think that modern democratic societies need to accept body art as a form of individual style because it does not harm anyone or limit anyone's freedom. Piercings, tattoos or coloured hair may be shocking to some people; however, outfits and clothing styles are personal decisions that need to be accepted. After all, everyone likes some styles and dislikes others, which means everyone needs to be tolerant of others in one way or another.

Übungsaufgaben

Task 1

Diese Aufgabe bezieht sich auf den Lesetext "Boy Who Was Bullied All of His Short Life" (siehe Seite 22).

Read the tasks carefully. Write complete sentences and use conjunctions to link your ideas. Make sure to write about all the aspects in the task.

1. **Describe** how Karl was bullied and how he reacted to the bullying.

2. **Describe and explain** how Karl's parents reacted to the bullying and to his suicide.

3. You have a choice here. Choose **one** of the following tasks:

   a) **Write an article** for your school magazine in which you (1.) describe what bullying is and (2.) suggest possible ways of dealing with the problem of bullying.

   b) Very often teachers are blamed for not noticing or not responding to bullying. What do you think? Are the teachers to blame? **Find arguments for and against** this view and **state your personal** opinion.

Task 2

Diese Aufgabe bezieht sich auf den Lesetext "A Lost Person in a Lost Place" (siehe Seite 23).

Read the tasks carefully. Write complete sentences and use conjunctions to link your ideas. Make sure to write about all aspects in the task.

1. **Describe** how the narrator's feelings and thoughts about the old lady develop in this story.

2. **Explain** the thoughts and emotions the old lady associates with the word "house" on the one hand and with the word "home" on the other (lines 51 – 52).

3. You have a choice here. Choose **one** of the following tasks:

   a) Shortly before the end of the scene the narrator says, "I did not really have any other options, or did I?". What do you think? Did he or did he not have any other options? **Find arguments for and against** the narrator's statement and **give your personal opinion**.

   b) **Write a possible ending to the story.** Include the narrator's thoughts and feelings about his decision to call the police as well as about what may have happened after he had called the police the day before.

Task 3

Diese Aufgabe bezieht sich auf den Lesetext "Life in the Slow Lane" (siehe Seite 25).

Read the tasks carefully. Write complete sentences and use conjunctions to link your ideas. Make sure to write about all the aspects in the task.

1. **Describe** the narrow boat in detail and explain what needs to be done before and while guiding a narrow boat.

2. **Explain** why this article is entitled "Life in the slow lane" and **give three examples** from the article illustrating the meaning of this title.

3. You have a choice here. Choose **one** of the following tasks:

   a) Imagine the parents of a girl (Amanda, 14 years old) planned to rent a narrow boat for a two-week holiday on Britain's historic canals. Amanda still lives with her parents and is not allowed to go on holiday alone or with her friends. The parents tell Amanda about their holiday plans. **Write the dialogue** between Amanda and her parents.

   b) For some people holidays on a narrow boat are the best holidays in the world. **Find arguments for and against** this view and **state your personal opinion**.

D. Sprache

Erklärung

Vorbereitung und Bearbeitung

Wenn du eine Fremdsprache lernst, ist es wichtig, dass du von Anfang an gründlich deine Vokabeln lernst. Die Vokabeln erst kurz vor einer Prüfung zu lernen, funktioniert meistens nicht besonders gut. Nur durch regelmäßiges Wiederholen prägen sich die Wörter in dein Langzeitgedächtnis ein.

Es gibt viele Tipps und Tricks, die dir das Vokabellernen erleichtern. Schreibe zum Beispiel schwierige Wörter oder solche, die du immer wieder vergisst, auf Karteikarten. Schreibe jeweils das englische Wort auf die Vorderseite der Karte. Als Merkhilfe schreibe dir einen Beispielsatz mit auf, denn viele Vokabeln lernst du besser im Zusammenhang. Auf die Rückseite der Karte schreibst du dann die deutsche Übersetzung. Mische die Karten zwischendurch und wechsle auch die Reihenfolge: deutsch-englisch und englisch-deutsch. Auch Grammatikregeln kannst du dir leichter merken, wenn du Karteikarten anlegst oder ein Grammatik-Poster machst.

Dein Wortschatz wird beispielsweise mit Lückentexten, Synonymfindungen oder Worterklärungen getestet. Du sollst also zeigen, dass du im Laufe deiner Schulzeit viele Wörter und Redewendungen gelernt hast und dass du diese auch anwenden und schreiben kannst. Bei den Wortschatzübungen unterscheiden sich manche Wörter teilweise nur durch einen Buchstaben. Sie bekommen dadurch aber eine ganz andere Bedeutung. Hier gilt es, besonders aufzupassen. Falls dir ein Wort nicht gleich einfällt, überlege, ob du ein anderes weißt, das fast dasselbe bedeutet.

Zum Überprüfen deiner Grammatikkenntnisse musst du zum Beispiel Sätze in die richtige Reihenfolge bringen, richtige Formen oder Zeiten in Lückentexte einfügen oder auch Personalpronomen oder Adjektive einsetzen. Bei Lückentexten solltest du erst den ganzen Text lesen, sodass du weißt, worum es geht. Dann fällt es dir auch leichter, das entsprechende Wort einzusetzen. Beachte auf jeden Fall die englische Satzstellung von Subjekt – Prädikat – Objekt, Prädikat und Objekt stehen immer zusammen.

Übungsaufgaben

I. Wortschatz

1. Vocabulary – Grammar

Read the sentences. Find words of the same word family to fit in.

a) She and her manager had an ______________________ **< argue >** over money.

b) There were ______________________ **< number >** people in the street.

c) She got ______________________ **< anger >** when she saw this mess.

d) She wondered who had made the ______________________ **< decide >** to come.

e) The ______________________ **< behave >** at the party was strange.

f) She did not ______________________ **< success >** in passing the crowd.

g) Some screamed because they were so ______________________ **< excitement >**.

h) There was no ______________________ **< explain >** for this.

i) It was all not really ______________________ **< necessity >**.

j) She could not find the ______________________ **< enter >** to the music hall.

2. Make nouns out of verbs.

a) to decide ____________________

b) to improve ____________________

c) to sell ____________________

d) to fly ____________________

e) to begin ____________________

3. Find the plural form of these nouns.

a) tree ____________________

b) century ____________________

c) foot ____________________

d) glass ____________________

e) knife ____________________

f) sheep ____________________

4. Find the missing words and fill in the gaps.

a) If you belong to a club, you are a ______________ of the club.

b) You can take your money to the ______________ if you don't need it now.

c) An ______________ acts in a play or a film.

d) You must show your ______________ when you arrive at a foreign airport.

e) California is a ______________ in the USA.

f) It doesn't rain very often in the ______________.

5. Read the definitions and find the words.

a) The line between one country or state and another: ______________

b) Something valuable which you get if you win a competition: ______________

c) A special place where Native Americans live today: ______________

d) You must go there if you are ill or if you had a bad accident: ______________

e) The room where you can cook meals or have lunch: ______________

f) The period of time between two lessons at school: ______________

6. Find words that mean the same and words that mean the opposite.

answer – clean – elect – dirty – cheap – old-fashioned – close – expensive – modern – reply – choose

same meaning	opposite meaning

7. Make nouns out of verbs and adjectives.

a) free ______________________

b) to hope ______________________

c) to act ______________________

d) poor ______________________

e) hot ______________________

8. Tick the correct form in the box below.

The procedures for renting an apartment in different countries or cities can differ widely, and ❶ knowing what to expect can help you in your apartment search. ❷ decide on the type of apartment you want to rent. How big ❸ it be? How much money are you willing to spend? Figure out the exact costs for renting an apartment and determine your budget. Is ❹ transportation available nearby? ❺ apartments are advertised in the local newspaper. These listings generally describe the size and location, and amenities of the place. Looking over these ads will give you a general idea of the ❻ of apartments available. Also ask people you know, if they can recommend any specific place to live. Be sure to carefully read and understand the terms of the rental agreement. Because once you sign you ❼ bound to uphold the terms of the contract. Ignorance is no excuse. Can you keep pets in the apartment? Is smoking allowed? How much notice do you need to give the ❽ before you move out? Better ask questions, if you aren't sure.

1.
- ☐ but
- ☐ although
- ☐ therefore
- ☐ even

2.
- ☐ Secondly
- ☐ First of all
- ☐ Finally
- ☐ At last

3.
- ☐ should
- ☐ shall
- ☐ does
- ☐ shouldn't

4.
- ☐ open
- ☐ official
- ☐ pedestrian
- ☐ public

5.
- ☐ Many
- ☐ Lot
- ☐ Much
- ☐ Amount of

6.
- ☐ types
- ☐ races
- ☐ species
- ☐ models

7.
- ☐ would be
- ☐ will be
- ☐ should be
- ☐ were

8.
- ☐ lord
- ☐ housekeeper
- ☐ landlord
- ☐ maid

9. Tick the correct form in the box below.

Gold Rush in California

In 1848, gold was ❶ at Sutter's Mill, about 100 miles east of San Francisco and the first gold-rush began. There hadn't been so many white people in California before, but ❷ a year 100 000 newcomers arrived at the west coast among ❸ only 8000 were women. If the diggers ❹ what expected them there some of them would have turned ❺ at once. Rooms were expensive as were tools, guns, wagons and food. In the wilderness you could only survive if you knew how to make a living on your own. On the ❻ it was a dangerous business. Law and order broke down and the hangman was always fast with his rope slung over the ❼ of a tree. Some of these stories can still be seen ❽ TV in the numerous "westerns", made about this adventurous period of American history.

1.
- ☐ made
- ☐ found
- ☐ bought
- ☐ given away

2.
- ☐ while
- ☐ within
- ☐ meanwhile
- ☐ between

3.
- ☐ which
- ☐ of
- ☐ these
- ☐ whose

4.
- ☐ knew
- ☐ would know
- ☐ know
- ☐ had known

5.
- ☐ round
- ☐ over
- ☐ along
- ☐ down

6.
- ☐ hole
- ☐ hall
- ☐ whole
- ☐ hold

7.
- ☐ top
- ☐ branch
- ☐ roots
- ☐ twig

8.
- ☐ on
- ☐ inside
- ☐ with
- ☐ in

10. Find the corresponding nouns.

a) astonished ______________________

b) important ______________________

c) successful ______________________

d) furious ______________________

e) obsessed ______________________

11. Find the opposites of the following words.

a) cheap ______________________

b) peace ______________________

c) ask ______________________

d) easy ______________________

e) wonderful ______________________

12. Complete the sentences by using these words in their correct forms.

difficult – important – to pollute – to produce – limited – electricity

a) The wind and sun as sources of energy are of special ________________.

b) The ________________ of electricity often costs a lot of money.

c) ______________ light is used in almost every home today.

d) Energy from the wind and the sun has no ________________.

e) The ________________ of the world has to be stopped.

f) We're having ________________ in finding cheap ways to replace oil and coal.

13. Homophones

In the following sentences, two words are missing in each line which are pronounced the same way, but spelt in a different way.

a) At the airport, we had to wait for __________ luggage for more than half an _________.

b) He is blind in one __________, my brother could not help him nor could __________.

c) I need two pounds of __________ for the cake. The rose is a beautiful __________.

d) We buy __________ at the butcher's. I'll __________ him at the station.

e) Our sailing trip was perfect: the sky was __________, and the wind __________ gently.

14. Add the correct ending: -ar, -or, -er

a) A man who plays in films is an act_____.

b) A person who breaks into houses is a burgl_____.

c) Someone who doesn't tell the truth is a li_____.

d) A person who goes to museums is a visit_____ there.

15. Write down the plural forms of the following words.

a) industry ________________ b) half ________________

c) hero ________________ d) life ________________

e) bus ________________ f) proof ________________

g) radio ________________ h) dress ________________

i) woman ________________ j) toy ________________

II. Grammatik

16. Put these sentences into negative forms.

a) Lisa and Tina are good friends. ________________________________

b) Mike will go to New York next week. ________________________________

c) My parents went to Paris last weekend. ________________________________

d) Tom plays football on Fridays. ________________________________

e) Our cat sleeps on the kitchen floor. ________________________________

f) Mr Burns has lived in Scotland for 25 years. ________________________________

17. Fill in the correct form.

a) A few years ago young people ______________ **< to prefer >** team sports.

b) But now they ______________ **< not to want >** to train regularly.

c) If you ______________ **< to be >** a member of a fitness club you can __________ **< go to >** there whenever you ______________ **< to want >** to.

d) But ______________ **< not to expect >** muscles like Arnold Schwarzenegger within a few weeks or you ______________ **< to be >** disappointed.

e) He ______________ **< to need >** years of training before he ______________ **< to become >** Mr Universe.

18. Use the correct tense.

a) Bobby was already 6 years old but he ________________ **< never speak >** a word in his life.

b) One evening, at dinner, he ________________ **< say >** very clearly:

c) "I don't want spinach! Please ________________ **< give >** me beans instead."

d) "We thought you ____________ **< can >** not ________________ **< talk >**," his father said.

e) "Why ________________ **< you, not, ever, say >** a word before?"

f) "Well," answered Bobby, "up to now, everything ________________ **< be >** fine."

19. If-clauses

a) If a racing driver does not get enough sleep, he __________ **< not able >** to concentrate.

b) If he wanted to win he __________ **< have to >** train hard.

c) If he had a serious accident, he __________ **< be >** afraid to drive again.

d) He __________ **< drive >** more carefully if it had rained.

e) If he __________ **< use >** too much gas, he would have to stop more often.

20. Write the sentences again using reported speech.

Parents talked about home-schooling.

Mrs Jenkins: "My kids must write test papers once a month."

Mr Brown: "My wife has more patience than I do so she teaches our kids."

Mrs Jenkins said … ____

Mr Brown said … ____

21. Reported speech

At the basketball camp the coach was a tough one. Here is what he said: "I've no room for lazy people, so you will have to train every day. Everybody must get up at five. You are not allowed to have breakfast until you have run five miles. There is no time to relax." Here's part of a letter Neal wrote to a friend. Use reported speech to complete the letter.
I had a very hard time at the camp. Our trainer was really tough. On the first day he told us that ...

a) ____________ no room for lazy people.

b) ____________ every day.

c) He said everybody ____________ at five.

d) We ____________ breakfast until

e) ____________ five miles.

f) He made it clear ____________ no time to relax.

22. Use direct speech.

a) The doctor said that he had proved that many kids were too lazy.
The doctor said, "____."

b) A trainer said that children had had more exercise 20 years ago.
A trainer said, "____."

c) A friend promised that he would ride his bike more often.
A friend promised, "____."

d) A health expert said that schools were starting sport programmes for kids.
A health expert said, "____."

23. You read an advert of a Health Farm. Fill in the missing -ing-form or infinitive.

a) Do you have trouble ____________ **< keep >** fit?

b) Do you find it difficult ____________ **< run >** after a bus?

c) Would you like ____________ **< play >** basketball again?

d) It's no good ____________ **< say >** I'm too old for sports.

e) We promise ____________ **< make >** you feel fit and healthy again.

f) If you enjoy ____________ **< walk >** or feel like ____________ **< jog >**, we have forests and hills not far away.

g) It's worth ____________ **< visit >** us.

24. Underline the correct word.

An eye witness is telling a news reporter what she saw when two cars crashed.

"The driver of the family car had stopped **correct/correctly/correctness** in front of the red traffic lights when a new sports car **crashed/crashing/crash** into it. The driver of the sports car is **well-known/know/knowing** in town for **drive/driven/driving** at **high/height/heightened** speeds. He hasn't lost his **drive/driver/driving** license yet. Every year the **own/owner/owning** of the sports car buys a new car which is **extremely/extreme** expensive. I was **deep/deeply/deeper** shocked when I saw how he tried to blame the driver of the family car for the accident. The poor man could **hard/hardly/harder** defend **himself/him/his**. The police arrived **fast/ faster** than I had expected and I told them everything."

25. Change the given words into the correct forms.

Voluntary worker Jasmina Begum (17), from London

When I started secondary school in London there a) ______________ **< be >** gang fights between people of different b) ______________ **< race >** origin.

When our teacher told my class about an anti-racism project in Belfast we c) ___________ **< decision >** to go there. There we learned that the fights were not because of d) ______________ **< difference >** skin colour or culture but because of e) ____________ **< religion >** beliefs.

Every day the kids from my class and I visited schools in Belfast to talk to kids there about their f) ______________ **< live >** and problems. We also told them about g) _________ **< oneself >**.

Back in London we h) ______________ **< trained >** together to work as peer counsellors[1] at our school. When talking about problems we had to be i) ___________ **< complete >** honest and nobody was allowed to get angry. We all learned more about each other and our school became a much j) ______________ **< friendly >** place.

[1] counsellor: *hier:* Streitschlichter

26. Fill in the correct form.

Broadway,

one of the greatest streets in the world, had a very simple a) _____________ **< begin >**. The story of Broadway is the story of New York b) ____________ **< oneself >**. It had been an Indian trail before white c) ____________ **< man >** reached the Island of Manhattan. In the days of the Dutch it had grown into a country road called Breedeweg. The name Broadway or Breedeweg had its d) _____________ **< original >** in the broad way that e) _____________ **< lead >** from the f) _____________ **< enter >** of the old Fort up to the gate at Wall Street. The street g) _____________ **< be >** wide enough to give the soldiers room to drill. When a wall was put around the little town, Breedeweg brought you h) ____________ **< direct >** to the city gate. And i) _____________ **< in/for/since >** nearly a hundred years it had been the only road j) ______________ **< connect >** one end of Manhattan to the other. With the coming of the British, Breedeweg changed quite k) _____________ **< natural >** from a Dutch to an English through road and l) ___________ **< become >** Broadway.

27. Make sentences and use all the words.

a) at 9 pm / They / at Hogwart's School / eat / always

____ .

b) Harry / Why / go / does / to Hogwart's School

____ ?

c) ever / a / Have / seen / wizard / in / real / you / life

____ ?

d) watch / and / Harry Potter movie / to the cinema / Let's go / the new

____ .

e) one / is / best / Hermione / friends / of Harry's

____ .

28. Fill in the adjective or adverb.

Firemen have a a) __________ **< dangerous >** job. They must work b) __________ **< fast >** and c) ____________ **< careful >**. They are d) __________ **< brave >** men who e) ________ **< unselfish >** risk their own lives to help f) ___________ **< desperate >** people. They do their job g) __________ **< good >** but very often people still die h) __________ **< tragic >**.

29. Bring the adjectives into the right form.

Ben is quite _______________ **< good >** at languages, but unfortunately he is _______________ **< bad >** than average in mathematics. He hasn't spent _________________ **< much >** time on his homework recently and he has made _________________ **< many >** mistakes.

Can't his _______________ **< old >** brother help him with his homework? I think it is the _______________ **< easy >** way to get better results. Ben should not wait until it is too ________________ **< late >**. It is always the same: the longer you wait the ______________ **< much >** time and energy you have to invest.

30. Who or which? Complete the sentences.

a) Football is a game _______________________ is very popular.

b) Dan is a boy _______________________ is crazy about football.

c) A fast car is something _______________________ many people would like to have.

d) Someone _______________________ never laughs cannot be truly happy.

e) The dog _______________________ always comes to our door for food is really cute.

f) _______________________ wants to sit in the first row at the concert?

31. Fill in the correct pronouns.

my – mine – your – yours – his – hers – it – its – our – ours – their – theirs

"Can I have _____________ math book? I've forgotten _____________," asked Christina. "And Linda hasn't got _____________. She hasn't done _____________ homework and we must give _____________ to Mr Smith today." "No, I haven't," said David. "But I know what we can do. Let's look for Max and _____________ brother. They'll have _____________ because they have got math today. But we mustn't forget _____________ books tomorrow."

Hörverstehenstexte

1. Four Teenagers Killed in Car Accident

(Audiotrack: QR-Code rechts / Aufgaben S. 14)

Four teenagers had been killed in a terrible crash. The court case was yesterday. Alana S., one of the girls, who survived told the court that she and her girlfriend Maggie, who had survived too, had told Mike, the driver, to drive as fast as he could. They had not asked their boarding school teachers for permission to leave school; therefore they wanted to be back for supper so that no one would notice. Mike drove too fast and lost control in a bend. The overloaded car with its six passengers crashed into a tree. The driver, his friend Tim, and two girls on the rear seats were killed instantly. The court heard from Alana that Mike had tried to show off. He wanted to impress the girls. He had accelerated and braked to throw the passengers around. The girl admitted that they all had teased Mike except Tim. They had laughed and joked about his driving, so that Mike had gone on driving foolishly. Tim had told him to stop being so silly, but the girls had gone on teasing him, and Mike had continued to drive dangerously. Four teenagers had to die because of this reckless driving. Alana admitted that she had teased Mike as well and felt guilty of having caused the death of her classmates. Maggie B. was not yet able to be heard by the court. She has not yet recovered from her major injuries. The trial will continue next week.

2. Hunger in Afghanistan

(Audiotrack: QR-Code oben / Aufgaben S. 15)

Afghanistan is a mountainous country located in Central Asia. Its history and culture goes back over 5000 years. Afghanistan is a heterogeneous nation. While the majority of the Afghans belong to the Islamic faith, there are also small groups of Sikhs, Hindu and some Jews. The capital of Afghanistan is Kabul. Unfortunately due to many years of war, the city has been nearly destroyed and the long period of war time has had a shattering effect on the population. "Six million out of 32 million people receive food aid," said Shiron, a merchant in Kandahar.

"The people are starving. The food prices rise and the poor and unemployed are desperate. Afghanistan doesn't grow enough and we have to import flour from Pakistan to bake bread. We are one of the poorest countries in the world. Our infrastructure has been destroyed. The food prices sometimes double within two weeks and are much too high compared to the people's income. Some are so desperate to help their families that they steal or threaten merchants to get food. The state bakeries have been closed and are not yet working again to supply the population with bread. Though the Afghanistan government has appealed for help from the World Food Program, the situation is miserable" says Shiron. He adds that food aid alone won't solve the country's problems. There has to be investment in agriculture, upon which the majority of the population survives. Farmers need seed and tools to increase the food production. Shiron complains that if no one donates grain, the situation will get even worse. There are no riots yet, but the growing hunger will increase desperation among the population.

3. Conversation about the Future

(Audiotrack: QR-Code oben / Aufgaben S. 16)

At Johnson College finals are just around the corner and the big question among students is: what to do after school? Helen, Cathy and Jason are talking about their plans for the future as well.

Helen: After school I want to spend a year in South Africa, working at a school. This will surely help me later with my plans to become a teacher.

Cathy: That sounds exciting. Have you already inquired about getting such a position?

Helen: I applied at an agency who will take care of everything for me. They will provide me with a host family and a school at which I'll be able to work. And they will help me with any problems I might have to face.

Cathy: Aren't you afraid of going to a country as dangerous as South Africa?

Helen: No, not really, but I think my mum is a bit worried about me. If it works out you could come and visit me.

Jason: That would be cool. I want to travel around for a bit after school, see something of the world and meet lots of new people. Maybe my travels will lead me to South Africa as well.

Helen: What's your first stop?

Jason: Mallorca, I'm going to party a lot and enjoy the sun. Berry and Tyler will be coming, too. After that I'll backpack through Australia and then I'll decide spontaneously.

Cathy: My, my, you've got it all planned out, haven't you? That's all too risky for me. I want to do something with animals.

Jason: Why don't you go to South America on a farm? Or to Ireland tending sheep?

Cathy: Why do I have to leave home at all? I'm not sure what I really want to do yet.

Helen: How about a volunteer's job at an animal shelter? There you can tend to and care for animals and see if it's something you might consider doing in your future.

Cathy: That's a really great idea, Helen. I'll try to find out tomorrow if there are any possibilities for me working.

As different as their interests were, on one thing they all agreed. After school they surely want to stay in contact. After all the others should know what had happened to their future plans in the end.

4. Interview

(Audiotrack: QR-Code S. 40 / Aufgaben S. 17)

Moderator: Good evening and welcome to "You and your health". Now, since 2003 there has been a sharp rise in obesity rates among young people in the United States. Children in this country are now fatter than they were five years ago. In the studio with me, I have Patrick Hoji, who is an expert in diet and fitness. Welcome to the programme, Patrick.

Patrick: Thank you.

Moderator: We often hear that it's unhealthy for children to be overweight. So, how can they lose weight?

Patrick: Well, first of all, if someone is overweight they really need to change the way they eat. They need to eat less unhealthy food and more healthy food.

Moderator: Okay. But which foods are unhealthy and which foods are healthy?

Patrick: Well, unhealthy foods usually have lots of fat and sugar in them. But they often taste great, too. For example, chocolate.

Moderator: Oh, I love chocolate.

Patrick: Yes, everyone loves chocolate. But it has lots of fat and sugar in it. And so if you eat too much of it, you put on weight. Of course, you can eat some chocolate without getting fat. So it is okay to eat a small amount once a week. But don't eat chocolate every day.

Moderator: Hmm, that's okay, I guess. What other foods are unhealthy?

Patrick: Well, fast foods like hamburgers and fries are also not very good for you. They have lots of fat and salt in them. And salt is bad for your heart.

Moderator: Okay, so what foods are healthy, then?

Patrick: Well, fruit is low in fat and has lots of vitamins in it. Vitamins are really good for your body. I tell children to eat fruit every morning for breakfast. It doesn't matter what fruit you choose.

Moderator: I usually have a bread roll for breakfast or a bowl of muesli. Is that healthy?

Patrick: Yes, it is. Bread and muesli are part of a group of foods called carbohydrates. Carbohydrates give us energy. And when we don't have enough energy we feel very tired. It's important to eat carbohydrates in the morning, so that we have enough energy for the day ahead. And you can make your muesli even healthier by adding some fruit to it.

Moderator: Great. What else can obese children do to lose weight?

Patrick: Well, sport is very important. In the modern world we don't move as much as we did fifty years ago, because many people have cars and so they don't walk very much. Children often don't do much sport, either. They watch television or play computer games, instead.

Moderator: So, how can we add more sport into our lives?

Patrick: Well, an easy way is to walk or cycle everywhere. Walk to school, walk to the shops. Or take up a sport you enjoy, like dancing. It can be fun to learn something new.

Moderator: Great, thanks Patrick. Those are really useful tips. Now, over to you, what do you think about diet and exercise? Send us an e-mail to …

5. A Long Weekend

(Audiotrack: QR-Code S. 40 / Aufgaben S. 18)

A long weekend was coming and Bob and Brad were thinking about what they could do with all that free time.

Bob: Where should we go this weekend, the weather will be great.

Brad: Well, we could go hiking. We haven't done that for a long time.

Bob imagined himself climbing with a way too heavy backpack, the sun burning down on them. That particular picture didn't excite him much.

Bob: I'd rather we go to the lake. We could have a barbecue and maybe find some girls to chat with.

Brad: That does sound good. Although I don't think Moira would like it, if I chatted up other girls. But maybe she could ask her sister to come along. Then we could go as a foursome. I'm sure that would be fun.

Bob: No, thanks. Neither do I want a blind-date nor am I interested in watching you two flirting with each other the whole time.
Brad: Oh come on, Bob. Don't be like that. You don't have to marry her right away, you know. Lisa is really nice. She could be your type.
Bob: Is she a redhead, too?
Brad: No, she's not. I know you don't like redheads. She's got short black hair and is quite sporty. Let's just try at least. After all, if you don't like it, you can still leave.
Bob: Well okay, you persuaded me. When should I come to pick you up?
Brad: Let's say around three o'clock.

On Saturday Bob had to admit, he was quite impressed with Lisa. She wasn't at all like her sister Moira, who he found a bit boring. Lisa was fun to be with and he was glad he had agreed to come.

Lisa: Hey Bob, you want to come swimming with me? Moira and Brad have been away for a long time. It's about time they remember they're not alone.
Bob: Sure.
Lisa: They are over there in that little boat. Come on we'll swim up to them and turn it over. Surely they need some cooling down by now.
Bob: Good idea. Maybe we'll get something to eat then. I'm starving.

After they tipped over the boat there was a big water fight and later they were so hungry that they prepared the grill and barbecued lots of steaks, burgers and sausages. At the end of the evening as they were driving home they all agreed that it had been a great outing and they really should do it again.

6. Detention[1]

(Audiotrack: QR-Code S. 40 / Aufgaben S. 19)

On a normal Thursday morning Laura and her mum were having breakfast. Laura's brother was asleep, her father was already in the office and Laura was still a bit sleepy. She wasn't very keen on talking, but her mother certainly was. She was practically waiting to bother Laura with her questions.

Mum: Laura, where were you yesterday evening?
Laura: I was at the movies with Sara. I told you that already.

Laura was hoping that her mother wouldn't question her further, but her mum was just getting started.

Mum: No, you were not, your brother saw you at the park hanging around with some guys. Why are you lying?

Laura just rolled her eyes and yawned. She was sixteen and her mother was still treating her like a little child.

Laura: I didn't lie to you. Before going to the cinema with Sara I met with a few friends in the park to get our maths homework. I just didn't tell you that.
Mum: Why didn't Sara give it to you?

Now the one thing Laura had wanted to prevent was happening, her mother was inquiring further and further. There wasn't much she could do but to tell the truth.

Laura: Because we were both at detention[1] when our teacher gave them out.

Shocked her mother just stared. Her daughter in detention, she just couldn't believe it.

Laura: Before you freak, it wasn't that bad really. Sara and I just hid Mr Smith's glasses. And without them he couldn't see so well, which is why he bumped into the shelf where the goldfish bowl was. The bowl fell and broke, the fishes and water were all over the floor and the whole class was laughing. It really was quite funny.

Her mother's shock grew with every word Laura said. She didn't quite know what to say. And so Laura just went on.

Laura: Of course we saved all the fishes and gave Mr Smith his glasses back. But he has no sense of humour whatsoever, and that's why Sara and I got detention.
Mum: I really don't know what to say. You always complain about us not treating you like an adult and then you go and behave like a child. How could you possibly think one can take you seriously? You're grounded for the next week.

[1] detention – das Nachsitzen

Erster Prüfungsteil: Hörverstehen – Leseverstehen

Aus urheberrechtlichen Gründen wurde der Teil Hörverstehen durch gleichwertige Musteraufgaben ersetzt.

1. Hörverstehen Teil 1

Conversation between Tom and Mary
(Audiotrack: QR-Code rechts / Hörtext S. 88)

You are going to hear a conversation between a radio show host and a caller.

- ▶ First read the tasks.
- ▶ Then listen to the conversation.
- ▶ While you are listening, tick the correct box **or** write down the information needed.
- ▶ At the end you will hear the conversation again.
- ▶ Now read the tasks. You have **90 seconds** to do this.

▶ Now listen to the conversation and do the tasks.

1. Tom, the radio show host, ...
a) ☐ remembers the thrilling holiday experience he had in New Zealand last week.
b) ☐ can give his listeners some tips for exciting holidays on the African continent.
c) ☐ tells his listeners where South Africa is located on the African continent.

2. Together with her parents, Mary ...
a) ☐ went to Cape Town during her summer holidays.
b) ☐ went to Cape Town during the South African summer, which was wintertime in Britain.
c) ☐ had a great time on the sandy beaches and in the crystal clear water of the Pacific Ocean.

3. In the hotel ...
a) ☐ Mary met a person from a company offering paragliding flights over Cape Town.
b) ☐ Mary read about a company offering paragliding flights over Cape Town.
c) ☐ Mary saw a paraglider flying past a company building in Cape Town.

4. When paragliding ...
a) ☐ you feel like sailing through the open air without any walls or windows around you.
b) ☐ you can open the windows to let the wind blow right in your face.
c) ☐ you can sail through both air and water.

5. Describe the argument that Mary's father uses to convince her mother that paragliding is not dangerous for Mary.

____

____

____

6. Describe a) why the paragliding flight did not take place on Saturday and b) why it did take place on Sunday.

a) ____

b) ____

7. Which of the following statements best describes Mary's feelings before and during the flight?

a) ☐ She was a bit scared directly before the flight, but as soon as she was in the air, she was really enthusiastic.

b) ☐ She felt uneasy when her feet had lost contact with the rocks, and even after that it took a while for her to relax and enjoy the flight.

c) ☐ From the very first moment she started running towards the cliff until the end of the flight she felt fantastic.

8. Table Mountain ....

a) ☐ is a very famous mountain in South Africa which is about 800 meters high.

b) ☐ is the place where you can buy picture postcards of the most photographed sights in South Africa.

c) ☐ is one of the most famous tourist attractions in South Africa.

After listening to the **whole** interview, complete this task.

9. This interview is about ...

a) ☐ most of the important tourist attractions that South Africa offers.

b) ☐ a teenager's account of a thrilling holiday experience.

c) ☐ the dangers of paragliding.

2. Hörverstehen Teil 2

Wildlife Safari in Africa

(Audiotrack: QR-Code S. 43 / Hörtext S. 89)

You are going to hear a story about a father going to Africa where he participates in a Wildlife Safari.

- ▶ First read the tasks.
- ▶ Then listen to the story.
- ▶ While you are listening, tick the correct box **or** write down the information needed.
- ▶ At the end you will hear the story again.
- ▶ Now read the tasks. You have **90 seconds** to do this.

▶ Now listen to the story and do the tasks.

1. Andrew's dad ...

a) ☐ had always dreamed of going on an 8-week railway trip through South Africa.

b) ☐ was asked to go to Johannesburg on business for 8 weeks including one week of holidays.

c) ☐ had always dreamed of going on a wildlife safari but could not do so because he didn't have the money.

2. Andrew ...

a) ☐ learned about his dad's opinion that wild animals should be observed in nature rather than in zoos.

b) ☐ does not like zoos because the animals are locked up in cages there.

c) ☐ felt bad about his father's plan to go on a safari.

3. The safari group consisted of ...

a) ☐ three men and three women.

b) ☐ two men, two women and Peter, the safari ranger.

c) ☐ four men and two women altogether.

4. Name the kind of animals that Andrew's dad took pictures of a) on the first day of the safari and b) the next few days after the first day.

a) ______________________________

b) ______________________________

5. The safari group ...

a) ☐ were taking photos next to the car, at a distance of about 100 meters from the lion family.

b) ☐ were standing about 100 meters away from the car while taking pictures of the lions.

c) ☐ had to run to the car for about a 100 meters when the male lion had stood up.

6. The lion ...

a) ☐ walked around the car, roared and jumped onto the roof of the car.

b) ☐ walked back to his family after Peter had looked angrily at him through the windscreen.

c) ☐ tried to get inside the car in several ways, but finally he walked back to his family because it was impossible for him to enter the car.

7. When was it possible for Peter to fix the car, and where were the other participants of the safari while Peter was fixing it?

____

____

____

8. Andrew ...

a) ☐ suggested going to the zoo with his dad because he still prefers to see wild animals in cages.

b) ☐ accepted his dad's invitation to go on a safari together in two weeks' time.

c) ☐ found his dad's joke about preferring to see caged animals in a zoo quite amusing.

3. Leseverstehen

New, Multiracial Beginning in Story of "Madam & Eve" John Murphy (Baltimore Sun)

JOHANNESBURG, South Africa – The doorbell rings at the home of Madam Gwen, but Eve, the black maid, refuses to answer it.

Madam reluctantly pulls herself up from the sofa and opens the door. "I don't think I've ever seen you answer the door before," says the startled[1] visitor, a neighbor.

"I wouldn't let Eve have time off to see her Uncle Joe, so now she's getting back at me," says Madam.

"By making you answer the door?"

"Forget about the door. She's protesting by not doing her work. She's on a go-slow."

"A go-slow? How slow is she going to go?"

Eve enters from the kitchen, walking at an exaggeratedly slow pace as if her feet are stuck in glue. She delivers tea to a displeased Madam and her guest.

"Well, at least she made you tea," says the visitor.

"I asked her last night," Madam says wryly[2].

So goes the first episode of "Madam & Eve," a popular South African sitcom to hit television screens.

Based on a popular comic strip of the same name, "Madam & Eve" explores the awkward relationship between a wealthy white woman and her black maid as they try to make their way in post-apartheid South Africa.

Signs of political and social change are everywhere in the new South Africa, but there are few places like television to understand how South Africans see themselves – or would like to see themselves.

Under Apartheid, a show such as "Madam & Eve" would have had no chance of getting on the air.

But since the democratic elections in 1994, television producers are turning to multiracial sitcoms as an entertaining way to deal with the country's uncomfortable past and perhaps show a path to the future.

South Africans want to look at South African life comically. They like to laugh at themselves. But behind the laughter, "Madam & Eve" delivers its share of social commentary.

Sitcoms are allowed to play with cultural stereotypes, such as the rich madam, the poor maid, the old racist Afrikaner and the Zulu grandmother, freeing the show's writers and viewers to explore the contradictions and complexities of South Africa today.

What sets South African television apart from its American and British counterparts is that by law, all shows must include as many of the country's 11 official languages as possible.

To an outsider, it makes for strange, often confusing, viewing. In "Madam & Eve," for instance, Eve speaks Zulu with the family's black gardener but will talk with the Madam in English. Sometimes viewers are provided subtitles; other times, viewers are expected to understand the conversation within context or with repetition.

Some critics view the visual humor – the funny faces, the objects falling on peoples' heads and toes as a way of reaching across a multilingual audience.

Fearing that it would be a dangerous, perhaps revolutionary technology, television was banned by Apartheid leaders until 1976, when the first government-owned station, the South African Broadcasting Corp., went on the air with tightly controlled news, sports and entertainment programs.

Early on, a black person could not appear in the same frame as a white person. Half of the programs were in English and half were in Afrikaans. Native African languages were rarely heard. But over the years, the restrictions were relaxed somewhat as the government launched two more stations broadcasting in black tribal languages.

In 1994, South African television was liberated from its Apartheid restrictions. Viewers now have their choice of the state-run South African Broadcasting Corp.'s three channels with programming in all 11 languages, independent e-TV[3] and several pay channels with home-grown shows. American, British and other foreign imports make up nearly half of all shows on television. Audiences, however, still prefer anything made in South Africa, because the shows reflect their own experiences.

[1] startled – here: confused, surprised
[2] wryly – showing that you are both amused and disappointed or annoyed
[3] e-TV – South Africa's biggest independent TV channel

Adapted from: John Murphy, http://articles.latimes.com/2001/mar/07/entertainment/ca-34178, The Baltimore Sun, March 07, 2001

"Madam & Eve" is based around the theme of a middle-class white woman and her black maid. Theirs is a relationship of friendly quarrelling.

▶ Tick the correct box **and** give evidence from the text.

1. The introductory scene of *Madam & Eve* is funny because ...

a) ☐ the maid is on strike.

b) ☐ a stranger opens the door.

c) ☐ Madam treats her guest rudely.

Evidence from the text: ______________________________

2. The storyline of *Madam & Eve* was invented for a TV series.

This statement is ... ☐ true ☐ false

Evidence from the text: ______________________________

3. TV is seen as a good way to reflect on South African identity.

This statement is ... ☐ true ☐ false

Evidence from the text: ______________________________

4. Today's South African TV productions ...

a) ☐ limit satirical programmes.
b) ☐ treat Apartheid with humor.
c) ☐ favour sensitive over funny broadcasts.

Evidence from the text: ______________________________

5. Shows like *Madam & Eve* work with clichés to help understand South Africa.

This statement is ... ☐ true ☐ false

Evidence from the text: ______________________________

6. South African TV must represent several African languages.

This statement is ... ☐ true ☐ false

Evidence from the text: ______________________________

7. During Apartheid, watching TV was restricted because of ...

a) ☐ poor financial resources.
b) ☐ outdated technical equipment.
c) ☐ concerns about bad influences.

Evidence from the text: ______________________________

8. Discrimination on TV showed in the underrepresentation of ...

a) ☐ black people.
b) ☐ African languages.
c) ☐ native programmes.

Evidence from the text: ______________________________

9. Today, South African viewers give priority to international TV imports.

This statement is ... ☐ true ☐ false

Evidence from the text: ______________________________

Zweiter Prüfungsteil: Wortschatz – Schreiben

4. Wortschatz

"A South African experience"

Michelle Faul and her mixed-race family experienced racist incidents in South Africa in the early 60s, forcing them to leave the country for England. Today Michelle Faul is Chief Africa correspondent for "The Associated Press". She looks back at what life was like in South Africa during Apartheid.

▶ Fill in suitable words or tick the correct box.

1. My widowed mother had driven us from our ______________________________ in Zimbabwe, which was then called Rhodesia, to visit family in her native South Africa.

2. There was racism in Rhodesia, too, but it was nothing like the laws in South Africa that made blacks subhuman because they had to ...

a) ☐ suffer b) ☐ hurt c) ☐ experience d) ☐ feel

in the most horrible ways.

3. We did not take the train because halfway through the trip, passengers would have to get out of the Rhodesian Railway compartment and ______________________________ to old and run-down black-only South African carriages.

4. The car trip presented its own challenges. Hotels ______________________________ only whites and everywhere you could see signs declaring places and facilities "for whites only".

5. Only whites were allowed inside the stores. So we had to carry piles of food and drinks from home because our mother ______________________________ to go to the back door of shops.

6. Being white meant you could live where you wanted. However, ...

a) ☐ circles of b) ☐ crowds of c) ☐ cliques of d) ☐ clouds of

blacks were caged in townships, if they could get jobs in the city.

7. If they didn't get jobs, their urban shacks – poor homes – were ______________________________ so that black South Africans had nowhere to live. They were then moved by force to unproductive "homelands".

8. My experience was more of absurd trivialities of Apartheid, rather than brutal ...

a) ☐ attack b) ☐ strike c) ☐ violence d) ☐ storm

used to uphold it.

9. If you were white, you had ...

a) ☐ access to b) ☐ entrance to c) ☐ arrival to d) ☐ reception to

jobs denied to blacks.

10. The only black professionals were teachers, like my mother, lawyers like Mandela and nurses and doctors, who could only ______________________________ black patients.

11. My mother spoke English. But to guarantee white superiority even at school, black learners should be taught to speak Afrikaans, the ______________________________ of the Apartheid regime.

12. Today, South Africa is a democratic country where everybody has the right to ...

a) ☐ choose b) ☐ elect c) ☐ vote d) ☐ select

so that their voices may be heard.

13. It is a tribute to Mandela's efforts that today, I and others forgive but do not ...

a) ☐ forget. b) ☐ lose. c) ☐ remember. d) ☐ suppress.

The gun by Beverley Naidoo

Esi and his parents are faithful and valued employees at the Mackay game farm[1] at the time of the South African Apartheid regime. When their boss Mackay has to leave one day, he asks his future son-in-law Williams to take charge until Mackay's return.

Early the following afternoon, there was the familiar sound of Mackay's Land Rover entering the camp. Esi saw immediately that it was being driven by the young man Williams – and he was alone. When he jumped down from the driver's seat, he was carrying Mackay's gun. Although he could only be a few years older than Esi, there was something in his manner that reminded Esi of the sneering[2] officer in the Mapoteng[3] attack. His bush-green eyes narrowed on their target.

"What're you staring at? You've seen me before, haven't you? Go get your boss-boy[4] for me. Be quick about it, jong[5]!"

Esi could feel his face going hot, but he turned rapidly and sprinted off. Even Mackay never spoke to him like that, always calling him by his name.

Esi accompanied his father as he walked forward to greet the white man. He wanted to see how Papa would react.

"You remember me? … Boss Williams. Boss Mackay has asked me to come and look after his place, so we better get on, you and me. I don't want any trouble from the other boys either, OK?" He turned to Esi.

"You can get my bags out the back and carry them to my room." Papa simply gave a little nod. It was impossible to tell what he was thinking. His lined face remained quite passive as father and son carried the young white man's cases.

Before long it was clear that Williams assumed Esi to be his personal servant. Up till now Esi had taken instructions either from his father or Mackay, who had known him since he was little. But this man's manner was different. He didn't seem to care at all who Esi was. It was as if he was just a thing to be used.

Much of the time Williams would sit on the veranda outside Mackay's room, legs stretched out on a stool, a can of beer at his side, while cleaning or playing with Mackay's gun.

"Hey, come clean my boots!"

"You can wash the truck now!"

"Make my bed properly, jong! Don't just pull the sheets up like that!"

"Do you call these boots clean? If you were in the army I'd donder[6] you! Do them again!"

"Go call the girl! I want her to do my washing this morning."

At the last order, Esi had to fight to control himself. Who did this man think he was? Didn't he know that "the girl" was Esi's own mother, old enough to be the white man's mother? When Esi found her, busy collecting wild spinach, his anger spilled out. She tried to calm him. His temper would get him into trouble. He should try to be like his father.

"Papa just lets them push him around. I don't want to be like that!"

"Ha! What else can you do my young man?"

And with that his mother began walking slowly, steadily, toward the camp to collect the dirty washing.

[1] game farm – a farm with wild animals
[2] sneering – unpleasant, arrogant
[3] Mapoteng – a South African village
[4] boss-boy – insulting expression for an adult man who is in charge of something
[5] jong – expression from Afrikaans meaning ‚boy'
[6] donder – expression from Afrikaans meaning ‚hit' or ‚bully'

Adapted from: Beverley Naidoo, The Gun, in: Out of Bounds, Penguin Random House Children's Books, 2001

5. Schreiben

- ▶ Read the tasks carefully.
- ▶ Make sure to write about **all** the aspects presented in each task.

1. **Describe** Williams' behaviour towards Esi and his parents and how it compares to that of Boss Mackay.

2. **Explain** how Williams' behaviour is reflected in the language he uses and the reaction it causes in Esi.

3. You have a choice here. Choose **one** of the following tasks.

   a) Esi's mother tolerates Williams' behaviour and states: "What else can you do?" **Comment** on this statement and remember that this story is set during the Apartheid regime.

   or

   b) Esi cannot accept his mother's attitude. When Williams calls Esi again and bosses him around, Esi cannot control himself any longer. **Write down** how the story goes on.

   Include the following aspects:
   - ▶ Esi's reaction
   - ▶ Williams' reaction
   - ▶ the consequences for everybody

Erster Prüfungsteil: Hörverstehen

Aus urheberrechtlichen Gründen wurde der Teil Hörverstehen durch gleichwertige Musteraufgaben ersetzt.

Hörverstehen Teil 1

Graduation Speech

(Audiotrack: QR-Code rechts / Hörtext S. 90)

You are going to hear the speech of a school headmistress at a graduation ceremony.

- ▶ First read the tasks.
- ▶ Then listen to the speech.
- ▶ While you are listening, tick the correct box **or** write down the information needed.
- ▶ At the end you will hear the speech again.
- ▶ Now read the tasks. You have **90 seconds** to do this.

▶ Now listen to the speech and do the tasks.

1. The reason for the meeting in the assembly hall ...

a) ☐ is to celebrate the opening of the recently built Nelson Mandela Memorial School.

b) ☐ is to hand over high school diplomas to 46 students as well as to celebrate their graduation.

c) ☐ is to congratulate 46 young teachers on their successful graduation in their teacher training programme.

2. The headmistress of the school ...

a) ☐ is sure that the students have had both happy and sad times during their 12 years at school.

b) ☐ is proud of being able to offer a broad variety of subjects like Maths and Sciences, History and Geography as well as Language and Arts.

c) ☐ assures the graduates that the mix of joyful and frustrating experiences will end forever as a result of their graduation.

3. The headmistress ...

a) ☐ advises the graduates to keep on studying at university because then their lives will be smooth and joyful journeys.

b) ☐ advises the students not to go on a boat trip when the weather is rough and stormy.

c) ☐ compares people's individual lives to the ups and downs that towns, cities and even whole countries go through as well.

4. Up until more than 25 years ago ...

a) ☐ there was widespread discrimination against black people of South Africa in all spheres of everyday life.

b) ☐ South Africa was a good example of respect people can have for one another in every sphere of everyday life.

c) ☐ South Africa had not yet been in the grip of the horrible system of Apartheid.

5. Name (at least) two things that the headmistress says about Nelson Mandela.

____

____

____

6. Today ...

a) ☐ there is an amazing feeling of hope for a better future throughout South Africa.

b) ☐ there are no more social problems in South Africa because of the progress and improvement the country has achieved in the last 25 years.

c) ☐ South Africa is a better country than it was 25 years ago despite the fact that it still has some social problems.

7. According to Nelson Mandela, what should people never ever lose in their struggles for a better future?

____

____

____

8. The headmistress says ...

a) ☐ that the graduates will definitely make the world a better place, no matter how they will live their lives.

b) ☐ the students have to find their own guiding principles – not the one that Nelson Mandela lived by – in order to make the world a better place.

c) ☐ that it is not important how big an individual's contribution is to making the world a better place.

Hörverstehen Teil 2

Conversation between Rachel and her siblings

(Audiotrack: QR-Code S. 51 / Hörtext S. 90)

You are going to hear a conversation between Rachel and her siblings about Brexit.

- ▶ First read the tasks.
- ▶ Then listen to the conversation.
- ▶ While you are listening, tick the correct box **or** write down the information needed.
- ▶ At the end you will hear the conversation again.
- ▶ Now read the tasks. You have **90 seconds** to do this.

▶ Now listen to the conversation and do the tasks.

1. Rachel's brother Edward ...

a) ☐ likes Mr MacElroy because he is a very modern teacher.

b) ☐ thinks that it is a serious mistake for Britain to leave the EU.

c) ☐ does not share Mr MacElroy's modern political views.

2. After Britain leaves the European Union ...

a) ☐ Ireland will be divided into two parts, namely Northern Ireland and the Republic of Ireland.

b) ☐ Northern Ireland will also have to leave the EU, while the Republic of Ireland will still be a member of the EU.

c) ☐ there will be no more border controls between Northern Ireland and the Republic of Ireland.

3. In 2014 ...

a) ☐ only 55 % of the Scots voted for Scotland's independence from Britain in a referendum.

b) ☐ 45 % of the Scots voted for Scotland's independence from Britain in a referendum.

c) ☐ 55 % of the Scots voted for Brexit.

4. Rachel's sister Linda ...

a) ☐ does not see the connection between Brexit and a possible second referendum about Scotland's independence from Britain.

b) ☐ is unsure about why the majority of Scots voted for independence from Britain in the 2014 referendum.

c) ☐ is unsure about why the majority of Scots should vote for Brexit the next time.

5. According to Rachel ...

a) ☐ England and Wales have always been much less in favour of EU membership than Scotland.

b) ☐ England and Wales have always been much more supportive of EU membership than Scotland.

c) ☐ Scotland will not have to leave the EU after Brexit because it is independent.

6. According to Rachel, why might the majority of Scots vote for Scotland's independence from Britain in a future referendum?

____

____

____

7. Which of the following statements best describes what Rachel tells her brother and her sister about large banks and insurance companies in London?

a) ☐ Some of those banks and insurance companies are currently leaving London or have already left it.

b) ☐ Almost all of those banks and insurance companies have already relocated from London to Frankfurt, Paris or Dublin, for example.

c) ☐ A lot of those banks and insurance companies are thinking about relocating to other parts of Europe, but so far none of them has actually left London.

8. Rachel's brother Edward ...

a) ☐ says that Brexit may cause Britain to lose lots of jobs.

b) ☐ is still proud of his country for showing the rest of Europe that Britain does not need the EU and can manage quite well on its own.

c) ☐ feels that he needs to rethink his view of Brexit after the chat with his sister.

Zweiter Prüfungsteil: Leseverstehen – Wortschatz – Schreiben

Aus urheberrechtlichen Gründen wurde der Teil Leseverstehen durch gleichwertige Musteraufgaben ersetzt.

Leseverstehen

Siku app helps Inuit to survive climate change

TECHNOLOGY • GLOBAL WARMING

As sea ice thins, indigenous[1] Arctic communities are learning to combine traditional knowledge with high tech. By John Bilstein

1 MORE PEOPLE are falling through thinning ice in the Arctic. There are no statistics available on the subject, but last year there were at least five such incidents in Alaska alone, according to Vice Media. Most of the victims are members of the Inuit community, whose ancestors[2] have lived and worked in the region for thousands of years. Inuit know more about how to move safely on the ice in the Arctic than anyone else. But their tradition, which relies on collective knowledge gathered over many centuries, is being challenged by rapid climate change.

2 With the Arctic warming at twice the rate of other parts of the world, a new app called Siku is proving to be a lifeline[3] for local communities. Under normal conditions, the sea ice off Alaska and Canada is strong enough to support snowmobiles and even trucks from October through April, but in recent years it has become more dangerous. Melting ice leads to more moisture in the air, which in turn generates more wind, rain and snow. These changes are also affecting the land itself, which is no longer protected by ice sheets and permafrost. Snowmobiles and other pieces of heavy equipment can fall through the surface, sometimes with passengers inside.

3 The Siku app, named after one of many Inuit words for sea ice, was developed with support from the Arctic Eider Society[4]. The multimedia platform combines ancient Inuit know-how, GPS data, and modern weather forecasting to give users up-to-the-minute information about ice safety. Ice conditions can be loaded on Siku's GPS atlas in the form of tags which can be viewed by area. Users can also upload their own videos and messages to exchange news, like where hunters can find walrus, seals and whales. Such animals have provided the Inuit with food as well as raw materials to make clothes, tents and kayaks for millenia. But climate change has also affected the Inuit hunting tradition.

4 The animals that the Inuit normally hunt need the ice and cold conditions to survive. Due to global warming, those animals are now migrating to new areas. Walrus have moved hundreds of miles away, and seals and narwhal are all changing their habits. It is hoped that the Siku app will make it easier for the Inuit to hunt in places unfamiliar to them because the safe areas are clearly marked on Siku's GPS maps.

5 One traditional aspect of Inuit culture is making a comeback because of climate change though: the dog sled[5]. Because of the new conditions, modern vehicles and snowmobiles often cannot be used. Many Inuit have gone back to using dog sleds not only because this traditional mode of transport is much lighter, but also because dogs are good at sensing danger.

[1] indigenous – people have always been in the place where they are
[2] ancestors – a member of a family/group who lived long time ago
[3] lifeline – a rope that is thrown to someone in the water who is in danger; here: a way to getting help to lead your life in a satisfactory way
[4] society – a large group of people who live together in an organized way
[5] sled – a small vehicle sliding over snow; here: pulled by dogs

Adapted from: Read On, Februar 2020, Carl Ed. Schünemann KG

Bild-Quelle: © Tyler Olson – stock.adobe.com

Rules of Conduct for Visitors of the Arctic

1. Respect the Arctic! Protect this fragile habitat and do not pollute the environment or damage the vegetation.
2. Do not fish or hunt endangered animals or buy products made of them.
3. Prefer non-motorised means of transport, or, even better, walk.
4. Respect potentially dangerous arctic species like polar bears, walrus or muskox. Keep your distance from them.
5. Do not treat sled dogs as pets and do not feed them.
6. Always use the right equipment, especially with regard to changing weather conditions.
7. As a visitor, you are a guest of the Arctic. Therefore, respect local culture and people.

You are doing some research for a school paper on *"Climate Change in the Arctic"*. You have come across the article *"Siku app helps Inuit to survive climate change"* and want to present the main points.

▶ Tick the correct box and give **one** piece of evidence from the text.

1. Last year,

a) ☐ many Inuit left the Arctic due to the thinning ice.
b) ☐ people fell through the thinning ice at least five times.
c) ☐ the thinning ice was no problem for the Inuit, who know how to move safely on the ice.

One piece of evidence from the text: ______________________________

2. The Inuit in the Arctic region

a) ☐ face many problems due to climate change.
b) ☐ have no idea how to cope with climate change.
c) ☐ asked Alaska's governor for help.

One piece of evidence from the text: ______________________________

3. In order to help the Inuit, the Arctic Eider Society engaged in developing an app.

This statement is … ☐ true ☐ false

One piece of evidence from the text: ______________________________

4. The Siku app

a) ☐ is a multimedia platform which combines ancient Inuit know-how and modern technology.
b) ☐ was only developed for hunting walrus, seals and whales.
c) ☐ is named after the Inuit word for climate.

One piece of evidence from the text: ______________________________

5. The Inuit have been living and working in the Arctic for only several hundreds of years.

This statement is … ☐ true ☐ false

One piece of evidence from the text: ______________________________

6. Thanks to the Siku app, the Inuit now are enabled to better cope with changing ice conditions.

This statement is … ☐ true ☐ false

One piece of evidence from the text: ______________________________

7. The climate change

a) ☐ prevents the Inuit from further using dog sleds.
b) ☐ forces the Inuit to use modern vehicles such as snowmobiles.
c) ☐ has revived the Inuit tradition of dog sleds.

One piece of evidence from the text: ______________________________

8. Your big dream is to travel to the Arctic one day. Visitors of the Arctic are requested to follow some rules of conduct.

▶ Match the titles (A – G) to the 7 rules of conduct from the text. There is one more title than you need.

	Title	rule of conduct
0	**Example: Experience of dangerous species only from a distance**	**4**
A	Respectful behaviour towards the inhabitants of the Arctic	
B	Rough weather demands suitable equipent	
C	Environment-friendly transport means are to be preferred	
D	Sled dogs are no cute pets	
E	No pollution of the Arctic environment	
F	Hiking – only in groups	
G	Protection of animals facing extinction	

Wortschatz

The Rights of the Child

All children have the same rights. These rights are listed in the UN "Convention on the Rights of the Child". It is very important that each child knows about his or her rights, so have a look below.

▶ Fill in suitable words **or** tick the correct box.

1. As you grow up, you have more responsibility to make …

a) ☐ options b) ☐ choices c) ☐ opportunities d) ☐ selections

and exercise your rights.

Here are some excerpts from the UN Convention:

2. All children under 18 have these rights. No child should be treated ______________________________, no matter who they are, where they live or whether they are a boy or a girl.

3. All adults should do what is best for you. When adults make decisions, they should think about how their decisions will …

a) ☐ affect children. b) ☐ look after children.

c) ☐ care for children. d) ☐ see after children.

4. The government has the ______________________________ to make sure your rights are protected.

5. You have the right to have a name. Your name should be …

a) ☐ proudly b) ☐ sensibly c) ☐ secretly d) ☐ officially

recognized by the government.

6. You have the right to find out things and share what you think with others, by talking, drawing, writing or in any other way unless it harms or ______________________________ other people.

7. You have the right to the best care possible, to drink safe water, to eat …

a) ☐ fast b) ☐ modified c) ☐ healthy d) ☐ low-calorie

food, a clean and safe environment, and information to help you stay well.

8. You have the right to a good education. You should be ______________________________ to go to a school and learn.

9. Your education should help you discover and develop your talents and …

a) ☐ certificates. b) ☐ abilities. c) ☐ subjects. d) ☐ grades.

10. You have the right to express your ______________________________: say what you think! Adults should listen to you and take you seriously.

11. You have the right to protection from any kind of ______________________________.
Nobody has the right to act against your will.

12. You have the right to legal …

a) ☐ organisations b) ☐ consequences
c) ☐ development d) ☐ help

and fair treatment in the justice system that respects your rights.

13. You have the right to know your rights! Adults should know about these rights and help you to ______________________________ about them too, so that you are well informed.

First earning extract from *No turning back* by Beverley Naidoo

Sipho is a 12-year-old black South African boy who runs away from home and now lives on the streets in Hillbrow, a poor neighbourhood of Johannesburg, South Africa.

A few of his new friends, all homeless like himself, were hanging out near the supermarket. When someone came out of the shop, each boy held out an open hand. Another boy was pushing a trolley and another was loading boxes into a car.

Sipho's new friend Jabu led the way inside the supermarket.

"Sometimes security people chase us like dogs. But other times they let us right in."

He took Sipho towards a till[1]. "Watch me," he whispered.

There were packers helping the customers load their trolleys at the tills. A lady was ready to leave and Jabu moved forward.

"Ma'am?" he offered, putting a hand out towards the trolley.

The lady shook her head with a frown[2], almost hitting him with the trolley. Jabu jumped back. A man was next in the queue. Sipho thought he too would send Jabu away, but instead he let the boy take the trolley from him and push it out. Jabu winked[3] across at Sipho as he left.

Sipho stood back for a minute, looking into the shop. Here were white people, black people, everybody. It was like that outside but suddenly, inside the shop, he noticed it more. In the township there were very few white people.

At one of the tills, a small boy was crying to his mother that he wanted 'sweeties'.

"Still here?" Jabu was back already. "You have to move quickly if you want a job", he said.

Jabu kept his eyes on the tills and soon enough he was again in charge of a trolley. Sipho gave himself a little shake, now ready to follow Jabu's example. The lady with the little boy was paying and about to leave. The child had slipped through the tills and was beginning to run around.

"Robbie! Come back here!" his mother called angrily.

But the little boy took no notice and as the mother let go of the trolley to get him by the hand, Sipho stepped forward to take hold of the trolley.

"All right! You can take it to the car for me," said the woman.

"I want to push the trolley!" cried the little boy.

Sipho had to smile as the child tried to reach the handlebar. He pushed the trolley slowly so the little boy didn't trip over. When they reached the car, Sipho helped unload the shopping, then stood waiting by the trolley as the mother put the child into the car. With her back to Sipho, she looked in her bag before turning around and holding out a twenty-cent coin.

"You were very helpful," she said with a smile.

Sipho shyly murmured his thanks as she dropped the coin into his open hand. It wouldn't buy much but it was the first coin he had earned in Hillbrow. He was learning fast. He didn't wait to see the car drive off, but quickly pushed the trolley back down the hill, ready to find another customer.

[1] till – a cash desk in a supermarket
[2] a frown – a look of dislike
[3] to wink at somebody – to quickly close and open one's eye

Adapted from: Beverley Naidoo, No turning back, Penguin Books London, 2016

Schreiben

- ▶ Read the tasks carefully.
- ▶ Make sure to write about **all** the aspects presented in each task.

1. **Describe** the situation Sipho is in and how he deals with it one day.

2. **Explain** how Sipho's behaviour changes in this situation and what it tells you about him.

3. You have a choice here. Choose **one** of the following tasks.

   a) The UN Convention on the Rights of the Child says that *"all children have the right to care and protection, no matter who they are and where they live"*.

   Comment on this right.

   Also include your thoughts on …
   - ▶ Sipho's situation as a homeless black child,
   - ▶ why support from adults is or is not important for young people.

   or

   b) At the end of an exciting day, Sipho settles down in the evening and thinks about what he has experienced that day. Imagine you are Sipho.

   Write Sipho's **diary entry**.

   Include …
   - ▶ his feelings and thoughts about living on the street and earning money,
   - ▶ his relationship with Jabu,
   - ▶ his aims / wishes for the next day.

Erster Prüfungsteil: Hörverstehen

Aus urheberrechtlichen Gründen wurde der Teil Hörverstehen durch gleichwertige Musteraufgaben ersetzt.

Hörverstehen Teil 1

The Presentation

(Audiotrack: QR-Code rechts / Hörtext S. 91)

You are going to hear a pupil speaking about a presentation for English.

- ▶ First read the tasks.
- ▶ Then listen to the story.
- ▶ While you are listening, tick the correct box **or** write down the information needed.
- ▶ At the end you will hear the story again.
- ▶ Now read the tasks. You have **90 seconds** to do this.

▶ Now listen to the story and do the tasks.

1. The narrator ...

a) ☐ advised his student to give a presentation in class to avoid getting a bad mark in English.
b) ☐ was given a chance by his teacher to avoid a very bad final mark by preparing an oral presentation in class.
c) ☐ hated his English teacher Mr Harris because his presentations were so boring.

2. The narrator ...

a) ☐ was not thrilled by the topic of his presentation at first, but the longer he researched it the more he began to like it.
b) ☐ was forced by Mr Harris to collect information for his presentation.
c) ☐ gradually realised that the websites focussing on his topic were all boring.

3. According to the narrator ...

a) ☐ William Shakespeare is a boring old writer.
b) ☐ a lot of Shakespeare's plays contain thrilling events as well as spooky creatures and characters.
c) ☐ he did not enjoy reading passages of Shakespeare's plays at all due to the old language the writer uses.

4. Name (at least) three elements that are typical of Gothic novels.

____

____

____

5. Frankenstein ...

a) ☐ is a spooky and brutal monster that was created from dead body parts.
b) ☐ is the title of a famous Gothic novel written by Bram Stoker in the 19th century.
c) ☐ is the name of a character in a novel written by Mary Shelley.

6. The Harry Potter novels ...

a) ☐ are full of typical elements of a Gothic novel, namely spookiness and mystery.

b) ☐ were written way back in the past.

c) ☐ are set in the late 20th century and early 21st century.

7. The narrator describes some elements of the spooky setting in the Harry Potter novels. Give (at least) two examples of those elements.

____

____

8. The next day ...

a) ☐ the narrator is going to actively participate in his English class by listening to, and replying to, as many of his teacher's questions as possible.

b) ☐ the narrator might be able to frighten both his teacher and his classmates with the help of his presentation.

c) ☐ the narrator will continue to prepare his presentation so that some time next week he will be able to give the best presentation his teacher and his classmates have ever seen or listened to.

Hörverstehen Teil 2

Interview in Cape Town

(Audiotrack: QR-Code S. 59 / Hörtext S. 92)

You are going to hear an interview by a British travel company in Cape Town.

- ▶ First read the tasks.
- ▶ Then listen to the interview.
- ▶ While you are listening, tick the correct box **or** write down the information needed.
- ▶ At the end you will hear the interview again.
- ▶ Now read the tasks. You have **90 seconds** to do this.

- ▶ Now listen to the interview and do the tasks.

1. The new advertising campaign of the British travel company ...

a) ☐ is meant to make Britain a more attractive destination for South African tourists.

b) ☐ includes video clips of the streets in Cape Town.

c) ☐ is intended to make the company more profitable in the future.

2. Julia says ...

a) ☐ that there are more gorges in Cape Town than in many other parts of the country.

b) ☐ that you can see quite a large variety of wild animals in South Africa without having to go to a zoo.

c) ☐ that lions, giraffes, elephants and other wild animals in South Africa have very natural habits.

3. Allison ...
a) ☐ describes some examples of South Africa's gorgeous sea life and hiking trails.
b) ☐ disagrees with Julia, arguing that South Africa's beaches and wildlife are by far not as beautiful and stunning as its sea life and hiking trails.
c) ☐ says people living along the coastline of South Africa are often amazingly rich.

4. Name two species of South Africa's amazing sea life and two breathtaking landscapes with hiking trails in South Africa.

____

____

5. After listening to Julia and Allison the interviewer ...
a) ☐ says that both the British viewers and he himself have a huge appetite and would therefore really like to eat something.
b) ☐ says that both the British viewers and he himself would now like to watch the video clip.
c) ☐ expresses his gratitude to the two young ladies and says goodbye to them.

6. The gentleman in the grey business suit ...
a) ☐ takes pride in sharing his first name with Nelson Mandela.
b) ☐ is Nelson Mandela, the famous South African national hero.
c) ☐ is in a hurry because he is on his way to his lawyer.

7. What does Nelson say about the diversity of black Africans, the largest section of South Africa's population?

____

____

8. Which of the following statements best describes what Nelson says about all those other groups of the population in South Africa which are not black Africans?
a) ☐ They are descendants of the first settlers who colonised the country.
b) ☐ They have European, Asian or mixed ethnic roots.
c) ☐ They are descendants of migrants who came to South Africa as cheap labour in the 19th century.

Zweiter Prüfungsteil: Leseverstehen – Wortschatz – Schreiben

Leseverstehen

Please, Sir – sit! The story of a learning support dog

More and more schools now employ furry little helpers.

When rubbish at Huntington School in York got out of control recently, staff managed to solve the problem pretty much overnight – not by replacing detentions with collecting rubbish, but by employing their newest, cuddliest colleague: Rolo, the school dog.

They made a short video for assembly, showing what a state the schoolyard was in. “Rubbish, isn't it?” was the headline, followed by: “Do you know what would be really rubbish? If Rolo had to leave because of rubbish.” This clever tactic of emotional blackmail[1] pictured the five-month-old, chocolate-brown Labrador. He was chewing on a plastic bottle and sniffing other rubbish in the schoolyard, while looking up into the camera with big brown eyes.

“The effect was incredible,” says the headteacher, John Tomsett. Within a week of ‘Operation Rolo Says No’, the school grounds were spotless, as the 1,500 students had worked together to clean it up.

Just as a flag is raised when the Queen is at Buckingham Palace, a sign on top of one of the bookshelves in the school library shows when the puppy is at school. The words ‘Rolo is in’ create a lot of excitement among pupils who would never normally be seen in the library. “People stand in a queue to see him – he's like a celebrity,” says Abbie Watson, 13. He has his own name tag, ‘Mr Rolo’, just like any other member of the staff.

Rolo's job title is “learning support dog” – a phenomenon which can be found more and more in modern classrooms, states Tracey Berridge of the charity *Dogs Helping Kids (DHK)*, which trains school dogs. “In the last two or three years the number of dogs in schools has exploded in a really big way,” she says.

Tracey Berridge is convinced of the benefits for pupils, but she is worried that too many dogs are unprepared for classroom life and have no proper training. “It is not right for all dogs,” she warns.

“There are probably hundreds and hundreds of dogs in schools across the country now, many not properly trained.”

The *Department for Education* has no idea how many dogs are currently working in classrooms and does not require schools to register or train their animals.

Classroom dogs not only improve pupils' reading and writing skills, but also have a calming effect, *DHK* claims – something headmaster Tomsett says is true. Sometimes Rolo follows Tomsett to small classes, and Tomsett settles him in a corner on his blanket. “He's fabulous. He just goes to sleep and the children don't want to wake him so they are really quiet,” he says.

Rolo is learning how to become a “listening dog” who will help children read aloud more confidently.

He will put his head on their knees and listen without judgement, encouraging them to turn a page.

[1] blackmail – the act of putting pressure on a person

Quelle: Helen Pidd, The Guardian, https://www.theguardian.com/education/2017/mar/28/teaching-support-dog-school-teach-read, 28.03.2017

Bildquelle: Robert Bosch Stiftung, © dpa, picture alliance / Robert Bosch Stiftung/dpa

Your British partner school employs a dog to create a better learning environment. You really like this idea and want to convince the school community to introduce a school dog programme at your school, too. The following text provides you with the necessary background information.

▶ Tick the correct box **and** give evidence from the text by quoting short passages from the text.

1. Thanks to Rolo, a difficult school situation could be stopped very quickly.

This statement is … ☐ true ☐ false

One piece of evidence from the text: ______________________________

2. Rolo raised the pupils' awareness of the situation because he …

a) ☐ had to leave to stay safe.

b) ☐ swallowed trash and became ill.

c) ☐ made them feel badly about their behaviour.

One piece of evidence from the text: ______________________________

3. Rolo managed to create a feeling of common responsibility among the pupils.

This statement is … ☐ true ☐ false

One piece of evidence from the text: ____________________

4. Rolo's presence at school is …

a) ☐ indicated by a notice.
b) ☐ announced in advance.
c) ☐ organised by fixed schedules.

One piece of evidence from the text: ____________________

5. Rolo hasn't become a real part of the educational team yet.

This statement is … ☐ true ☐ false

One piece of evidence from the text: ____________________

6. Having a dog at school is ...

a) ☐ a recent trend in the UK.
b) ☐ still an exception in the UK.
c) ☐ usually forbidden in the UK.

One piece of evidence from the text: ____________________

7. Dog trainers are concerned about …

a) ☐ the dogs' well-being.
b) ☐ the pupils' behaviour.
c) ☐ the teachers' qualifications.

One piece of evidence from the text: ____________________

8. The ministry is observing the school dog situation very closely.

This statement is … ☐ true ☐ false

One piece of evidence from the text: ____________________

9. School dogs encourage an atmosphere of silence during lessons.

This statement is … ☐ true ☐ false

One piece of evidence from the text: ____________________

10. School dogs help pupils to ...

a) ☐ make friends.
b) ☐ accept criticism.
c) ☐ believe in their abilities.

One piece of evidence from the text: ____________________

Wortschatz

The British school system

Spending some time in a school in the UK is a once-in-a-lifetime experience and guarantees life-long memories. Check out this basic information on the British school system.

▶ Fill in suitable words **or** tick the correct box.
▶ Give only one solution.

1. Children's education in the UK is normally …

a) ☐ isolated into
b) ☐ divided into
c) ☐ segregated into
d) ☐ cut into

two separate stages: primary education at the age of five, and secondary school where they stay until they reach sixteen, seventeen or eighteen years of age.

2. In the UK, 93 % of children in England and Wales ______________________ "state schools". Although state schools are free, parents are expected to pay for their child's school uniform and items of sports wear.

3. Schools in the UK are almost always …

a) ☐ diverse,
b) ☐ varied,
c) ☐ different,
d) ☐ mixed,

i.e. for both girls and boys.

4. Nearly 88 % of secondary school pupils in the UK go to comprehensive schools, as do all pupils in Wales. These take children of all …

a) ☐ abilities
b) ☐ skills
c) ☐ know-how
d) ☐ gifts

and provide a wide range of secondary education.

5. Grammar schools are …

a) ☐ open
b) ☐ free
c) ☐ selective
d) ☐ undemanding

and only take the best-qualified pupils in their academically oriented education.

6. This is why entrance is based on a/an ______________________ to find out if the children are up to the standards the schools expect. It's called CE, the Common Entrance.

7. Children have to ______________________ the Common Entrance (CE) at the age of 11 (girls) or 13 (boys). Without it pupils don't get accepted.

8. Most schools in England require uniforms. The British government believes that uniforms play an important role in supporting the school's …

a) ☐ identity.
b) ☐ character.
c) ☐ recognition.
d) ☐ identification.

9. However, there are many ______________________________ for school uniforms. They must be fair for both genders, available at a reasonably low cost, and respect religious freedoms (such as wearing a turban).

10. Most secondary schools in the UK …

a) ☐ work from
b) ☐ run from
c) ☐ continue from
d) ☐ go on from

8.30 a.m. to 3.30 p.m., Monday through Friday.

11. Most teachers in British schools offer time before or after school when students can ask questions or ______________________________ extra help.

12. Almost all British secondary schools offer a wide range of ______________________________ including sport teams, music and art clubs, cultural clubs, and academic groups.

13. In addition, most secondary schools have many artistic programmes including music, dance, theatre, and visual arts that students can …

a) ☐ carry out.
b) ☐ complete.
c) ☐ exercise.
d) ☐ participate in.

14. In the UK, PE is ______________________________ for all students until the age of sixteen, after which time they can quit. Sports culture is very strong in boarding and independent schools in the UK.

Schreiben

Jessica's speech extract from *Separation* by Babette Brown

In the early 1990s, 15-year-old Jessica is sent to live with her granny in London by her parents because of the situation in Cape Town, South Africa. There is a lot of violence between anti-apartheid activists and supporters of the regime.

"Jessica. Mr Herbert wants to see you right away."

With everyone staring at me, I rushed from the room. Mr Herbert was the principal and only called people to his office if they'd done something really bad.

I knocked at the door.

"Come in."

"You wanted to see me, Sir?"

"Yes. Sit down, relax, no need to look like a frightened rabbit. I'm going to ask you to do me a favour."

How weird was that? What could he possibly want me to do?

"I would like the pupils in this school to have the opportunity to hear about South Africa from somebody who has lived there. At next Friday's assembly I was wondering if you would tell them about what's happening to your friends."

I wouldn't know what to say, I'd never done anything like it in my life. I was going to refuse, when a thought hit me: Ben and Daisy would want me to do it.

"Sounds really scary, but I'll have a go."

The time flew by. I was scared, but I'd thought a lot about what I was going to say. It would be good to get it over with.

Mr Herbert invited me to come on to the platform and introduced me. Hundreds of eyes looked up expectantly. My heart thundered, my legs shook and my mind went blank[1]. Words tumbled out of my mouth.

"One of the hardest things about leaving South Africa was leaving my best friend, Daisy, and the love of my life, Ben. We didn't even get the chance to say goodbye. He's in prison, in solitary confinement which means he's all alone in a very small and empty cell."

A shocked murmur echoed around the hall. "I have no idea where Daisy is because she's in hiding. The cops want to arrest her not because she's stolen anything, hurt anyone, been in a fight or anything like that. Her "crime" and Ben's is that they, like millions of others, want to get rid of[2] the government and its apartheid laws. Because of these laws Daisy and I have never travelled together on a bus, tram or train. We've never been to a cinema, theatre, pub, restaurant, café, or park. Do you know why? All those places, and many others, are for whites only and Daisy's black."

My words provoked gasps[3] and shaking heads. "Ben and I are white. Our comfortable homes are in tree-lined suburbs; all our neighbours are white. I visited the township where Daisy and hundreds of black families are forced to live. They don't have running water or electricity in their homes.

On my first day at this school, I was really surprised. Black and white pupils in the same class! It couldn't happen in South Africa, but Daisy and Ben are hoping it will one day. The good news is that we can do something to help it happen. The black people in South Africa are asking us and our parents, family and friends, to stop buying fruit, cigarettes, wine, anything that is grown or made in South Africa. If people in this country and in lots of other countries boycott South African goods, we will all be helping to get rid of apartheid sooner rather than later."

Dead silence and then a loud burst of applause. A smiling Mr Herbert came over and congratulated me. "Thank you Jessica. I think I speak for everyone in this hall when I say you have given us a most interesting and moving account of what is happening to your friends and others in apartheid South Africa."

Turning to face the rest of the school he said, "I want you all to remember what Jessica told us about the boycott." More supportive clapping. I returned to my seat feeling rather pleased with myself.

[1] to go blank – to be suddenly unable to think
[2] to get rid of sth – to make yourself free of sth that you do not want
[3] a gasp – a quick deep breath, usually caused by a strong emotion

- ▶ Read the tasks carefully.
- ▶ Make sure to write about **all** the aspects presented in each task.

1. **Summarize** what you get to know about Jessica's life and the political situation in South Africa.

2. **Explain** what you get to know about Jessica's character. Look at her behaviour and her relationship to her friends.

3. You have a choice here. Choose **one** of the following tasks.

a) The text is an extract from the book *Separation* by Babette Brown.

Comment on why the title *Separation* fits.

Base your comment on the following questions:
- ▶ Who is separated from whom in the text?
- ▶ Why are these people separated?
- ▶ Why do you think the author has chosen this title?

or

b) Back in the classroom, Jessica is surrounded by her classmates.
Write the **continuation** of the story.

Include …
- ▶ how the classmates behave towards Jessica after her speech,
- ▶ their ideas to raise awareness about apartheid,
- ▶ what they want to do to fight apartheid,
- ▶ how Jessica experiences the situation.

Start like this: *I was really surprised – everybody …*

Erster Prüfungsteil: Hörverstehen

Aus urheberrechtlichen Gründen wurde der Teil Hörverstehen durch gleichwertige Musteraufgaben ersetzt.

Hörverstehen Teil 1

Teil 1: Radio Podcast "Pros and cons of living in Dublin"
(Audiotrack: QR-Code rechts / Hörtext S. 93)

You are going to hear a podcast about living in Dublin.

- ▶ First read the tasks.
- ▶ Then listen to the story.
- ▶ While you are listening, tick the correct box **or** write down the information needed.
- ▶ At the end you will hear the story again.
- ▶ Now read the tasks. You have **90 seconds** to do this.

- ▶ Now listen to the story and do the tasks.

1. Holly ...
a) ☐ comes from a small town called Trinity.
b) ☐ is happy to live in a big city now.
c) ☐ thinks that the countryside on the west coast of Ireland is absolutely boring.

2. According to Holly, the west of Ireland primarily consists of three things. Name these three things.

____

____

3. Trinity College ...
a) ☐ is a very important tourist attraction in Dublin.
b) ☐ is a place in Dublin where a lot of priests live.
c) ☐ is one of the most beautiful summer camps in Europe.

4. Holly ...
a) ☐ was unhappy because she had nowhere to live in the middle of her teenage years.
b) ☐ would have liked to have more opportunities of going to Irish folk music concerts when she was a teenager.
c) ☐ was taken to a lot of concerts by her father, who played in an Irish folk music band.

5. What makes the music scene in Dublin so fascinating? Name (at least) two details.

____

____

6. Adam ...
a) ☐ argues that driving children to school and collecting them again in the afternoon is very time-consuming for parents in Dublin.
b) ☐ thinks that most schools in Dublin are not good at all.
c) ☐ is happy that his daughter can cycle to her school.

7. Jennifer, the show host, ...
a) ☐ does not share Adam's opinion about traffic in Dublin.
b) ☐ thinks that there are too many terrible accidents in the city centre.
c) ☐ is happy that she can use public transport to get to work.

8. Adam and his wife ...
a) ☐ are happy that they both have good jobs so that they can afford two kids and two cars.
b) ☐ believe that moving to a small town would make life affordable for them again.
c) ☐ are thinking of moving to a small town to be able to meet each other again more often.

Hörverstehen Teil 2

Teil 2: Martha's Audio File

(Audiotrack: QR-Code S. 67 / Hörtext S. 94)

You are going to hear a pupil speaking about her experiences with the British.

- ▶ First read the tasks.
- ▶ Then listen to the story.
- ▶ While you are listening, tick the correct box **or** write down the information needed.
- ▶ At the end you will hear the story again.
- ▶ Now read the tasks. You have **90 seconds** to do this.

- ▶ Now listen to the story and do the tasks.

1. Martha ...
a) ☐ has changed her opinion about school uniform during her stay in Leeds.
b) ☐ argues that students at German schools do not try to outdress anybody else.
c) ☐ does not believe that school uniform creates a sense of togetherness, identity and team spirit.

2. Martha ...
a) ☐ has noticed that the British often apologise in a wrong and inappropriate way.
b) ☐ dropped all the things she was carrying when she bumped into Mr Hopkins.
c) ☐ is convinced that she would not have been given an apology after bumping into a teacher in Germany.

3. What Martha finds really surprising about the British is the fact that ...
a) ☐ they queue almost everywhere except for bus stops and tube stations.
b) ☐ they tend to form a queue everywhere and usually stay very calm and friendly in it.
c) ☐ they have a quick chat everywhere: at bus stops, in tube stations and in front of shops etc.

4. During Martha's stay in her British host family ...
a) ☐ she was recommended to drink tea unless told otherwise.
b) ☐ she was offered tea both before and after school by her host parents.
c) ☐ she was given a lot of tasks by either of her host parents.

5. Describe the different kinds of tea the British drink in the morning and in the afternoon.

____

____

6. In Britain ...

a) ☐ people often have long discussions about whether or not to pour milk into a cup of tea.

b) ☐ it is quite common for people to say that they do not like Chinese tea.

c) ☐ the significance of tea in everyday life is illustrated by a number of English phrases which include the word tea.

7. According to Martha, ...

a) ☐ the weather is a topic that you can hear British people talk about very often.

b) ☐ in Britain it rains almost anywhere and in any situation imaginable.

c) ☐ in Britain people often arrange a meeting at a bus stop to talk about the weather.

8. Describe different weather conditions one can often experience in Britain within a couple of hours. Name (at least) three of those conditions.

___

___

Zweiter Prüfungsteil: Leseverstehen – Wortschatz – Schreiben

Leseverstehen

The family that is enough by Juliet Rix

"If you want to hang out with my brothers you have to be in top form or you'll be destroyed," says Eoin (pronounced 'Owen') Colfer, the second of five boys and author of the hugely successful *Artemis Fowl* books (often described as James Bond with fairies). His relationship with his brothers, he believes, explains the quick, dry humour in his books. His writing style has put his books at the top of many bestseller lists, and so Eoin, who used to work as an Irish primary school teacher, became an international celebrity.

Born in 1965, Eoin grew up in the seaside town of Wexford, Ireland. The household was large, loving and loud. Eoin's father used to take his sons on historical trips. "To keep us from fighting, my dad would tell us all stories about fairies and dragons. He had to keep going because whenever he stopped, me and my brothers were at each other's throats[1]."

Eoin loved comic books, invented his own characters and drew and wrote his own comics when he was young. His interest in writing continued as a love of drama: He used to help his mother (a drama teacher and local actress), learned her lines with her and had parts in Wexford Opera Festival productions.

It is perhaps not surprising that when Eoin started to write books, his brothers became the characters. All five boys are part of the story. In the second *Artemis Fowl* book, four goblins[2] have a fight. Their names are almost identical to those of Eoin's brothers.

Eoin had written three other children's books while teaching at the local primary school in Wexford. He thought that his *Artemis* books would also become successful but only in Ireland. But when his wife Jackie read the manuscript, she knew it was different. She asked Eoin's brothers to take him to a pub and make him promise to get an agent[3]. Convincing their brother was really difficult, but it paid off.

The money was not as big as has been reported, but fame came fast and bigger money followed later. Didn't that change things? "Not as much as you would expect," says Eoin. In Ireland everyone is a writer and people in Wexford aren't interested in wealth and fame: "They've known me for decades, so they don't care." The brothers keep his feet on the ground too, Eoin adds.

Colfer's kids have changed his writing. "My son Finn, for example, is very funny," says Eoin. "He comes up with some great funny remarks and I get a lot of material straight from him." When Finn argues in the back of the car, Eoin doesn't tell stories to stop him. Instead, he tries to remember it for his books.

The realisation that his children would one day read his books also made him think about the violence. "There is a huge fight in the first book. I decided there was no need for that really … Now there are struggles but not much actual violence." The amorality[4] of his hero – the criminal boy *Artemis Fowl* – worried the new father in him too. Over the next four books, *Artemis* develops a feeling for right and wrong. "I don't know how much longer he will stay interesting as a character," admits Eoin. "Once he turns completely good, that's it."

[1] to be at each other's throat – to argue angrily
[2] goblin – a small scary, fantastical creature
[3] agent – *here:* a person who is paid to advertise and sell someone's books
[4] amorality – a lack of moral principles

The Guardian https://www.theguardian.com/lifeandstyle/2006/oct/14/familyandrelationships.booksforchildrenandteenagers

You are doing a reading project in your English class. All the students have to present a famous English-speaking author who writes books for young adults. You have come across Irish author Eoin Colfer, creator of the famous Artemis Fowl *books. Who is this man? Find out more about him in the online article.*

▶ Tick the correct box **and** give evidence from the text by quoting short passages from the text.

1. Eoin Colfer grew up as an only child.

This statement is … ☐ true ☐ false

One piece of evidence from the text: ______________________________

2. Colfer's way of writing is influenced by his …

a) ☐ family.
b) ☐ former job.
c) ☐ favourite book.

One piece of evidence from the text: ______________________________

3. Colfer grew up in a household with …
a) ☐ peace and quiet.
b) ☐ little entertainment.
c) ☐ lots of fantastic tales.
One piece of evidence from the text: ______________________________

4. Growing up, Colfer showed little creative talent.
This statement is … ☐ true ☐ false
One piece of evidence from the text: ______________________________

5. Figures in the *Artemis Fowl* books are based on family members.
This statement is … ☐ true ☐ false
One piece of evidence from the text: ______________________________

6. When Colfer wrote the *Artemis Fowl* books he …
a) ☐ kept them secret from his family.
b) ☐ already had some experience in the job.
c) ☐ hoped they would become an international hit.
One piece of evidence from the text: ______________________________

7. The *Artemis Fowl* books made Colfer rich overnight.
This statement is … ☐ true ☐ false
One piece of evidence from the text: ______________________________

8. Because of Colfer's success the people in his town …
a) ☐ began to ask him for money.
b) ☐ kept their distance from him.
c) ☐ behaved like they had before.
One piece of evidence from the text: ______________________________

9. Despite his success as a writer, Colfer has remained a fairly normal person.
This statement is … ☐ true ☐ false
One piece of evidence from the text: ______________________________

10. Daily-life situations with his children are an inspiration for Colfer's books.
This statement is … ☐ true ☐ false
One piece of evidence from the text: ______________________________

11. Because of his children, Colfer's stories have become …
a) ☐ gentler.
b) ☐ simpler.
c) ☐ more exciting.
One piece of evidence from the text: ______________________________

12. Colfer plans to stop writing the series once *Artemis Fowl* is too …

a) ☐ old.

b) ☐ nice.

c) ☐ strict.

One piece of evidence from the text: ______________________________

Wortschatz

Welcome to "Thinkuknow"

Using the Internet can be very helpful but it can sometimes also be dangerous. Explore the advice of the "Thinkuknow" websites about staying safe when you're on a phone, tablet or computer.

- ▶ Fill in suitable words **or** tick the correct box.
- ▶ Give only one solution.

1. With every new photo or comment we ______________________ on the Internet, we add lots of information about ourselves which stays online.

2. This is called a …

a) ☐ numerical b) ☐ statistical

c) ☐ digital d) ☐ valued

footprint. People who know us, and people who don't, can see and learn more about us.

3. These footprints can show us in our most positive moments – but sometimes they reflect thoughts or experiences that we later wish had been kept ______________________ and not visible for everyone.

4. When you put something online, who can see it? Think about who you're …

a) ☐ parting b) ☐ dividing

c) ☐ splitting d) ☐ sharing

the information with.

5. Don't forget: it's easy for other people to copy, change and ______________________ that information to others without you knowing it.

6. Most apps and social networks have 'privacy settings'. These help you to …

a) ☐ control b) ☐ govern

c) ☐ direct d) ☐ command

who can see what.

7. It's easy to lie online. Some people set up ______________________ profiles on social networks.

8. If you use social networks, always think about what personal information your footprints …

a) ☐ give away. b) ☐ let out.
c) ☐ carry out. d) ☐ show off.

9. If you ______________________________ to someone via social media, don't tell them anything which could help them find you in the real world – things like your full name, school, email address or even photos.

10. Be careful! It can be ______________________________ when you meet people online: Some people could threaten you if you don't do what they say.

11. If you stop using an app or a social network, remember to delete your …

a) ☐ organisation. b) ☐ participation
c) ☐ account. d) ☐ society.

12. Are you worried about something that's happened on the Internet? Most sites will let you …

a) ☐ guard b) ☐ block
c) ☐ arrest d) ☐ catch

people if you don't want to talk to them online anymore.

13. *The Mix* is a service which provides free, personal support for young people 24/7. If you're experiencing any painful emotion or are in crisis, you can send a ______________________________ to *The Mix*.

Schreiben

Click'd by Tamara Ireland Stone

Teenager Allie Navarro has participated in a special summer camp on computers: Code Girls Camp. At the end of the summer camp, she presents her result to a jury, parents and participants.

She took a deep breath.

And then she began.

"On the first morning here at Code Girls Camp, our instructor told us we had a whole summer to create any kind of app or game we wanted. Anything.

Something just for fun. Something that would solve a real-life problem. I loved that."

"But I admit," Allie continued, "on that first morning, I wasn't sure I was ready for that kind of challenge. I was much too terrified. Because I didn't know a single person."

Allie began walking up and down the stage. Her legs were shaky and she hoped the audience wouldn't notice.

"I kept looking around the room at these girls – nineteen total strangers I'd be spending my whole summer with – and wondering who they were. Did we like the same music? Did we read the same books? Did they have sisters or brothers?"

"And that's when the idea hit me. Why not an app that could help you make new friends?"

Allie waved her phone in the air. "For my summer project, I created a game called *Click'd*."

"Let me demonstrate how it works. This auditorium[1] seats two hundred and twenty people. I assume most of you don't know each other," she said jokingly, and she could see people looking around and shaking their heads.

"What if I told you there was one person in this room right now who had more in common with you than with anyone else? Of course, you could leave this room and never know who that person is, but ... Allie leaned forward. "Wouldn't it be more fun to find out?"

"We're going to use that *Click'd* app you installed when you came in, so, everyone, please pull out your phones and play along."

Allie took a deep breath. "Ready, everyone?" she asked as the screen behind her filled with four scenic[2] photographs. "Which do you prefer: the ocean, the forest, the desert, or the mountains?

Select A, B, C, or D."

Allie looked down at her screen. She could see the data collecting in the app she'd built specifically for this demonstration. It used the same system as *Click'd*, taking all the information the audience entered and immediately matching people with similar interests.

"Let's do some more so we have lots of information to work with," Allie said, and she clicked through seven more slides.

"When you're done with the quiz, *Click'd* figures out how you scored against each person, but it doesn't immediately tell you who your top friends are, because that wouldn't be as much fun," she said with a wink[3]. "Instead, *Click'd* uses sounds, lights, and clues to help you find your top ten friends."

As she walked across the stage, she noticed her legs weren't shaking anymore.

Allie tapped on her screen, and one of the phones in the back of the room let out a sound that startled[4] its owner. "Sir, would you please stand?" She tapped another button, and a phone in the front row on the opposite side of the auditorium sounded. A woman held her phone in the air and then stood and turned around.

"Congratulations! If you two were playing *Click'd*, you'd be in each other's high score lists." They waved at each other from across the auditorium.

"That's basically how my game works."

Everyone clapped as the man and woman took their seats.

Allie looked back at the audience, feeling on top of the world!

[1] auditorium – a room for a large audience
[2] scenic – showing beautiful countryside
[3] with a wink – to shut one eye briefly as a signal
[4] to startle – to surprise s. o. suddenly

Quelle: Stone, Tamara Ireland: Click'd, Herausgeber: Little, Brown Books, 2017

▶ Read the tasks carefully.
▶ Make sure to write about **all** the aspects presented in each task.

1. **Describe** Allie's product, how it works and why she has created it.

2. **Explain** how Allie's feelings change during the presentation.
   To do this, look at how she acts and speaks at the beginning, in the middle and at the end of her presentation.

3. Here you can choose between three different options. **Do only ONE of them!**

   a) What do you think about *Click'd*? **Comment** on Allie's product.

   Include the following aspects:
   ▶ risks or chances of Allie's product,
   ▶ the role social media play in your life,
   ▶ your opinion on personally using *Click'd*.

   or

   b) Imagine you were in the audience and listened to Allie's presentation. You have to write an article on it for the summer camp's magazine.

   Write this article.

   Include the following aspects:
   ▶ things to know about *Click'd*,
   ▶ the audience's possible reactions to *Click'd*,
   ▶ your view on computer summer camps for teenagers.

   You can start like this:

   Have you been "Click'd" yet?

   16-year-old Allie Navarro is the winner of this year's Code Girls Camp. She has demonstrated her product in a convincing presentation to …

or

c) Imagine that Allie is the first speaker at the *Code Girls Camp's* opening event one year later. She is talking to the new participants about her experiences over the last year.

Write Allie's speech.

Include the following aspects:
- how *Click'd* has changed her and her life,
- how she feels about the summer camp in general,
- her advice for the new participants.

You can start like this:

Hi everyone, I'm happy to be back here at Code Girls Camp. I can't believe it's already been a year. So much has happened since …

Erster Prüfungsteil: Hörverstehen

Aus urheberrechtlichen Gründen wurde der Teil Hörverstehen durch gleichwertige Musteraufgaben ersetzt.

Hörverstehen Teil 1

Teil 1: British TV Game Show "How well do I really know the UK?"

(Audiotrack: QR-Code rechts / Hörtext S. 95)

You are going to hear the audio track of the TV game show "How well do I really know the UK?".

- ▶ First read the tasks.
- ▶ Then listen to the game show.
- ▶ While you are listening, tick the correct box **or** write down the information needed.
- ▶ At the end you will hear the audio file again.
- ▶ Now read the tasks. You have **90 seconds** to do this.

▶ Now listen to the audio file and do the tasks.

1. Before the third round of the game ...

a) ☐ Kevin is in the lead with three points.
b) ☐ Kevin has more points than Lizzy but fewer points than Jane.
c) ☐ Kevin occupies the second place with a score of six points.

2. Name the subject matter and the difficulty level of Kevin's question as well as the city that has the lowest population size.

____

____

3. Jane ...

a) ☐ picks a question about the Royal Family which is neither easy nor hard.
b) ☐ will not be able to regain the lead after her next answer, no matter what difficulty level she will choose for her question.
c) ☐ picks an intermediate question from the area "Geography".

4. The Queen ...

a) ☐ is the official owner of several species of marine life living within a certain distance from UK shores.
b) ☐ has a strong longing for swans.
c) ☐ technically owns several species of sea life living more than three miles off UK shores.

5. Lizzy ...

a) ☐ chooses a one-point question about "politics".
b) ☐ chooses a three-point question about "politics".
c) ☐ is sure that her next question about "politics" will not be hard.

6. Lizzy ...

a) ☐ wants to keep the peace between Kevin and Jane.
b) ☐ hopes that Kevin and Jane will not choose three-point questions again.
c) ☐ tries to make sure she does not fall behind too much in comparison to Kevin's and Jane's scores.

7. Lizzy's question is about …
- a) ☐ the constitution of the UK.
- b) ☐ a famous Member of Parliament.
- c) ☐ the size of constituencies in the UK.

8. What information does Lizzy give about her husband? Name two details.

____

____

Hörverstehen Teil 2

Teil 2: Podcast "Dublin and Belfast: travel account"
(Audiotrack: QR-Code S. 76 / Hörtext S. 96)

You are going to hear the podcast "Dublin and Belfast: travel account".

- ▶ First read the tasks.
- ▶ Then listen to the podcast.
- ▶ While you are listening, tick the correct box **or** write down the information needed.
- ▶ At the end, you will hear the podcast again.
- ▶ Now read the tasks. You have **90 seconds** to do this.

- ▶ Now listen to the podcast and do the tasks.

1. Rebecca ...
- a) ☐ suspects that her listeners may find a trip to Ireland less interesting than other trips she has covered in some of her previous podcasts.
- b) ☐ cannot wait to finally make trips to all four corners of the earth in the future.
- c) ☐ is looking forward to the short trip to Ireland she will be making within the next couple of months.

2. Rebecca ...
- a) ☐ wanted to explore both the natural beauty of Ireland and Ireland's two major cities, Dublin and Belfast.
- b) ☐ says that Orla and Liam, the managers of the car rental office at Dublin Airport, were very warm-hearted people.
- c) ☐ drove to a B&B run by two people called Orla and Liam right after picking up her rental car at Dublin Airport.

3. In Dublin ...
- a) ☐ Rebecca explored the famous Book of Kells, which can be found in one of Dublin's two most imposing churches.
- b) ☐ Rebecca drank a pint of what is probably the most famous Irish beer in a building called the Guinness Storehouse.
- c) ☐ Rebecca was served excellent gourmet food in one of the amazing Temple Bar restaurants.

4. During the car ride from Dublin to Belfast ...

a) ☐ Rebecca found it quite annoying that the speed limits and the petrol prices were very different in the two parts of Ireland.

b) ☐ Rebecca crossed a hardly noticeable border between the EU und the UK.

c) ☐ Rebecca was surprised that the landscape was so different in the two parts of Ireland.

5. When Rebecca ordered some food in the fish and chips shop in Belfast, all the customers started to look at her. Which thoughts went through her mind then? Describe (at least) one of those thoughts.

____

____

6. In the fish and chips shop ...

a) ☐ some of the other customers reacted to Rebecca in a hostile way.

b) ☐ some of the other customers told Rebecca that several relatives of theirs were born in British cities like Sheffield, Liverpool, or Manchester.

c) ☐ Rebecca was surprised by the friendly way in which some of the other customers treated her.

7. Rebecca was shown a number of very famous sights as well as a number of lesser-known places in Belfast. Name two very famous sights and two lesser-known places.

____

____

8. Rebecca ...

a) ☐ hopes that her travel account may be helpful for her listeners in case they plan to take a trip to Dublin and/or Belfast in the future.

b) ☐ is not sure yet where her next trip will take her, but her listeners can find out about that in her next podcast.

c) ☐ says that Belfast and Dublin are both worth a visit, but she thinks that a trip to Dublin has some advantages over a trip to Belfast.

Zweiter Prüfungsteil: Leseverstehen – Wortschatz – Schreiben

Leseverstehen

The power of traditional beliefs

A group of young people are sitting around a table when one of them scratches his nose. "Ah, my nose is itchy[1]," he says. Then he hits his mates lightly and everything is fine again. If you know something about Irish superstitions[2], you'll understand that traditionally an itchy nose is a sign of an upcoming fight, and that a fight for fun should be carried out to make sure that a real fight will not happen. Many of us hear superstitions like these in the schoolyard or around the family dinner table and carry them on into adult life.

How many others can you remember, now you're thinking about it? Itching on the inner side of your hands – a sign of money to come. Itching on the temples[3] – something will make you cry.

But it's not all about itching. A gap between the front teeth is a sign of a beautiful singing voice. A black spot on the tongue is a sign of telling lies. Many Irish parents who want their children to tell the truth, tell them: "Stick your tongue out so I can see if you're lying". If your ears are "burning", someone is talking about you. If it's the right ear that feels extremely warm, people are talking about you positively, but if it's the left ear, the talk is negative.

In Ireland, the word for superstition is *piseog*, but the word does not only describe simple sayings and unusual beliefs. In old stories everything connected with magic is believed to be a *piseog*.

A classic *piseog* was connected to *May Day*[4] morning. For Irish people *May Day* was the turning of the year from winter into summer, a time for changes. An unkind person could go out on this particular morning and hide old meat in the hay, or old eggs everywhere on your farm. If you didn't find these things, your luck would turn bad. *May Day* was also a time for good changes – washing one's face with dew[5] on this morning would provide people with fresh beauty throughout the year.

These old beliefs, or superstitions, may seem silly to us now, thinking about them in the light of modern science, but they show our psychological needs. And they show how we as humans have thought, felt, and interacted with the world around us and with each other.

Though we can understand the logic behind the origins of some *piseogs*, they survived because of repetition, not because they made sense. When something is done again and again, down through the generations, it becomes not a superstition but a tradition. Traditions are links to the past and a connection through the generations. Based on them, each new family creates their own rituals.

Maybe the old *piseogs* save us from bad luck and bring about good luck, or maybe they don't. We don't know for sure, so it's up to you to decide what to believe in.

[1] itchy – making you want to scratch
[2] superstition – the belief that something can bring good or bad luck
[3] temples – the flat parts of your head between your eyes and ears
[4] May Day – 1st May, a traditional spring festival celebrated in many countries
[5] dew – drops of water that form outside during the night

Your English class is doing a project on the strange things people in the English-speaking world believe in. You decide to take a closer look at Ireland. The online article above gives you some information.

▶ Tick the correct box and give **one** piece of evidence by quoting short passages from the text.

1. In Ireland, an itchy nose stands for future …

a) ☐ joy.
b) ☐ trouble.
c) ☐ friendship.

One piece of evidence from the text: ____________________

2. In Irish belief, itching can also mean future wealth.

This statement is … ☐ true ☐ false

One piece of evidence from the text: ____________________

3. In Ireland, you ask someone to stick their tongue out to check for …
a) ☐ illness.
b) ☐ honesty.
c) ☐ bad thoughts.
One piece of evidence from the text: ______________________________

4. Your ears can tell you what …
a) ☐ the weather will be like.
b) ☐ path your future will take.
c) ☐ other people think of you.
One piece of evidence from the text: ______________________________

5. The Irish expression *piseog* stands for something that is real.
This statement is … ☐ true ☐ false
One piece of evidence from the text: ______________________________

6. People played tricks on other people on *May Day* to …
a) ☐ make fun of them.
b) ☐ force them to clean up.
c) ☐ cause problems for them.
One piece of evidence from the text: ______________________________

7. Today we know that old beliefs tell us a lot about people.
This statement is … ☐ true ☐ false
One piece of evidence from the text: ______________________________

8. Old beliefs still exist today because they …
a) ☐ make sense to us.
b) ☐ explain lots of things.
c) ☐ are practised regularly.
One piece of evidence from the text: ______________________________

9. How people practise these beliefs can vary.
This statement is … ☐ true ☐ false
One piece of evidence from the text: ______________________________

10. Finally, the author wants the reader to …
a) ☐ choose what to think.
b) ☐ pass on the old beliefs.
c) ☐ forget about superstition.
One piece of evidence from the text: ______________________________

Wortschatz

Food as a cultural experience

One way to experience the culture of a foreign country is through food. Find out how the food we eat influences us.

▶ Fill in suitable words **or** tick the correct box.
▶ Give only one solution.

1. There is a bigger …

a) ☐ union b) ☐ connection
c) ☐ touch d) ☐ contact

between food and culture than you may think.

2. On a personal level, we grow up eating the food of our family's culture. For many of us, warm feelings and good memories …

a) ☐ arrive at b) ☐ get to
c) ☐ come to d) ☐ go for

our minds when we think about food from our childhood.

3. Almost every one of us has his or her favourite food. What is yours? Surely just thinking about the ______________________________ of your favourite food might make you feel hungry.

4. A lot of food is also known for getting you back up on your feet again when you are feeling ______________________________. Sometimes having a cup of tea or a hot soup will definitely make you feel better.

5. Many ______________________________ from all over the world change our food today. So you don't need to travel to foreign countries, because you can enjoy all kinds of different food in your hometown.

6. Indian, Thai, Turkish, Italian or Chinese food is available everywhere. There is such a big …

a) ☐ difference b) ☐ description
c) ☐ change d) ☐ variety

you can choose from.

7. Nowadays, traditional food is often mixed with food from other countries when immigrants bring the food of their countries with them to keep their ______________________________ alive.

8. When people move from one country to another, making food from their hometown is often a way for them to …

a) ☐ guide b) ☐ govern
c) ☐ manage d) ☐ command

homesickness and to feel connected to their native country.

9. Many people also open their own ______________________________ to sell food and to introduce local people to other cultures.

10. For example, Indian curries such as chicken tikka masala are now …

a) ☐ generally b) ☐ only
c) ☐ daily d) ☐ rarely

regarded as typical British food.

11. Or think about your own cuisine! Turkish kebabs or Italian pizza and pasta are now ________________________ ________________________ in many street food restaurants all over the world.

12. You've been out for lunch and had some ____ Thai food. Get the recipe and try to cook it at home!

13. You see, food can be a great way of getting to know other cultures and people, and it …

a) ☐ creates b) ☐ unites
c) ☐ combines d) ☐ meets

us in more ways than one.

Schreiben

Do you speak chocolate extract from *Do you speak chocolate?* by Cas Lester

Jaz, a British girl, is explaining how she has made friends with Nadima, a refugee from Syria.

Outside, on the steps by the canteen, everyone crowded around Nadima. On the one hand to make her welcome, but on the other hand mostly because they didn't want to miss anything.

Kara was right in the centre of the crowd.

"Hi! I'm Kara," she said, "Where are you from?"

Nadima smiled as if she was sorry.

"I don't think she understands you," I said.

Kara shot me an angry look. "You don't say," she said. Then she repeated the question more slowly and … much louder.

"I don't think she's deaf," I said.

Kara ignored me and went on. "Do … you … speak … English?"

But before Nadima could even answer Chloe said, "How long have you been in England?"

And Lily said, "Where do you live now?"

They showered her with questions. It was absurd! Nadima just did a lot of smiling and nodding. But she was starting to look a bit confused.

"Seriously!" I cried. "Give her a break. It's obvious she can't understand a word you're saying."

"Well, that's just racist! Thinking she can't speak English!" declared Kara.

"No, it's not!" I said angrily. "Mrs C told us Nadima doesn't speak much English!" I said.

Nadima looked at me when I mentioned her name. I suddenly felt embarrassed, like we were all talking about her as if she wasn't there.

"Wait! I've just had a brilliant idea," said Kara. She took out her phone from her back pocket.

"We can use Google Translate!"

"Good idea," cried Lily, getting her phone out too.

"Yes!" agreed Chloe and Elly, grabbing theirs. I didn't bother. Honestly, me and Google Translate?

I have enough trouble reading English.

Kara's "brilliant" idea turned out to be a complete failure. The basic error in her plan was that we didn't actually know which country Nadima was from. And, when we tried asking her, she didn't understand.

She just stood there looking puzzled. I gave her a big smile and raised my shoulders in a big comedy shrug. She smiled and did a big shrug back.

As soon as Kara realised it was going to be impossible to actually talk to Nadima she got bored and went away – taking Lily with her of course. So everyone else followed them too.

Soon I was the only one left with Nadima.

There was a long, horrible silence while we both looked at each other in embarrassment.
"Um … Parlez-vous français[1]?!" I said. Nadima just looked at me.
"Er … Deutsch?" I tried.
She looked worried. I took that as a no. Just as well really, since I don't speak French or German anyway.
There was another, even more unpleasant silence. Then, I had a brilliant idea. I dug into my bag and took out a bar of chocolate, broke off a bit and offered it to Nadima.
"Do you speak chocolate?" I said.
Her eyes seemed to come to life. She took the chocolate, but before putting it into her mouth she searched around in her school bag and gave me something that looked like *Turkish Delight*[2].

[1] Parlez-vous français? – French for "Do you speak French?"
[2] Turkish Delight – a type of sweet

- ▶ Read the tasks carefully.
- ▶ Make sure to write about **all** the aspects presented in each task.

1. **Describe** the situation Jaz and her classmates are in and how they deal with it.

2. **Explain** what you get to know about Jaz' character. Look at what she does and says.

3. Here you can choose between three different options. **Do only ONE of them!**

a) At the end of the extract, Jaz has found a way of dealing with the situation.
Comment on the gesture Jaz chooses at the end of the extract when she offers some chocolate to Nadima.

Include …
- ▶ how Nadima might feel about Jaz' behaviour,
- ▶ why the chocolate plays an important role in the text,
- ▶ what you think about Jaz' action in this situation.

or

b) After the incident at school, Jaz and Nadima become close friends. One Friday after school, Jaz invites Nadima home for dinner. Jaz' parents are curious to meet their daughter's new friend.

Write how the story continues during dinner.

Include …
- ▶ how everyone tries to deal with the communication problem,
- ▶ how Jaz helps Nadima to feel more comfortable,
- ▶ how Nadima has won everybody's sympathy by the end of dinner.

You can start like this:

Mum and Dad were already busy setting the table. Nadima just stood in the doorway to our kitchen. I saw Nadima taking a deep breath and …

or

c) After her meeting with Nadima, Jaz wants to organise a school food bazaar. She decides to write an article for the school homepage to inform all the students about her idea.

Write her article.

Include …
- how Jaz got the idea to organise the food bazaar,
- how food can play a role in bringing different cultures together,
- how Jaz wants to organise the food bazaar at school.

You can start like this:

Bringing cultures together through food

When I first met Nadima, the new girl from Syria at our school, we had trouble communicating with words, but "talked" to each other through food. This made me think …

Notizen

Hörverstehenstexte 2017

Teil 1: Conversation between Tom and Mary
(Audiotrack: QR-Code rechts / Aufgaben S. 43)

Listen to the weekly British radio show "Your very best holiday experience". Every Friday afternoon, the show host Tom Logan invites teenagers to call into his show in order to talk about the best holiday experience they ever had. Each time the show focuses on a particular country.

Tom: Hello everyone. My name is Tom Logan. Welcome to our weekly programme "Your very best holiday experience". Last week we focused on New Zealand, and I still remember the holiday experiences you told our listeners about. Some of them were quite thrilling indeed. This week our focus is on South Africa. So if you have ever spent your holidays in this beautiful country at the southern tip of the African continent, please call us on 020-334466 and tell us about the experience you had there. And our first caller today is Mary, I believe. Hello Mary, how are you doing?

Mary: Hi Tom, very well indeed, thank you.

Tom: Mary, please tell us about your South African holiday experience.

Mary: Last winter, my parents took me on a family trip to Cape Town in the Christmas holidays. You know, South Africa lies on the southern half of our planet. When it is winter in Britain, it is summertime in South Africa. So it was really hot when we were there. We went swimming quite often because, well you know, Cape Town is located on the Atlantic Ocean. They have very nice sandy beaches with crystal clear water there.

Tom: So the experience you want to tell us about has to do with water.

Mary: No, quite on the contrary. It has to do with air. You see, in the hotel that my parents and I were staying in I came across a flyer by a company offering paragliding flights over Cape Town.

Tom: I think you have to explain to some of our listeners what paragliding is.

Mary: Well, paragliding is like sailing. It's just that you do not sail on the water but through the air. However, you are not in a sailplane with a closed cabin and windows but in an open glider, which means that you can actually fly through the air, with the wind blowing right in your face.

Tom: When you saw the flyer, did you decide right away to give paragliding a try?

Mary: Well, at first I thought that I would be too scared to give it a try. But then my dad said that he had tried it once on Gran Canaria and that he had found it very thrilling and not scary at all.

Tom: So your dad obviously encouraged you to do it. But what about your mother? What did she say?

Mary: To be honest, she wasn't happy about it at first. But then my dad told her that paragliding was not dangerous at all because beginners never fly on their own but always together with an instructor. So in the end even my mother allowed me to do it if I really wanted to do it that much. Eventually, my dad called the company and booked a flight for me for the coming Saturday.

Tom: So what was the flight like? I'm sure our listeners can't wait for the details.

Mary: Well, let me first tell you that the flight did not take place on Saturday due to bad weather conditions. It was too windy, which is why the flight was cancelled by the company for safety reasons. However, the next day it was less windy, so the company offered to do the flight then.

Tom: But now you do have to give our listeners an account of your experience in the air. They really want to hear about the flight. And so do I, to be honest.

Mary: I have to admit that I had an uneasy feeling when the instructor and I were running towards the cliff. But once my feet suddenly had no contact with the mountain rocks anymore and we actually started to fly in the air, the feeling changed immediately. It was just fantastic. You cannot compare that to flying on a plane, for example. It is so much more thrilling. It is mind-blowing, that's what it is.

Tom: How was the view from up there?

Mary: It was breathtaking. We were flying about 800 meters above the centre of Cape Town. Everything was so small: the houses, the streets, the cars. But one thing that we passed during our flight was not small at all. In fact, it was much higher than the height we were flying at. What I'm talking about is "Table Mountain", which is a very famous mountain that marks the southern end of Cape Town. It is so famous that you can see it on a lot of picture postcards in South Africa. In fact, it is one of the most photographed sights in South Africa.

Tom: Mary, do you know why it is called "Table Mountain"?

Mary: Yes, I do. Table Mountain is almost 3 km wide and has a very flat top all across. When you see it from a distance, it really looks like a huge table. That's why it is named "Table Mountain".

Tom: Mary, that was quite an exciting holiday experience indeed. Thank you very much for that, and all the best to you. Well, now it's time for our next caller ...

Teil 2: Wildlife Safari in Africa

(Audiotrack: QR-Code S. 88 / Aufgaben S. 44)

My dad had always dreamed of going on a wildlife safari in Africa, and he had told my mum and me countless times about that dream of his. And then, in late September last year, this dream finally seemed to come true. The company my dad worked for had asked him to go to South Africa on an 8-week business trip. His knowledge and advice as an expert on high-tech railway construction were needed in Johannesburg.

"They want me to go to Johannesburg as early as mid-November. And my boss said that I could take a week off between Christmas and New Year's Day to see some of South Africa as well. Can you believe that?", dad shouted excitedly when we were at dinner that night. My mum stopped eating and said, "I am really happy for you, George, but you make it sound as if you can't wait to get away from Andrew and me as quickly as possible." Dad was surprised at my mum's reaction and said, "Carol, you know perfectly well that I don't mean it like that. It's just that I will have a chance to go on a wildlife safari at last. And the two of you know very well how long I have been dreaming of that." I felt happy for my dad, but all I was able to say was, "Aren't you afraid of that, dad? After all, it's a lot of wild animals like lions, leopards and elephants you will see from a very short distance, without any cages protecting you like in a zoo." Dad just laughed and answered, "No, Andrew, I'm not afraid at all. Quite on the contrary, I hate zoos for the very reason that they have cages there. I want to see those wild animals in their natural environment."

From that day in September up until dad got on the plane to Johannesburg in November, the safari was nearly the only thing he talked about. He had booked a 5-day safari between Christmas and New Year's Day in Kruger National Park, which is a famous wildlife reserve not far away from Johannesburg.

The safari began on 27th of December. I still remember the first message dad sent my mum and me with his smart phone late that day. He wrote that his safari group consisted of 6 people: 3 men and 2 women plus Peter, their safari ranger. On that first day he had already seen about 20 giraffes, about a dozen rhinos as well as hundreds of exotic birds. Dad was thrilled, which was probably why he attached dozens of pictures of those animals to his message. The next few days mum and I received similar messages, often with attached selfies of dad smiling in front of hippos, zebras, buffalos or elephants.

It was on New Year's Eve, however, that mum and I did not receive a text message as usual but a phone call from dad. "Carol, Andrew, I need to tell you about what happened on our safari today", he said in a nervous and somewhat frightened voice. Then he continued, "Peter, our ranger, had spotted a family of lions resting in the hot sun next to the bushes. He drove our Range Rover closer to the lions. Finally, we were standing next to the car about 100 meters away from the lions, taking pictures. All of a sudden the male lion stood up and started running towards our Rover. Peter asked all of us to get in the car immediately. However, when he tried to start the engine, it wouldn't work. Fortunately, we had all managed to sit in the car and shut the windows before the lion reached us. The lion walked around the car, roaring and scratching the outside with his paws. Then he jumped on to the front of our car, showing his huge teeth and looking angrily at us through the windscreen. Peter told us to stay calm, but we were all scared to death." Mum looked quite worried and asked, "What happened next? How did you manage to get out of this?" Dad answered, "When the lion realised that he couldn't get inside the car, he eventually decided to walk back to his family."

Listening to dad's story with great interest, I asked him, "But what about the car? How did you manage to get it fixed?" Dad replied, "We had to wait in the car for another two hours until the lion family walked off into the bushes. Then Peter was able to get out of the car to fix it. But he asked the rest of us to stay in the car at all times." At that point my mum started crying and said, "Oh, George, I'm so glad nothing happened to you. And I really can't wait for you to come back home as soon as possible." In fact, it was not only mum missing him. I was anxious for dad to come back home as soon as possible, too. Then dad said, "It is just another two weeks before I fly back to England. I'm also looking forward to seeing you." And then he added with a laugh, "And Andrew, would you like to go to a zoo with me once I'm back home? I think I'd prefer to see some animals in cages for a change." Now I had to laugh, too, and I answered, "Yes, dad. I would love to do that. See you in two weeks' time."

Hörverstehenstexte 2018

Teil 1: Graduation Speech

(Audiotrack: QR-Code rechts / Aufgaben S. 51)

Dear colleagues, dear parents, and, above all, dear students,

We are meeting in this beautiful school assembly hall today to celebrate those 46 graduates who have recently passed their final exams at our Nelson Mandela Memorial School. Let me begin by congratulating each and every one of those 46 students on their successful graduation, for which they will today receive their high school diplomas.
As the headmistress of our magnificent school I would like to point out that I am very proud of you and that you can all be very proud of yourselves for what you have achieved. In the past 12 years you have studied subjects like Maths and Sciences, History and Geography, Language and Arts, to name just a few. I am sure that each one of you has experienced moments of success and joy, but also moments of failure and frustration in those years. Well, to be honest, from personal experience as a 45-year-old woman I can assure you that this mix of positive and negative experiences will not end for you today because, I am afraid, this mix is just what life is about at all stages of our lives.
You will soon enter the world of adulthood. You may, for example, decide to keep on studying at university, to start an apprenticeship or to look for a job right away. However, no matter what you decide to do, you will inevitably experience that life can sometimes be a smooth and joyful journey, but a rough and stormy voyage at other times. But then, why shouldn't it be? After all, our individual lives are like mirrors of what happens in small towns, in large cities or even in whole countries. Our beautiful country, South Africa, is certainly a good example in this respect. Up until more than 25 years ago, our country was in the grip of the horrible system of Apartheid, which meant that black people in South Africa were discriminated against in every sphere of everyday life. Miraculously, however, in the 1990s, our great black freedom fighter Nelson Mandela, after whom our school is named, was released from prison after 27 long years behind bars. And a couple of years later he even became the first black president of South Africa, and, as a result, Apartheid was abolished once and for all. At that time, there was an amazing feeling of hope for a better future throughout our country after those long years of discrimination, racism and hatred against black people.
Of course, even today our country still has quite a few social problems because life simply is not perfect. But let us not forget that there has nevertheless been a lot of progress and improvement in our country in the last 25 years. And it is the next generation – in other words: you, dear graduates – that will have to continue the struggle for a better future. And a struggle it is, no doubt about that. There is one thing, however, that I would like to remind you of. Please never ever forget what Nelson Mandela taught this country before, during and after his presidency: No matter what you struggle for or against, never ever lose your respect for your neighbour, for your fellow citizen, or for any human being, for that matter. My dear graduates, if you live your lives with this guiding principle in mind – a principle that Nelson Mandela lived by throughout his entire life –, you will definitely make the world a better place, no matter how small your individual contribution will actually be. Thank you for your attention.

Teil 2: Conversation between Rachel and her siblings

(Audiotrack: QR-Code oben / Aufgaben S. 52)

16-year-old Rachel O'Connor lives in Edinburgh with her parents, her 17-year-old brother Edward and her 14-year-old sister Linda. Unlike her older brother, Rachel is very interested in, and knowledgeable about, politics. Her younger sister Linda does show some interest in politics, too, but she knows far less about politics than Rachel. In the evening Rachel has a chat with her older brother and her younger sister.

Rachel: Edward, Linda, last week Mr MacElroy started a new topic in our "Government and Politics" class. It is all about the pros and cons of Brexit. It's really interesting.

Edward: Okay, Rachel, let me guess. Your super-modern teacher Mr MacElroy thinks that it is a serious mistake for Britain to leave the European Union and that the British people will pay dearly for Brexit in the end. Am I right?

Rachel: Edward, come on. Stop criticising Mr MacElroy all the time just because you do not share his political views and because you think he is not conservative enough.

Linda: Edward, please do not argue with Rachel about politics again. Let her first tell us what they discussed in class.

Rachel: Thank you, Linda. Well, Mr MacElroy told us that Brexit may have all kinds of political, economic and social consequences. Did you know, for example, that there may be border controls again between Northern Ireland and the Republic of Ireland? That is because the Republic of Ireland, which is an independent country, is part of the EU, but Northern Ireland, which is part of the United Kingdom, will leave the EU with Brexit. Isn't that crazy? It took several decades to finally achieve free travel between the two parts of Ireland, but as a result of Brexit the Irish may have to set up a so-called "hard border" between those two separate parts again.

Edward: Well, to be honest, I don't really care about the Irish. Let them solve their own problems. That's none of our business. We are Scottish, so we'd better care about Scotland.

Rachel: But Edward, don't you see that this might affect Scotland, too? You may remember that there was a referendum in Scotland in 2014 in which only 55% of the Scots voted against Scotland's independence from Britain. What do you think would be the result if there was another referendum on Scottish independence now that Brexit has been decided on?

Linda: But Rachel, why should the majority of Scots vote for independence from Britain the next time? And what has this got to do with Brexit?

Rachel: Linda, Scotland has always been more supportive of EU membership than England and Wales. Brexit means, however, that Britain will leave the EU. As Scotland is part of Britain, it will have to leave the EU as well. I am quite sure that a lot more than 50% of the Scots would not like to see Scotland leave the EU. So, in a future referendum, they might vote for Scottish independence from Britain to give Scotland a chance to stay in the European Union.

Edward: Oh dear, I have never really thought about that. That sounds horrible. Can you imagine Scotland not being part of Britain any more?

Rachel: In class we also talked about some other possible consequences of Brexit, for example economic ones. As you know, London is the biggest financial centre in Europe with all its large banks and insurance companies. Mr MacElroy told us that a lot of those banks and insurance companies are thinking about relocating from London to Frankfurt, Paris, Dublin or elsewhere in Europe to continue enjoying the EU's advantages of free trade and free travel after Brexit. In fact, some of them are leaving London just now or have already left it.

Linda: Really? But that means Britain will lose a lot of jobs. This will be a big blow for the British economy.

Edward: I'm afraid you are right, Linda. I must admit that I will have to think this whole Brexit thing over again. So far I have really been proud of our country for showing those bureaucrats in Brussels, Berlin, Paris and elsewhere in Europe that Britain does not need the EU and will be able to manage quite well on its own. However, after what you've just told us, Rachel, I am not so sure any more.

Hörverstehenstexte 2019

Teil 1: The Presentation

(Audiotrack: QR-Code rechts / Aufgaben S. 59)

The first thing that came to my mind was: "Oh, my goodness, why me?" Mr Harris, our English teacher, had just told me that I had been way too lazy throughout this school year and that I could only avoid getting a very bad final mark by giving an oral presentation in class. But I just hated English because it was so boring. And now I was to prepare a presentation in class? That was horrible! And to make things even worse, the topic Mr Harris gave me for the presentation sounded so terribly uninteresting: "Spooky, creepy and mysterious elements in British literature today and in the past".

However, now that I have almost finished preparing my presentation I must admit that the topic is really very interesting. At first, I had to force myself to start collecting information for my presentation. But once I had found some websites focussing on this topic, I gradually realised that it was not boring at all. Having done a good deal of research into the topic, I decided to start my presentation with our greatest national poet: William Shakespeare. Before preparing this presentation, I had always thought that Shakespeare was just a boring dead old writer, but, in actual fact, he is not. In his plays you can find all kinds of creepy ghosts and witches as well as a great many other spooky creatures and events. What I found out about Shakespeare during my Internet research even encouraged me to read some original passages of his plays, which was great fun indeed. It is true that the 16th century language he uses is sometimes hard to understand, but the storylines and characters in a lot of his plays are really creepy, mysterious and thrilling.

Continuing my research, I found out that part of British literature after Shakespeare is also full of mystery and spookiness. Quite a number of British novels written in the 18th and 19th centuries, for example, are set in old, and often haunted, castles or monasteries with secret passageways, mysterious chambers and hidden trapdoors. There is even a name for this category of novels. They are called Gothic novels. Some Gothic novels also include supernatural beings, mysterious events and scary characters. Two Gothic novels, *Frankenstein* by Mary Shelley and *Dracula* by Bram Stoker, are still very well known today and have been turned into famous movies several times. Interestingly, many people think that the monster in Shelley's novel is called *Frankenstein*, but it is actually the last name of a scientist who creates a human being from parts of dead bodies. Later in the novel Frankenstein's creature turns into a brutal and horrifying monster. An even scarier example of the Gothic novel, however, is Bram Stoker's *Dracula*, in which there are vampires who drink human blood and sleep in coffins.

Many people think that spookiness, creepiness and mystery are predominantly elements of literary works that were written way back in the past. However, if you examine the hugely successful Harry Potter novels, for example, which were

written by J. K. Rowling around the end of the 20th century and the beginning of the 21st century, you realise that a lot of those spooky and mysterious elements are still quite popular in modern-day British literature, too. To begin with, the hero of the series, a young boy called Harry Potter, belongs to the world of wizards and witches who can work magic and who time and again have to defend themselves against evil supernatural forces or creepy creatures like Lord Voldemort, for example. Second, Hogwarts, the school the young wizards and witches attend, is an old castle with secret chambers, hidden passageways and a wide range of magical powers. Third, the castle is surrounded by a forest called *The Forbidden Forest*, which is populated by all kinds of creepy, mysterious or dangerous beings. Last but not least, the adventures the main characters experience in these novels are all extremely spooky and thrilling.
Well, tomorrow I will have to give my presentation in class. So far in this school year I really have not contributed to, or actively participated in English classes at all. But tomorrow I am going to surprise them all. I am quite sure my presentation will be one of the best Mr Harris and my classmates have ever seen or listened to. Maybe I will even manage to scare all of them a little with my spooky presentation. That would be great fun.

Teil 2: Interview in Cape Town

(Audiotrack: QR-Code S. 91 / Aufgaben S. 60)

A British travel company that has specialised in trips to South Africa is running a new online advertising campaign in order to increase its sales. Part of that campaign includes video clips in which ordinary South Africans are interviewed in the streets of Cape Town about why they think South Africa is a wonderful destination for tourists. Listen to one of those interviews.

Interviewer: Hi, I'm Jack Roberts from the British travel company 'No Better Place Than South Africa'. We are currently running a new advertising campaign in Britain to enhance people's interest in South Africa as a tourist destination. Can I ask the two of you some questions about your home country?

Julia: Yes, sure, go ahead.

Interviewer: Well, first of all, may I ask your names?

Julia: My name is Julia, and this is my friend Allison.

Interviewer: Okay, Julia, let's start with you. If you had to convince our British viewers that a trip to South Africa is really worth taking, what would you tell them?

Julia: Well, the first thing I would tell them about is South Africa's beautiful nature and landscapes. For example, we have the most gorgeous beaches in the world, not only here in Cape Town but also in numerous other parts of the country. What's more, in South Africa you can go on safaris to see a wide variety of wildlife such as lions, giraffes, elephants, hippos, rhinos or zebras in their natural habitat.

Interviewer: Thank you, Julia. Now, what about you, Allison? Why would you recommend your home country to British tourists?

Allison: Well, I certainly agree with Julia that South Africa's beaches and wildlife are just stunning. And I would like to add two more things to Julia's list. First, along our coastline you can find an amazingly rich and beautiful variety of sea life which includes penguins, seals, dolphins, sharks, and whales. And second, South Africa boasts some of the world's most spectacular hiking trails through very diverse and breathtaking landscapes such as rugged mountains, lush green forests, dry deserts or deep canyons and gorges.

Interviewer: Wow, the two of you are really whetting my appetite for a holiday in South Africa. I'm sure our viewers will feel the same way when they watch this video clip. Thank you for taking the time to tell us about your terrific home country. Take care and bye-bye.
And now ... let us walk over to this young gentleman in the grey business suit. Hello, can you spare a few minutes for a short interview?

Nelson: Yes, I can, but it really has to be short because my lunch break will be over soon.

Interviewer: Of course. Now, I'm Jack Roberts from the British travel company 'No Better Place Than South Africa'. We are currently running a new advertising campaign in Britain to enhance people's interest in South Africa as a tourist destination. May I ask your name?

Nelson: Yes, of course. My name is Nelson.

Interviewer: Oh, that's interesting. Just like your famous national hero, Nelson Mandela.

Nelson: Yes, that's right. And I am very proud of that. You see, being a black person myself, if it hadn't been for Nelson Mandela, I would definitely not be a lawyer today, walking around in a business suit on the streets of Cape Town.

Interviewer: I'm sure you are right. Mandela did influence the history of South Africa like no one else in the last 30 years. Well, from your point of view, why would you encourage British tourists to come to South Africa?

Nelson: Well, I suppose most tourists come here because of South Africa's magnificent natural resources such as our wildlife, sea life and landscapes. However, what most people are not really aware of is the fact that

South Africa boasts a wide range of cultural treasures, too. For example, our population is a very interesting and colourful mix of different ethnic groups. The vast majority consists of black African people like myself although these black Africans are by no means a homogeneous cultural group. In fact, there are quite a number of different black tribes or communities in this country with their own social structures, traditions and cultures.

Interviewer: That is indeed interesting. What about the rest of the population?

Nelson: Well, we also have a white community, often with Dutch, German and British roots, since those were the first European settlers colonising the country. Then there is the group of the so-called 'Coloureds', who have a mixed racial background. Last but not least, we also have a significant Asian community; they are the descendants of Indian and Chinese migrants who came here as cheap labour in the 19th century. All these ethnic groups have their own festivals, cuisine, languages and religions.

Interviewer: I'm sure that those of our viewers who are particularly interested in learning about different cultures and traditions will be motivated to spend their next holidays in South Africa just because of your description of the rich cultural diversity that South Africa holds in store for them. Thank you very much, Nelson, for providing our viewers with such deep insights into the ethnic mix of South Africa's population.

Nelson: You're welcome. But I'm afraid I really need to go now.

Interviewer: Yes, of course. Have a nice day. Goodbye.

Hörverstehenstexte 2021

Teil 1: Radio Podcast "Pros and cons of living in Dublin"

(Audiotrack: QR-Code rechts / Aufgaben S. 67)

Listen to the Irish radio podcast "Pros and cons of living in Dublin". Each Thursday afternoon the show host Jennifer Cook asks people to call into her show, which is broadcast from a Dublin-based radio station. The callers are invited to voice their opinions about living in Dublin.

Jennifer: Hello everyone. My name is Jennifer Cook. Welcome to our weekly podcast "Pros and cons of living in Dublin". If you would like to contribute to our show by expressing your opinion about life in the Irish capital, please call us on 01-800-800-800. … And here is our first caller … Holly, is it? How are you doing, Holly?

Holly: I'm great, thank you.

Jennifer: Now, Holly, what would you like to share with our listeners about living in Dublin?

Holly: Well, I'm really thrilled about living in Dublin. You see, I come from a small town located on the west coast of Ireland. And now I'm a student at Trinity College here in Dublin. The countryside on the west coast is, of course, absolutely gorgeous, no doubt about that. But as a teenager there was hardly anything I could do in my free time because the west of Ireland primarily consists of lonesome beaches, small towns and cattle or sheep farms. That's why I was so glad when I finally got the place at Trinity last year.

Jennifer: What fascinated you most of all when you first arrived in Dublin?

Holly: Obviously, the very first thing I got to know about Dublin was Trinity. I still remember the first weeks as a student here. I just couldn't believe that I really got a place at such a prestigious university.

Jennifer: Yes, you are certainly right. Trinity College is undoubtedly one of Dublin's major sights. But now that you have been living in Dublin for more than a year, is there anything else about Dublin that you have grown fond of?

Holly: Oh, yeah. You see, just like my father, I have always been a big fan of Irish folk music. When I was a teenager, my father took me to any live concert in the area where we lived. However, there weren't many opportunities to do so because, as I mentioned earlier, we basically lived in the middle of nowhere.

Jennifer: Well, I suppose here in Dublin there are quite a few opportunities to attend live folk music gigs, aren't there?

Holly: You bet! Not only are there a number of big music locations here in Dublin, you can also go to a lot of pubs and clubs offering live music several days a week. And especially at weekends you can listen to dozens of street musicians.

Jennifer: The music scene is one of the things that fascinate me about Dublin, too. Holly, thank you very much for your contribution today. Take care.

Holly: Have a great day, Jennifer, and thanks for having me on your show.

Jennifer: Well, it's always nice to hear about people who enjoy living in Dublin. Now, our next caller is … Adam. Let's see if he is also happy about living here in Dublin. Adam, how are you?

Adam: Hello, Jennifer. I'm fine, thanks. Now, I'm afraid I do not share Holly's enthusiasm about Dublin at all.

Jennifer: Okay, Adam. Let us know why you are not so fond of Dublin.

Adam: You know, I'm 39 years old and I have two kids. Our daughter goes to secondary school and our son is still in primary school.

Jennifer: So it's the schools in Dublin that you are not happy about?

Adam: No, not at all. The schools are fine, but it takes my wife and me so much time to drive our kids to school in the morning and collect them again in the afternoon.

Jennifer: Are the two schools so far away from your place?

Adam: Well, our daughter's school is too far away for her to walk or even cycle there. And our son is still too young to walk or cycle to school on his own.

Jennifer: But this is a problem for parents all over the country, not only here in Dublin, isn't it?

Adam: That's true, but can you imagine what traffic is like in Dublin every morning and afternoon? The streets are so jammed that it's just stop-and-go driving all the time. That is certainly quite different in small towns and villages.

Jennifer: I perfectly agree with you. Traffic in Dublin is just horrible. Fortunately, I can go to work by tram, so I can avoid the terrible jams in the city centre.

Adam: Lucky you! What makes things even worse is the fact that we need two cars for our kids and our jobs. And with two kids we need quite a large flat. All this makes living in Dublin almost unaffordable for us, despite the fact that my wife and I both have good jobs. We are really thinking of moving to a small town to be able to make ends meet again.

Jennifer: Well, I really feel for you because I also think that living in Dublin is incredibly expensive, especially for families. Anyway, I hope you will find a good solution for your family, Adam. Take care. Right, let's now take a quick commercial break, but stay tuned for more listeners voicing their opinions about life in our capital city …

Teil 2: Martha's Audio File

(Audiotrack: QR-Code S. 93 / Aufgaben S. 68)

Two years ago 15-year-old Martha from Münster in North Rhine-Westphalia spent a year as an exchange student in Leeds, a city in the north of England. Three weeks before her return to Germany, Martha was asked by Mr Hopkins, the head teacher of her school in Leeds, to record an audio file for their school website. For this audio file Mr Hopkins encouraged Martha to describe things that struck her as confusing, surprising, amusing or strange aspects of British culture. Listen to Martha's audio file.

Hi, my name is Martha Petzold. I come from a city called Münster, which is located in the northwest of Germany. It is the middle of June and I have now spent almost a year at your school as an exchange student. The other day, Mr Hopkins asked me to create an audio file about things that have struck me in one way or another about Britain and the British during my stay here in Leeds.

I'll start with the very first thing that any German exchange student would probably find amazing about British schools: school uniform! I had already known for a long time that school uniform is compulsory in most British schools. However, I must admit that I was not really fond of the uniform at first because in Germany I had always been used to dressing the way I wanted to at school.

I have come to understand why school uniform is not really that bad. In contrast to what often happens at schools in Germany, in Britain no student tries to outdress anybody else. And there is no bullying about not wearing branded clothes or about failing to follow the latest fashion trends, either. What's more, school uniform tends to create a sense of togetherness, identity and team spirit which can rarely be found in German schools.

Another thing that I noticed right away when I arrived here last summer is that the British say "sorry" much more often than Germans do. In fact, sometimes the British even apologise when it was the other person who did something wrong or inappropriate. For example, a couple of weeks ago, I ran along the hallway at school because I was late for my Science class. When I dashed around a corner, I bumped straight into Mr Hopkins. As a consequence, he dropped all the things he was carrying, but before I could say anything he had already apologised to me twice. In Germany, every teacher would have reacted angrily.

What will also catch the eye of a foreigner coming to Britain is undoubtedly the preference of the British for forming a queue. It may sound like a stereotype, but from my personal experience I can confirm that the British really queue everywhere: at bus stops, in tube stations, in front of shops, cinemas, restaurants, banks, you name it. A queue in itself may not be extraordinary, but the orderly, polite and quiet behaviour of British people in a queue is just stunning.

What I still find surprising about Britain, too, has to do with tea. Before coming here, I'd had no idea how important a cup of tea can be. Both in the morning and right after school in the afternoon I was asked by either of my host parents whether I would like a cup of tea. But that is not the full story about the importance of tea in Britain. To begin with, in the morning the tea has to be strong and dark to help people wake up, whereas the tea served in the afternoon is milder and

lighter. Second, there can be long discussions in Britain about whether milk has to be added before or after pouring tea into the cup. Finally, the enormous importance of tea in British culture is also reflected in common English idioms such as "not my cup of tea" or "not for all the tea in China".
Last but not least, for a foreigner like me it is quite amazing how often the British talk about the weather. After spending a year in Britain, however, I think I have come to understand why the British seem to be so obsessed with talking about the weather. Here in Leeds, just like in other parts of Britain I suppose, the weather is much more changeable than in my hometown in Germany. Even during the summer, you can experience a sequence of morning fog, rainfall, stretches of sunshine and strong winds with clouds rushing by – even within a couple of hours.
Well, there are certainly a number of other things about Britain that I could enlarge on, but I think I'd better stop here. Thank you very much for listening.

Hörverstehenstexte 2022

Teil 1: British TV Game Show "How well do I really know the UK?"

(Audiotrack: QR-Code rechts / Aufgaben S. 76)

Listen to the audio track of a British TV game show which is called "How well do I really know the UK?". The show is hosted by Nick Cunningham. In the show three contestants have to answer "easy", "intermediate" or "hard" questions about one of four subject matters, namely "geography", "history", "politics" or "The Royal Family". The contestants can choose both the difficulty level and the subject matter. They can gain, or lose, one, two, or three points, respectively, depending on the level of difficulty they have chosen for each particular question.

Nick: Now, it's time to start the third round of our game. But before that, let me give you a quick update on the current score. After the first two rounds Jane is in the lead with a total of five points, followed by Kevin with three points. Lizzy has gained one point so far. But, Lizzy, please don't be discouraged by this score. We still have another six rounds to go, so nothing has been decided yet. Right … well, Kevin, I believe it's your turn to pick a subject matter and a difficulty level.

Kevin: Thank you, Nick. I think this time around I'll go for "geography".

Nick: Okay, and what about the difficulty level, Kevin?

Kevin: Hmm, give me a hard question for a change.

Nick: Right. Here is your question, Kevin. Put the following three cities in descending order of population size: Belfast, Sheffield, Edinburgh.

Kevin: Oh, God. That's a tricky one indeed. Now, let me think … I'm quite sure that Sheffield has the largest population of those three cities. But I can only guess about Edinburgh and Belfast, to be honest. Hmm, okay, with a fifty-fifty chance I'd say that Belfast is number 2 und Edinburgh number 3.

Nick: You were quite certain about Sheffield, and I can tell you straight away that you were right about that. The interesting thing is that your guess about Belfast and Edinburgh was right, too. Congratulations, your answer has won you three points.
Okay, who's next? Oh yes, it's your turn now, Jane. Mind you, Kevin has just managed to take the lead with a total of six points. However, you can regain the lead with your next answer, of course. Please pick a subject matter and a difficulty level.

Jane: Thanks a million, Nick. I'll try my very best with an intermediate question about the Royal Family.

Nick: Okay, let's see what question I've got for you … Here it is. The Queen is the official owner of some species of sea life which live within three miles of UK shores. Can you name at least two of those species?

Jane: Wow, what a bizarre question. I remember reading somewhere that all swans in the UK officially belong to the Queen. But I have never ever heard about any species of ocean life that the Queen technically owns. I'm sorry, Nick, but I really don't know the answer.

Nick: That's quite a pity, Jane because this means you are losing two points on this. Well, believe it or not, the Queen technically owns all dolphins, whales, porpoises[1], and sturgeons[2] living within 3 miles of UK shores. That is quite an amazing fun fact, isn't it? Let's now give Lizzy a chance to gain some points in this third round. Lizzy, what subject matter and difficulty level would you like to choose?

Lizzy: Considering that I have got only one point so far, I think I'll choose a hard question. About … politics.

Nick: Obviously, you want to keep pace with Jane and Kevin by choosing a 3-point question, right? I hope the following question will help you to do so. Here is your question. Which is the smallest UK constituency[3] by geographical area?

Lizzy: Well, interestingly, I happen to know the answer to that question. You see, my husband is a member of the Labour Party, and he has actively supported the Labour campaigns in the last two general elections. Hence I know from him that the smallest UK constituency has been held by one of the most famous Labour MPs for quite some time now. And this constituency is Islington North in London.

Nick: Well, Lizzy, I must admit that I'm quite impressed, not only because your answer is correct, but also because I suspect that only very few people know this. Congratulations, Lizzy ...Let's now check what the score is after our third round: Kevin is in the lead with six points, followed by Lizzy with four points. And Jane is now in third place with a total of 3 points.

1 porpoise = Schweinswal, Tümmler
2 sturgeon = Stör
3 constituency = Wahlkreis, -bezirk

Teil 2: Podcast "Dublin and Belfast: travel account"

(Audiotrack: QR-Code S. 95 / Aufgaben S. 77)

Thank you for listening to my podcast "Rebecca's travel accounts". Today I would like to tell you about a short trip to Ireland which I made last week. Compared with the various trips to all four corners of the earth which I have told you about in my podcasts over the last couple of months, Ireland may not seem to be the most exotic holiday destination. Nevertheless, my trip was really exciting and full of interesting impressions.
Let me begin by pointing out that I did not do what most tourists probably do in Ireland. I did not cycle, hike or experience Ireland's natural beauty in any other way. Instead, I wanted to immerse myself in the urban atmosphere of Ireland's two major cities, namely Dublin and Belfast. I started my trip on 2nd of August, flying from Manchester to Dublin. After arriving at Dublin Airport, I picked up a rental car and drove straight to the B&B I had booked online a couple of weeks before. The managers of my B&B, Orla and Liam, were the most warm-hearted people you can imagine. In a way they really confirmed what I had heard about the Irish all my life, namely that they are very cheerful, kind and hospitable people indeed. For the next three days I had planned to take in as many of Dublin's major sights and tourist attractions as possible. For example, I explored Trinity College with its beautiful campus and the world-famous Book of Kells. Second, I visited two of the most imposing churches in Dublin: Christ Church Cathedral and St. Patrick's Cathedral. Moreover, I took part in a guided tour of the Guinness Storehouse. This tour was rounded off by a pint of Guinness, which is arguably the best-known Irish beer, on the top floor of the building in a bar named 'Gravity Bar'. Last but not least, on my final night in Dublin I wanted to dive into the city's night life in the Temple Bar district. Most of the restaurants in that district may not really serve what I would call gourmet food, but the pubs are absolutely fantastic. There is live music in almost all of them, and the atmosphere in those pubs is just amazing.
The next day I left Dublin right after breakfast. I drove onto the motorway, heading north to Belfast. The drive from Dublin to Belfast takes about two hours. What is interesting about this drive is the fact that you cross the border between the Republic of Ireland, which is part of the EU, and Northern Ireland, which is part of the UK, without really noticing it right away. There are no border controls, and the landscape is very similar in both parts of Ireland. What you do notice, though, is that all of a sudden the speed limits on traffic signs are in miles rather than in kilometres per hour and that petrol stations display prices in pounds rather than in euros.
After arriving in Belfast, I checked into my hotel right away. As it was lunchtime, I decided to have a snack in a fish and chips shop around the corner. As soon as I opened my mouth to order my food, all the customers in the shop started to look at me. The first thought I had was that my British accent had caused them to do so. The second thought that went through my mind related to the fact that my hotel was located in a part of Belfast where more than 90% of the population are Catholics.
Then one of the customers came up to me and asked me what part of Britain I was from. I said that I was from Manchester, expecting some kind of hostile reaction. But what actually happened was quite the opposite. Some of the other customers, namely two men and two women, also came to my table, telling me all kinds of stories about their uncles, aunts, grandfathers or other relatives who had gone to Manchester, Sheffield or Liverpool to work or study there many years ago. They were all very friendly, and after a short chat they offered to show me some of the top tourist attractions in and around Belfast in the next couple of days.
The sights they showed me included some of the famous attractions like Belfast Castle, Belfast City Hall, Queen's University, the Botanic Gardens and the super-modern 'Titanic Belfast' museum. However, they also showed me some other places which you will not usually find on any tour guide's list of attractions. For example, they took me to the Cuban Sandwich Factory, where I ate the most delicious sandwich I have ever had in my entire life. Moreover, we went to the Belfast Gin School & Distillery, where you can learn to make your own bottle of gin that you may even take home. Finally, on the last night, we went to a live concert in a music venue[1] called Voodoo, which boasts a fantastic atmosphere.

This is where my travel account about my trip to Ireland ends. I hope you have enjoyed it and can take advantage of it if you decide to visit Dublin or Belfast, both of which are truly worth visiting. But now I need to continue organising my next trip to a destination that I am not yet giving away at this point. If you want to find out about it, just listen to my next podcast.

[1] venue = Veranstaltungsort

Notizen

Schule – und dann?

Tipps und Infos zum Start in den Beruf

- Bewerbungsunterlagen
- Anschreiben
- Lebenslauf
- Einstellungstests + Lösungen
- Assessment-Center
- Online-Tipps
- Bildungswege

Bewerbungsunterlagen

Auch, wenn die klassische Bewerbung per Post von vielen Firmen noch akzeptiert wird, so bevorzugen die meisten Betriebe inzwischen eine Online-Bewerbung. Dabei bieten große Unternehmen oft eigene Bewerbungsportale auf ihren Firmenwebseiten, in denen die Bewerber/-innen ein Onlineformular ausfüllen und ihre Unterlagen (Lebenslauf, Zeugnisse, ggf. weitere Nachweise und Bewerbungsfoto) hochladen können. Hat die Firma kein Bewerbungsportal, so verschickt der/die Bewerber/-in seine/ihre Bewerbung per E-Mail mit entsprechendem Anhang. Dabei empfiehlt es sich, die oben genannten Unterlagen in ein einziges Dokument zu packen, damit der/die Personalzuständige nicht lange suchen und nur eine Datei öffnen muss. Wichtig bei einer Online-Bewerbung (egal ob Bewerberportal oder E-Mail) ist jedoch immer eine seriöse E-Mail-Adresse, die Qualität der eingescannten Dokumente, das richtige Format (meist PDF) und die Dateigröße (max. 2 – 3 MB).

Für die Onlinebewerbung gelten die gleichen Maßstäbe wie für die klassische Bewerbungsmappe. Insbesondere das Anschreiben sollte die herkömmlichen Kriterien erfüllen (Briefkopf, Betreffzeile mit der ausgeschriebenen Stelle, die persönliche Anrede, das direkte Eingehen auf den angestrebten Ausbildungsplatz, korrekte Rechtschreibung und Zeichensetzung sowie einheitliches Layout, Grußformel und Unterschrift etc.) und dabei eine DIN-A4-Seite nicht überschreiten. Wird das Anschreiben als Anhang versendet, so sollte eine Kurzversion im Textfenster der E-Mail enthalten sein. Das Anschreiben kann aber auch Teil der E-Mail selbst sein.

Die folgende Liste gibt Ihnen einen wichtigen Überblick über die Unterlagen, die Ihre Bewerbung enthalten sollte:

Deckblatt (optional)

- Titel: Bewerbung für (Ausildungsplatz/Stelle)
- Kontaktdaten (Name, Adresse, Telefonnummer, E-Mail)

Bewerbungsfoto

- professionelles Bewerbungsfoto (bei Papierfoto: Name und Adresse auf Rückseite schreiben)
- Standard: Foto oben rechts im Lebenslauf oder auf dem Deckblatt

Anschreiben

- persönliche Kontaktdaten im Briefkopf aktuell und richtig
- Name und Adresse des Ansprechpartners richtig schreiben
- korrekte Betreffzeile, z. B. Bewerbung für/als (Ausbildungsplatz)
- Grund für Bewerbung angeben
- Bezug zwischen Anforderungen und eigenen Fähigkeiten formulieren
- nicht länger als eine DIN-A4-Seite
- fehlerfreie Rechtschreibung und Zeichensetzung; einheitliches Layout
- Grußformel und Unterschrift

Lebenslauf

- persönliche Angaben (Name, Anschrift, Telefonnummer und E-Mail-Adresse, Geburtsdatum, Staatsangehörigkeit)
- Schulbildung (besuchte Schultypen) und voraussichtlicher Schulabschluss
- Berufserfahrung: Praktika, Aushilfs- oder Nebenjobs, etc.
- außerschulisches Engagement (z. B. Ehrenamt)
- besondere Kenntnisse oder Fähigkeiten
- nicht länger als zwei DIN-A4-Seiten
- lückenlos, korrekte Zeitangaben
- Unterschrift

Anlagen

- Kopien von Zeugnissen, Referenzen, Zertifikaten

Anschreiben

Bevor Sie sich bei einer Firma bewerben, sollten Sie sich bei der dortigen Personalabteilung nach dem Namen der zuständigen Person erkundigen. Das Anschreiben sollte, so weit möglich, immer eine personalisierte Anrede enthalten; Formulierungen wie „Sehr geehrte Damen und Herren“ sollten vermieden werden. Es macht auch einen guten Eindruck, wenn Sie sich vorher schon einmal über das Berufsbild informiert haben und in Ihrem Anschreiben darstellen können, warum gerade Sie sich für diesen Beruf eignen.
Außerdem ist es wichtig, dass Sie sich über das Unternehmen informieren, bei dem Sie sich bewerben. Vermeiden Sie dabei Schreib- und Kommafehler und vergessen Sie Ihre Unterschrift nicht.

Beispiel für ein klassisches Anschreiben

Marc Schmidt
Bahnhofstraße 158
35889 Krielinghausen
Telefon 06456 445932
E-Mail marc.schmidt@mail.de

Bäckerei Herrlinger
Herrn Fritz Herrlinger
Backgasse 15
33886 Wieshain

Krielinghausen, 15. Oktober 2021

Bewerbung um einen Ausbildungsplatz zum Bäcker

Sehr geehrter Herr Herrlinger,

durch Ihre Mitarbeiterin, Frau Fischer, habe ich erfahren, dass Sie ab dem 1. September 2022 einen Ausbildungsplatz zum Bäcker anbieten. Dafür möchte ich mich bei Ihnen bewerben.

Der Beruf des Bäckers ist bereits seit Langem mein Traumberuf. Die handwerkliche Arbeit in einer Backstube und der Umgang mit Lebensmitteln haben mich schon immer interessiert. Als Kind habe ich mit meiner Mutter oft Kuchen und Plätzchen gebacken, inzwischen backe ich alleine und probiere auch gerne neue Rezepte aus. In einem örtlichen Gasthof habe ich bereits erste Erfahrungen gesammelt.

Im Juni beende ich die Schule mit dem Hauptschulabschluss. Danach würde ich gerne bei Ihnen ein Praktikum machen, damit Sie mich vorab besser kennenlernen können.

Über die Einladung zu einem Vorstellungsgespräch freue ich mich.

Mit freundlichen Grüßen

M. Schmidt

Marc Schmidt

Anlagen: Lebenslauf mit Foto, Zertifikat Praktikum, Schulzeugnis

Lebenslauf

Ein in Aufsatzform formulierter Lebenslauf ist heutzutage nicht mehr üblich. Arbeitgeber und Arbeitgeberinnen erwarten stattdessen einen Lebenslauf in Tabellenform – und zwar:

- ▶ chronologisch geordnet (die in Deutschland üblichere, traditionelle Variante)
- ▶ umgekehrt chronologisch geordnet mit den neuesten Daten am Anfang (die moderne internationale/EU-Variante)

Beispiel für einen chronologischen Lebenslauf

Lebenslauf
Marc Schmidt

Bahnhofstraße 158
35889 Krielinghausen
Telefon 06456 445932
E-Mail marc.schmidt@mail.de

Persönliche Daten	
Geburtstag und -ort	23. April 2007 in Krielinghausen
Staatsangehörigkeit	deutsch
Schulischer Werdegang	
09/2013 bis 07/2017	Grundschule Krielinghausen
09/2017 bis 06/2022	Gesamtschule Krielinghausen • voraussichtlicher Schulabschluss: Hauptschulabschluss • Lieblingsfächer: Mathematik, Werken Teilnahme an der Koch-AG
Betriebspraktikum	
02/2021 bis 03/2021	Frischmarkt AG, Winterhain Dreiwöchiges Schülerpraktikum • Einräumen der angelieferten Waren • Mitarbeit an der Kasse • Mitarbeit an der Brottheke
Aushilfstätigkeiten	
08/2021 bis 09/2021	Gasthof „Sonne“, Krielinghausen Vierwöchiger Ferienjob • Tätigkeit als Küchenhilfe • Mitarbeit im Service
Hobbys	Backen, Kochen, Musik
Seit 10/2017	Mitglied im Musikverein (Posaune)

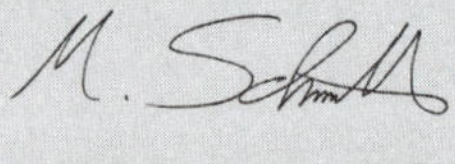

Krielinghausen, 15. Oktober 2021

Einstellungstests

Viele Schüler/-innen kennen die Angst vor Prüfungen. In der Schule hat man wenigstens den Vorteil, dass man ungefähr weiß, was drankommen kann. Berufseinstellungstests sind den meisten jedoch fremd und der Druck, sich gegen andere Bewerber/-innen durchzusetzen, verstärkt die Prüfungsangst meist noch.

Wir wollen Sie auf diese Situation vorbereiten und Ihnen die Angst vor dem Unbekannten nehmen. Dafür haben wir auf den nächsten Seiten einige Musteraufgaben zusammengestellt, wie sie in solchen Tests vorkommen können.

Es geht den Prüfer/-innen nicht nur darum, dass Sie alle Aufgaben korrekt lösen, sondern auch darum, wie Sie sich in einer solchen Situation verhalten und wo Ihre Stärken liegen.

Die Lösungen zu den Tests finden Sie auf Seite A14.

1. Logisches Denken

Zahlenreihen

Welche Zahl ergänzt die Zahlenreihe sinnvoll?

1. 2 6 12 20 30 ?

2. 16 23 28 38 49 62 ?

TIPP

Notieren Sie den Rechenschritt zur jeweils nächsten Zahl, dann kommen Sie meist schnell auf die Lösung.

Wortanalogien

1. Mehl verhält sich zu Kuchen wie Zement zu ...?

a) Bäcker b) Maurer
c) Haus d) Hefe

2. Schnecke verhält sich zu Ohr wie Knöchel zu ...?

a) Oberschenkel b) Fuß
c) Gartenhaus d) Pflanze

TIPP

Untersuchen Sie das vorgegebene Wortpaar und suchen Sie die bestehende Beziehung zwischen den Wörtern.

Beziehungen

1. Morgen ist Mittwoch. Welcher Tag war vorgestern?

a) Montag b) Dienstag c) Mittwoch d) Donnerstag
e) Freitag f) Samstag g) Sonntag

2. Es ist die Tochter deiner Großmutter, aber nicht deine Tante. Wer ist es?

a) Großmutter b) Nichte c) Cousine d) Tochter
e) Mutter f) Schwester g) Tante

Grafikanalogien

Bestimmen Sie aus den vier möglichen Grafiken diejenige, die die Bildgleichung sinnvoll ergänzt.

1.

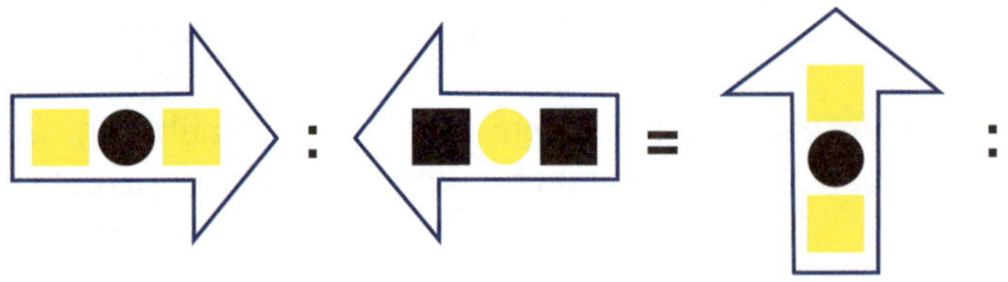

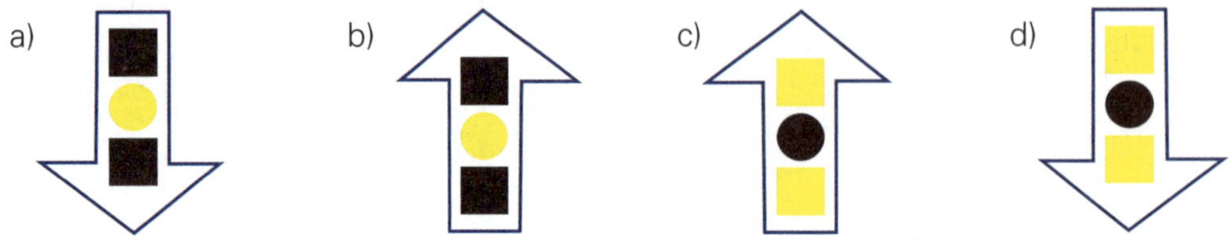

2.

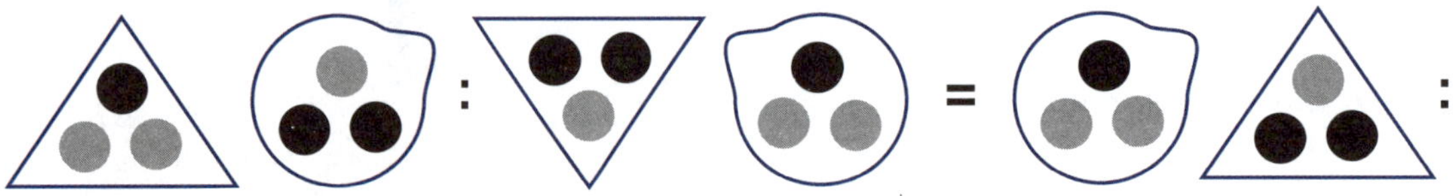

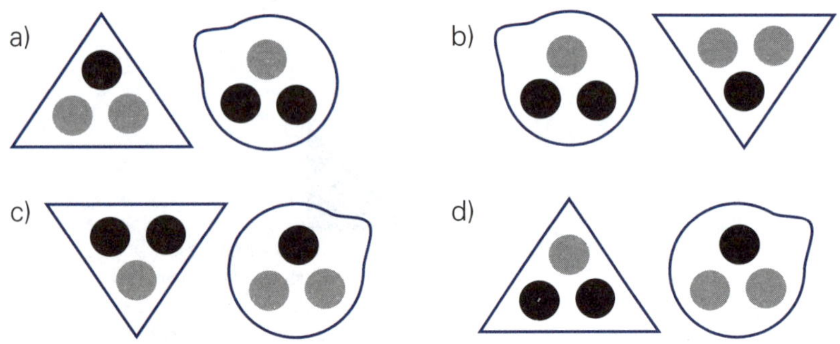

2. Konzentration

Die alphabetische Reihenfolge

Erkennen Sie die korrekten alphabetischen Buchstabenabfolgen von 3 bis 5 Buchstaben und unterstreichen Sie diese.

1. dhabanejdhenahjbekjabcdfgejndnansmjodnbdjwxyzjbdnrnmalmüppkdknshdkjklndhadnenduenduendopqrhzfunrucmchdtebnsmnaüskendhabezefghnmkelodhbezshynmnbabsebdnmeidjnantzbszxtgbsnxhzsstuvwb
2. hnsndnadhendnsjuvwxhdndnbdnmejdkalehijkdnmadnsomemaödefgnbdbanskjneksoxnaknbsjxonbshzebaisbelmanslmnopzehbaisjbajsnenakmslxpklmhjdamsidjendhijdnsmalsneisxnmamsrstudbansmensuaylxvn

Kopfrechnen

Geben Sie das Ergebnis folgender Rechnung an. Rechnen Sie Schritt für Schritt, die Rechenregel „Punkt vor Strich“ gilt hier nicht.

1. $6 + 6 - 3 + 7 - 5 \cdot 2 + 8 - 20 \cdot 2 + 7 =$
2. $81 : 9 + 7 + 5 + 3 : 2 + 13 \cdot 2 - 20 : 2 - 15 + 7 \cdot 2 - 6 \cdot 3 =$

Mosaik

1. In welchem Feld ist ein Mosaikbaustein falsch? Geben Sie an, ob A, B, C oder D richtig ist.

1 2 3

TIPP

Kreuzen Sie im Zweifelsfall die Antwort an, die Ihnen richtig erscheint.

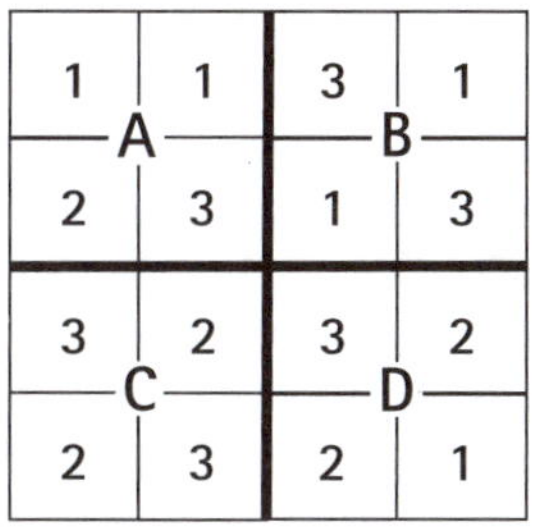

2. In welchem Feld ist ein Mosaikbaustein falsch? Geben Sie an, ob A, B, C, D oder E richtig ist.

1 2 3 4 5 6 7

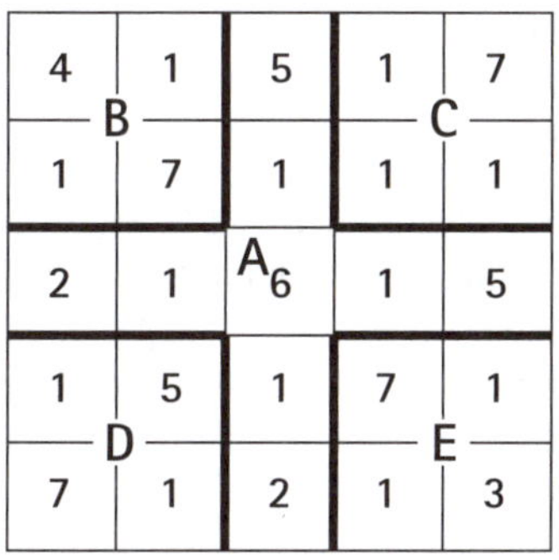

Additions-/Subtraktionsaufgaben

Rechnen Sie zuerst die obere und dann die untere Zeile aus. Ist das zweite Ergebnis kleiner als das erste, ziehen Sie es vom ersten ab und schreiben diese Differenz auf. Ist das Ergebnis der zweiten Zeile größer, müssen Sie beide Ergebnisse addieren.

1. 2 + 4 − 5
5 + 4 + 4

2. 7 + 8 − 3
4 + 5 − 2

3. 4 + 4 − 3
7 + 6 + 4

4. 4 + 5 + 4
9 − 8 + 7

5. 8 − 4 − 1
3 + 4 + 6

6. 3 + 8 − 3
4 + 3 + 2

7. 4 + 9 − 7
5 + 6 − 3

8. 9 − 2 + 7
3 + 2 + 4

9. 7 + 3 − 4
4 + 7 − 3

TIPP

Rechnen Sie jede Reihe für sich und schreiben Sie das Ergebnis auf. So verlieren Sie nicht die Übersicht.

3. Allgemeinwissen

1. Wie viel Liter Blut fließen durchschnittlich durch den menschlichen Körper?

a) 5 bis 6 Liter
b) 12 bis 14 Liter
c) 8 bis 10 Liter
d) 3 bis 4 Liter

TIPP

Wenn Sie sich nicht ganz sicher sind, gehen Sie nach dem Ausschlussverfahren vor und kreuzen Sie auf jeden Fall eine Antwort an.

2. Wie lautet das chemische Gegenstück zur Säure?

a) Salz
b) Oxid
c) Zucker
d) Base

3. Welche Einheit bezeichnet elektrischen Strom?

a) Hertz
b) Ampere
c) Watt
d) Pascal

4. Wie viele Seitenflächen hat ein Tetraeder?

a) 4
b) 6
c) 8
d) gar keine, es ist eine Kugel

5. Wie nennt man in der Informatik die kleinste Informationseinheit?

a) Chip
b) Unix
c) Link
d) Bit

6. Welches Wirtschaftssystem hat Deutschland?

a) Zentrale Marktwirtschaft
b) Soziale Marktwirtschaft
c) Kapitalistische Marktwirtschaft
d) Sozialistische Marktwirtschaft

7. An wie viele Länder grenzt Deutschland?

a) 6
b) 7
c) 8
d) 9

8. Wessen Interessen werden in der Kommunalpolitik vertreten?

a) Bundesländer
b) Bund
c) Landkreis und Gemeinde
d) Europäische Gemeinschaft

9. Wer war der erste Bundeskanzler der Bundesrepublik Deutschland?

a) Gerhard Schröder
b) Konrad Adenauer
c) Helmut Kohl
d) Ludwig Erhard

10. Unter welchem Namen schrieb der erste römische Kaiser Octavian Geschichte?

a) Caesar
b) Augustus
c) Romulus
d) Herkules

11. In welchem Drama Goethes wird die „Gretchenfrage“ gestellt?

a) Götz von Berlichingen
b) Faust I
c) Torquato Tasso
d) Egmont

12. Wer schrieb das Stück „Die Räuber“?

a) Johann Wolfgang von Goethe
b) Friedrich Schiller
c) Gotthold Ephraim Lessing
d) Wilhelm Hauff

13. Welcher Künstler malte die „Mona Lisa“?

a) Pablo Picasso
b) Michelangelo Buonarroti
c) Salvador Dali
d) Leonardo da Vinci

14. Wie heißen die Stimmlagen der Männerstimmen, absteigend nach der Höhe sortiert?

a) Sopran, Bass, Tenor
b) Tenor, Bariton, Bass
c) Bariton, Tenor, Bass
d) Alt, Tenor, Bass

15. Woraus besteht eine Nordische Kombination?

a) Skisprung und Skilanglauf
b) Skilanglauf und Schießen
c) Slalom und Abfahrt
d) Skiflug und Slalom

4. Sprachgefühl

Abkürzungen

Wofür stehen folgende Abkürzungen? Kreuzen Sie alle richtigen Antworten an.

1. a) Mofa = Montagefabrik
b) ABS = Autobahnschnee
c) FAZ = Frankfurter Allgemeine Zeitung
d) DIN = Deutsches Institut für Normung

2. a) IHK = Industrie- und Handelskammer
b) AGB = Angestelltengesetzbuch
c) USA = United States of America
d) EU = Europäische Universität

3. a) BASF = Badische Anilin- und Soda-Fabrik
b) PS = Pendelstrom
c) BVerfG = Bundesverfassungsgericht
d) VW = Volkswagen

Wortbedeutungen

Welches der vier Wörter passt nicht zu den anderen?

1.

a) Deutsch
b) Französisch
c) Schwäbisch
d) Englisch

2.

a) Fußball
b) Tennis
c) Basketball
d) Schwimmen

3.

a) Buchstabe
b) Zahl
c) Vokal
d) Konsonant

Fremdwörter

1. Was bedeutet das Fremdwort „heterogen"?

a) fremd
b) ungleichartig
c) stark erhitzt
d) keimfrei

2. Was bedeutet das Fremdwort „relativ"?

a) verhältnismäßig
b) sehr klein
c) sehr groß
d) verändert

Satzergänzungen

1. Das menschliche Verhalten wird von der … untersucht.

a) Biologie
b) Zoologie
c) Chemie
d) Psychologie

2. Im Straßenverkehr muss man besonders … sein?

a) aggressiv
b) mutig
c) schnell
d) aufmerksam

TIPP

Führen Sie zuerst die Aufgaben und Antworten zusammen, bei denen Sie sich sicher sind.

3. Der Stundenzeiger einer Uhr ist immer ... als der Minutenzeiger.

a) länger
b) kürzer
c) dicker
d) dünner

Sinnverwandte Sprichwörter

Welches Sprichwort hat eine ähnliche Bedeutung wie das vorgegebene?

1. „Jeder kehre vor seiner eigenen Türe."

a) Wer anderen eine Grube gräbt, fällt selbst hinein.
b) Wer im Glashaus sitzt, soll nicht mit Steinen werfen.
c) Der Lauscher an der Wand hört seine eigene Schand.
d) Reden ist Silber, Schweigen ist Gold.

2. „Das Glück ist mit den Dummen."

a) Die dümmsten Bauern haben die größten Kartoffeln.
b) Den Tüchtigen hilft das Glück.
c) Scherben bringen Glück.
d) Wer nicht wagt, der nicht gewinnt.

Groß- und Kleinschreibung

Welcher Satz ist richtig geschrieben?

1. a) Aber heute Früh habe ich wieder einen Arzttermin.
b) Aber Heute früh habe ich wieder einen Arzttermin.
c) Aber heute früh habe ich wieder einen Arzttermin.

2. a) Sie hatte fünf einsen im Zeugnis und war zweite im Weitsprung.
b) Sie hatte fünf einsen im Zeugnis und war Zweite im Weitsprung.
c) Sie hatte fünf Einsen im Zeugnis und war zweite im Weitsprung.
d) Sie hatte fünf Einsen im Zeugnis und war Zweite im Weitsprung.

3. a) Als die englische Königin abends in ihr Schloss kam, war das Licht schon aus.
b) Als die Englische Königin abends in ihr Schloss kam, war das Licht schon aus.
c) Als die Englische Königin Abends in ihr Schloss kam, war das Licht schon aus.
d) Als die englische Königin Abends in ihr Schloss kam, war das Licht schon aus.

Rechtschreibung

Welches Wort ist richtig geschrieben?

1. a) Dampflockomotive
b) Dampflockomotife
c) Dampflokomottife
d) Damflockomotive
e) Dampflokomotive

2. a) Renaissanse
b) Renaissance
c) Rennaissance
d) Rennaisance
e) Renaisance

TIPP

Stellen Sie sich die Wörter ausgesprochen vor und überlegen Sie, welches richtig klingt.

Bilden Sie den Plural folgender Wörter.

3. Visum
4. Globus
5. Pizza

5. Mathematisches Denken

Dreisatz

1. Ein Motorrad benötigt für eine 125 km lange Strecke 22,50 Liter Benzin. Welchen Verbrauch hat das Motorrad auf 100 km?

2. In einem Betrieb kommen 60 % der Männer und 50 % der Frauen mit dem Auto zur Arbeit. Wie viel Prozent kommen insgesamt mit dem Auto, wenn dort 60 % Männer arbeiten?

3. Vier Personen haben ein durchschnittliches Gewicht von 69 kg. Die erste Person wiegt 76 kg, die zweite 61 kg, die dritte 65 kg. Wie viel wiegt die vierte Person?

Maßeinheiten

1. Wie viele Stunden und Minuten sind 7200 Sekunden?

a) 120 Stunden
b) 2 Stunden
c) 5 Stunden
d) 1 Stunde 20 Minuten

2. Wie viele Hektar sind 55 000 Quadratmeter?

a) 5,5
b) 550
c) 55
d) 5550

3. Wie viele Kubikmeter sind 300 Liter?

a) 0,3
b) 30
c) 3
d) 300

Prozent- und Zinsrechnung

1. Die Mehrwertsteuer (19 %) beim Kauf eines Fahrrads beträgt 57 Euro. Wie teuer ist das Fahrrad inklusive Mehrwertsteuer?

a) 243 Euro
b) 357 Euro
c) 300 Euro
d) 414 Euro

2. Nach welcher Zeit sind 15 000 Euro auf 20 000 Euro angewachsen, bei einer jährlichen Verzinsung von 5 %?

a) 6 Jahre und 216 Tage
b) 6 Jahre und 260 Tage
c) 6 Jahre und 220 Tage
d) 6 Jahre und 8 Monate

Gleichungen

Ergänzen Sie die fehlenden Rechenzeichen bei den Gleichungen, um auf die vorgegebene Lösung zu kommen. Die Rechenregel „Punkt vor Strich" gilt hier.

1. 8 … 4 … 1 = 31
2. 2 … 60 … 12 = -3
3. 11 … 20 … 5 … 12 = 99

6. Räumliche Vorstellung

Drehungen im Raum

In welcher Position befindet sich der Buchstabe nach der Drehung, wie es die Pfeile der Reihe nach vorgeben? Die Drehungen sind jeweils 90 Grad um die Raumachsen.

a) ☐ 

b) ☐ 

c) ☐ 

d) ☐ 

e) ☐ 

Flächen eines Körpers

Bestimmen Sie die Gesamtzahl an Flächen der vorgegebenen Körper.

1. 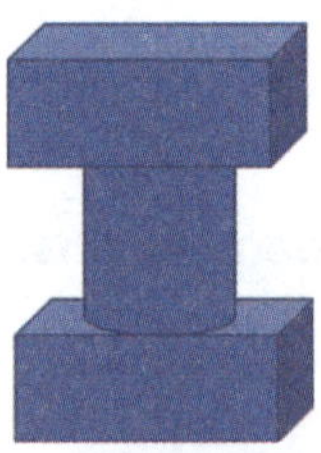

a) 15 b) 12 c) 14 d) 17

2. 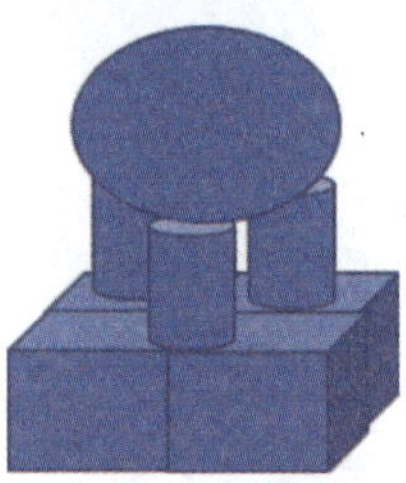

a) 32 b) 33 c) 34 d) 30

3. 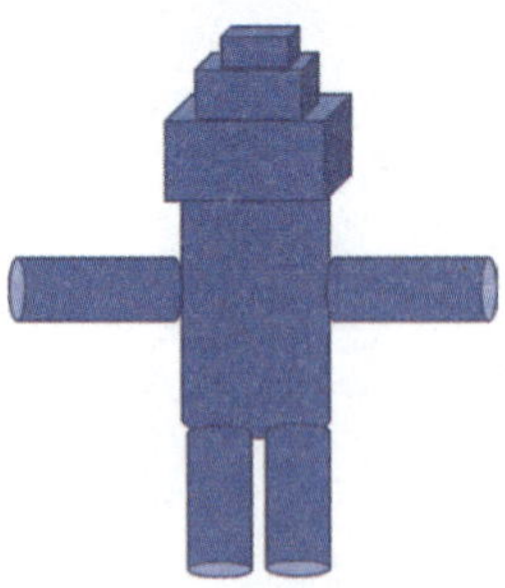

a) 31 b) 30 c) 29 d) 32

Spiegelbilder

Welche Figur passt nicht zu den anderen?

1. a) ☐  b) ☐  c) ☐ 

d) ☐  e) ☐  f) ☐ 

2. a) ☐  b) ☐  c) ☐ 

d) ☐  e) ☐  f) ☐ 

Würfelfaltung

1. Welcher Würfel lässt sich aus dieser Vorlage falten?

a) ☐  b) ☐  c) ☐  d) ☐ 

2. Aus welcher Faltvorlage lässt sich dieser Würfel falten?

a) ☐ 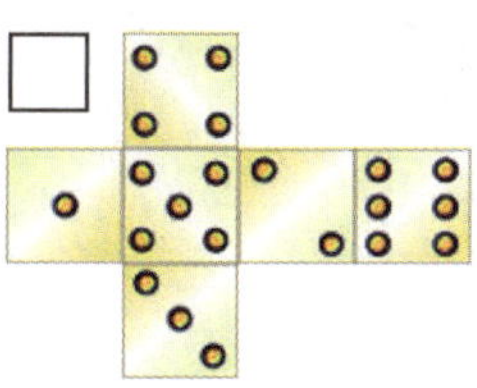 b) ☐ 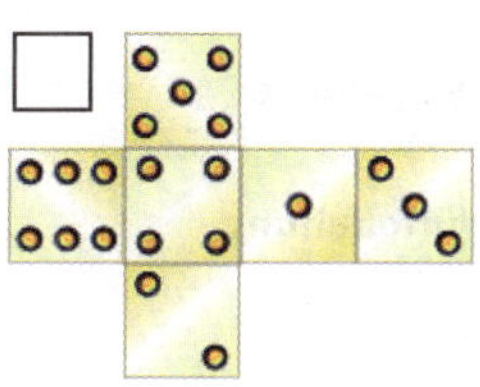 c) ☐ 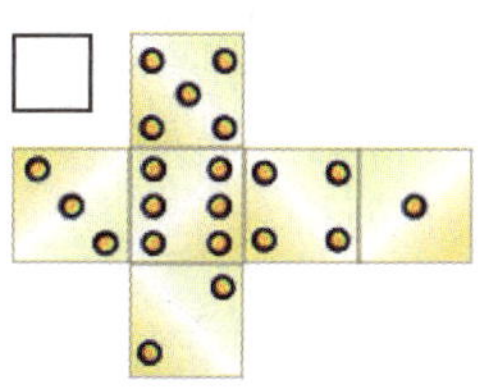 d) ☐ 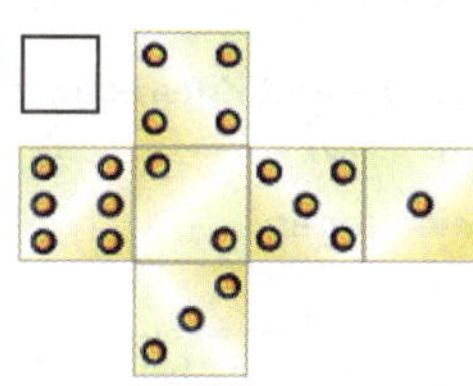

Lösungen Einstellungstests

1. Logisches Denken

Zahlenreihen

1. 2 $^{+4}$ 6 $^{+6}$ 12 $^{+8}$ 20 $^{+10}$ 30 $^{+12}$ **42**
2. 16 $^{+7}$ 23 $^{+5}$ 28 $^{+10}$ 38 $^{+11}$ 49 $^{+13}$ 62 $^{+8}$ **70**
(Quersumme addieren)

Wortanalogien

1. c) Haus **2.** b) Fuß

Beziehungen

1. g) Sonntag **2.** a) Mutter

Grafikanalogien

1. a)  **2.** b) 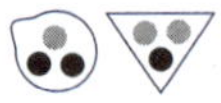

2. Konzentration

Alphabetische Reihenfolge

1. dhabanejdhenahjbekjabcdfgejndnansmjodnbdjwxyzjbdnrnmalmüppkd-knshdkjklndhadnenduenduendopqrhzfunrucmchdtebnsmnaüskendha-bezefghnmkelodhbezshynmnbabsebdnmeidjnantzbszxtgbsnxhzsstu-vwb
2. hnsndnadhendnsjuvwxhdndnbdnmejdkalehijkdnmadnsomemaödefgn-bdbanskjneksoxnaknbsjxonbshzebaisbelmanslmnopzehbaisjbajsnen-akmslxpklmhjdamsidjendhijdnsmalsneisxnmamsrstudbansmensuaylxvn

Kopfrechnen

1. 27 **2.** 24

Mosaik

1. D **2.** C

Additions-/Subtraktionsaufgaben

1. 14 **2.** 5 **3.** 22
4. 5 **5.** 16 **6.** 17
7. 14 **8.** 5 **9.** 14

3. Allgemeinwissen

1. a) 5 bis 6 Liter
2. d) Base
3. b) Ampere
4. a) 4
5. d) Bit
6. b) Soziale Marktwirtschaft
7. d) 9
8. c) Landkreis und Gemeinde
9. b) Konrad Adenauer
10. b) Augustus
11. b) Faust I
12. b) Friedrich Schiller
13. d) Leonardo da Vinci
14. b) Tenor, Bariton, Bass
15. a) Skisprung und Skilanglauf

4. Sprachgefühl

Abkürzungen

1. c) FAZ = Frankfurter Allgemeine Zeitung
d) DIN = Deutsches Institut für Normung
2. a) IHK = Industrie- und Handelskammer
c) USA = United States of America
3. a) BASF = Badische Anilin- und Soda-Fabrik
c) BVerfG = Bundesverfassungsgericht
d) VW = Volkswagen

Wortbedeutungen

1. c) Schwäbisch **2.** d) Schwimmen **3.** c) Zahl

Fremdwörter

1. b) ungleichartig **2.** a) verhältnismäßig

Satzergänzungen

1. d) Psychologie **2.** d) aufmerksam **3.** b) kürzer

Sinnverwandte Sprichwörter

1. b) Wer im Glashaus sitzt, soll nicht mit Steinen werfen.
2. a) Die dümmsten Bauern haben die größten Kartoffeln.

Groß- und Kleinschreibung

1. c) Aber heute früh habe ich wieder einen Arzttermin.
2. d) Sie hatte fünf Einsen im Zeugnis und war Zweite im Weitsprung.
3. a) Als die englische Königin abends in ihr Schloss kam, war das Licht schon aus.

Rechtschreibung

1. e) Dampflokomotive **2.** b) Renaissance
3. Visa oder Visen **4.** Globen oder Globusse **5.** Pizzas oder Pizzen

5. Mathematisches Denken

Dreisatz

1. 18 Liter **2.** 56 Prozent **3.** 74 kg

Maßeinheiten

1. b) 2 Stunden **2.** a) 5,5 **3.** a) 0,3

Prozent- und Zinsrechnung

1. b) 357 Euro **2.** d) 6 Jahre und 8 Monate

Gleichungen

1. 8 x 4 – 1 = 31
2. 2 – 60 : 12 = -3
3. 11 + 20 x 5 – 12 = 99

6. Räumliche Vorstellung

Drehungen im Raum

1. c)

Flächen eines Körpers

1. a) 15 **2.** c) 34 **3.** b) 31

Spiegelbilder

1. a) **2.** c)

Würfelfaltung

1. a) **2.** b)

pauker.

Abschluss2023

MSA Klasse 10 Nordrhein-Westfalen

Lösungen Englisch

Realschule Typ B · Gesamtschule EK · Sekundarschule

Trainingsteil

Originalprüfungen

10

hutt lernhilfen

pauker.

Abschluss2023
MSA Klasse 10 Nordrhein-Westfalen

Lösungen

Name: ______________________

Schule: ______________________

Klasse: ______________________

hutt lernhilfen

hutt.lernhilfen ist eine Marke der
Bergmoser + Höller Verlag AG
Karl-Friedrich-Straße 76
52072 Aachen

T 0241 93888123
F 0241 93888188
kontakt@buhv.de

Umsatzsteuer-Id.Nr.: DE 123600266
Verkehrsnummer: 10508
Handelsregister Aachen HRB 8580

Vorstand:
Andreas Bergmoser
Peter Tiarks

Aufsichtsratsvorsitz:
Holger Knapp

Autor:
Joachim Krick

Lektorat:
Hubert Bening, Simone Grohmann, Annika Leal Mayer

Gestaltung: Hanne Hutt

Umschlag:
Konzeption + Gestaltung:
Hanne Hutt
Fotografie:
Anna Leippe

Ausgabe 2022/2023

ISBN: 978-3-88997-872-1

klimaneutral Printprodukt
natureOffice.com | DE-077-178633

Inhaltsverzeichnis

Die Lösungsvorschläge im Teil „Schreiben" sind als Orientierungshilfen gedacht. Andere Lösungen werden dadurch keinesfalls ausgeschlossen.

A. Hörverstehen

Text 1 – Four Teenagers Killed in Car Accident

1. b)
2. She told the court that she and her girlfriend Maggie had told Mike, the driver, to drive as fast as he could.
3. b)
4. b)
5. He had accelerated and braked to throw the passengers around.
6. c)
7. She felt guilty of having caused the death of her classmates.
8. a)

Text 2 – Hunger in Afghanistan

1. c)
2. b)
3. c)
4. b)
5. The food prices sometimes double within two weeks and are much too high compared to the people's income.
6. a)
7. a)
8. Desperation among the population will increase.

Text 3 – Conversation about the future

1. b)
2. They will provide Helen with a host family. They will provide Helen with a school where she will be able to work. They will help her with any problems that she may have to face.
3. a)
4. He would like to see something of the world and meet lots of new people.
5. b)
6. Jason thinks that Cathy could either work on a farm in South America or tend sheep in Ireland.
7. c)
8. b)

Text 4 – Interview

1. There was a sharp rise in obesity rates among young people in the USA. In other words, children in the USA were fatter in 2008 than they were in 2003.
2. c)
3. If you eat too much chocolate, you put on weight. It is okay to eat a small amount of chocolate once a week because in this way you will not get fat. Do not eat chocolate every day.
4. a)
5. b)
6. b)
7. c)

Text 5 – A Long Weekend

1. Bob is not very fond of that idea because he does not want to climb with a heavy backpack in the burning sun.
2. b)
3. a)
4. Lisa is a nice girl. She could be Bob's type. She has short black hair. She is sporty.
5. c)
6. a)
7. c)

Text 6 – Detention

1. c)
2. Laura told her mother that she had been at the movies with Sara. After that she hoped that her mother would stop asking any further questions.
3. a)
4. c)
5. Laura's mother was shocked, which is why she only stared. She just could not believe it.
6. b)
7. a)
8. c)

B. Leseverstehen

Text 1 – Boy Who Was Bullied All of His Short Life

1. c) took an overdose of painkillers after being bullied for 12 years.
2. d) Karl does not mention the bullies.
3. b) it seemed that Karl had started to find a solution to the bullying.
4. d) usually waited for Karl before bullying him in different ways.
5. d) intends to set up a website where victims of bullying can find help.

Text 2 – A Lost Person in a Lost Place

1. b) false … "… and no one seems to care about either doing it up again or pulling it down."
2. c) at first had difficulty in recognising the person leaning out of the window. "Due to the darkness, I was not able at first to recognise exactly whether the figure was a child or an adult, a woman or a man."
3. b) did not seem to have noticed the narrator at first because she was staring into the distance. … "… and she was staring into the distance … She did not seem to have noticed me …"
4. b) false … "At first she did not respond at all, but a moment later she bowed her head down to the pavement where I was standing."
5. a) had a vague idea about how the old lady had come to the old house. … "'Could it be that you are talking about an old people's home where you were staying before you decided to come here?'"
6. b) false … "'This is my home.' As she finished the last sentence, she began to move her tearful eyes along the front wall of the run-down old house."
7. b) had mixed feelings for the old lady, ranging from utter pity to a deep sense of responsibility. … "I felt such utter pity for the woman. At the same time, however, I knew that I had to do something. I could not simply walk off, leaving the old woman in this cold and dark house all by herself."
8. a) true … "I must admit that I hated myself for what I had just said and even more for what I was about to do."

Text 3 – Life in the Slow Lane

1. c) show the people on the boat just how slowly their boat is moving.
2. a) because it is only 2.1 metres wide.
3. d) are very popular because they offer lots of different things you can do in your free time.
4. b) can be learned within a couple of hours if you get proper instructions and a short period of training on the boat by a member of the rental company.
5. b) means doing a lot of tiring physical work.

C. Schreiben

Task 1

Text 1: Boy Who Was Bullied All of His Short Life

1. From the age of four until he killed himself at 16, Karl Peart was bullied in a number of ways. The gang of bullies usually waited for him to attack him. To begin with, the bullies would beat him with sticks, or they would punch and kick him on his way home. Once the bullies held him against a wall by the throat, threatening to cut his face with a broken bottle. In another incident that happened during a school trip, Karl ended up having a broken finger after being attacked at an ice rink.
Sadly, Karl reacted to the bullying by blaming himself and finally even by killing himself. In a suicide note to his mother he explained that he thought the bullying happened because he was not a nice person. Moreover, he wrote that he was sorry he could not live up to his parents' expectations. Although he had planned to get a day-time job and start evening classes to get away from the bullies, in the end he just couldn't take it anymore and decided to take an overdose of painkillers.

2. Karl's mother was, of course, very sad about her son's suicide. She was absolutely sure that the terrible and mean bullying was the reason for Karl's suicide. She started to hope things might be getting better when Karl had begun to think about getting a day-time job and starting evening classes. Together with her husband, Karl's mother moved her son from schools to help him get away from the bullies. Now that her son committed suicide, Mrs Peart was sure that bullying is a big and common problem in schools and that there is not enough help or support for the victims. As she wants to help other victims of bullying as well as their parents, she intends to set up a website that victims of bullying can turn to for practical and moral support.

3. a) Recently there has been a lot of media coverage about bullying in schools because of a number of suicides by teenagers who were victims of bullying. In this article we try to give you some information about what bullying really is and what you can do about it.
Bullying means that someone is repeatedly threatened, psychologically terrorized and/or physically attacked by another person or, more commonly, by a group of other people. In most cases the bullies are also teenagers, and they are often, but not necessarily, a bit older than their victims. Bullying can take place in a great many ways. The victims are made fun of, punched, kicked, beaten, robbed, blackmailed, seriously injured or sometimes even killed. Sadly, the victims often have no one to turn to for help. They may be too embarrassed to tell their friends, parents or teachers that they are being bullied. Furthermore, they are simply too scared that the bullying might become even worse if they report it to their parents, friends or teachers. Unfortunately, the victim may still be helpless even after telling others about the bullying. Either their friends or parents do not believe them or they think that the "victim" is only exaggerating. Teachers may also react in this way, or they simply ignore the problem because they already have too much work and stress to deal with such a problem as bullying.
What can you do if you notice that another teenager is being bullied or if you are a victim of bullying yourself? If you see how another teenager is being bullied, it is probably useless or even dangerous to confront the bullies directly. In this way, you might end up being bullied yourself. What you should do, however, is tell somebody about what you saw. You might tell a teacher about it. You could also tell your parents or the victim's parents about it. If none of these people are willing or able to help, you might also report what you observed to the police. If you are a victim of bullying yourself, you can also try to turn to any of the people mentioned before. Last but not least, you can also go to any of the following websites where you can log on to contact someone who knows how to help you: …

b) When teenagers are bullied, their teachers are often blamed for either not noticing or not responding to it. Is putting the blame on teachers justified or is it unfair to them? In the comment at hand I will try to examine this question from various points of view in order to finally make a summarizing statement of my personal opinion.
First of all, it is necessary to look at the two parts of the question individually. It is one thing if a teacher does not notice that a pupil is being bullied, but it is a completely different thing if he or she does not respond to a case of bullying. It seems quite unfair to blame somebody for not doing anything about a problem that they have not even noticed. Teachers often have a large number of pupils because they usually teach between 3 and 7 classes at a time, depending on the kind of position they have and the way their school is organized. This means that it is almost impossible for them to be informed in detail about each and every one of their pupils. Furthermore, apart from teaching, a teacher's job consists of a number of other little jobs and duties. Therefore the time they are actually in personal contact with each of their pupils is very limited. There may be some very talented teachers who have an extremely good sense of even the smallest change in their students' behaviour. These few teachers would probably find out about and respond to a case of bullying very quickly. However, one simply cannot expect all teachers to have this kind of talent.
Not responding to bullying is, on the other hand, inexcusable because it means that a teacher does know about the bullying but nevertheless does not react to it in any way. Even if this teacher is very busy at the moment, he or she could still respond to the bullying by informing other people about it, for example the student's parents, a colleague, the head teacher or, in a very serious case, the police. Like parents, a teacher has a special responsibility for children or teenagers who still need and have a right to, receive special help and protection. Teachers who do not respond to bullying do not only act against the moral principles of their job, they should also be punished by law. After all, the special protection of children and teenagers under the age of 18 is fixed by laws in almost any country on our planet.
Summarising, the question of whether teachers are to blame in relation to bullying cannot be answered in general. If a teacher has indeed not noticed a case of bullying, they should not be blamed unless they have already lost interest in their pupils or their job entirely. However, teachers who notice a case of bullying but do not respond to it in any way should not only be blamed morally but should be punished by law. The legal protection of children and teenagers is very important and valuable; therefore, breaking these laws must result in serious consequences.

Task 2

Text 2: A Lost Person in a Lost Place

1. At the beginning of the story the narrator sees only a silhouette of a figure in the dark leaning out of a window of the old house. As he is not sure whether this figure is young or old, male or female, he is, understandably, a little frightened. As soon as he recognises that the figure is an old woman, however, he loses his fear. Instead, he begins to worry about whether the old lady might be in need of help, especially after he manages to take a closer look at her, realising that the woman is indeed very old. When the old lady asks the narrator not to take her back to the house with the other old people she has never seen before, his view of the woman changes again. The thought that springs to his mind right away is that the woman may be having a mental problem. However, shortly after that another vague idea starts to form in his mind about the old lady having come to the run-down house from an old people's home, which, he concludes, would mean that the lady is telling the truth rather than having hallucinations. Subsequently, the narrator's assumption about the lady having run away from an old people's home is indeed confirmed by the lady. What is more, it also turns out that the lady chose to come to the run-down old house because it used to be her home for some part of her life. At this point the narrator's feelings about the lady change again. He is torn between deep-felt sympathy and a sincere sense of responsibility for her. Last but not least, the narrator decides not only to lie to the lady about things being all right but also to call the police. However, he is by no means relieved or happy after taking this decision. He hates himself for what the phone call to the police will probably mean for the old woman. She will most likely be sent back to the old people's home. This is why he finally asks himself with some degree of doubt and uncertainty if he did or did not have any other option apart from calling the police.

2. When the old woman entreats the narrator not to take her back to the "house", the narrator is at first confused because he does not know what "house" the lady is referring to. Subsequently, the narrator concludes that the lady is probably referring to an old people's home and asks her if this is where she was before coming to the old house. The lady's reply reveals that her associations with the word "home" do not apply to institutions like old people's homes, which is why she calls her old people's home a "house". Apparently, for the old lady a "house" is just a lifeless building made of bricks, steel and concrete that cannot evoke any agreeable emotions, possibly because a mere building itself does not "come to life" without any personal relations or emotional connections among its tenants. When she explains that an old people's home should not be called a "home" because it is not a home, at least not a home for her, it becomes clear under which circumstances, in the old lady's view, a "house" truly deserves to be called a "home". To her a "home" is a place that is associated with emotions like togetherness, happiness, human warmth and a deep-felt sense of belonging. This is why she finally calls the old, run-down house her "home". This is the place where she probably felt happy and truly at home for a substantial part of her life.

3. a) The narrator's decision to call the police most likely means that the old lady will be taken back to the old people's home that she ran away from. The question of whether or not the narrator had any other options in this situation is not easy to answer because there are arguments for and against it.
Analysing other potential options for the narrator, one has to take a very close look at what consequences each option may have had for the old lady. If, for example, the narrator had just walked off without taking any action at all, the old lady may have starved or frozen to death in the old house. Even if the narrator had decided not to call the police but to provide the old lady with food, drink and a heater instead, it is not clear how long he would have been able to continue this. Moreover, being very old, the old lady would, at some point, probably have needed some kind of medical help which the narrator would not have been able to provide. Another option the narrator may have had is to try and find members of the old lady's family to ask them for help. However, the fact that the lady was staying in an old people's home, perhaps even against her will, indicates that whatever family members the lady may still have, they would probably have been unwilling to take her into their homes. Consequently, the lady's relatives would most likely have sent her back to the old people's home anyway.
In conclusion, most of the other potential options the narrator may have had in terms of helping the lady in one way or another would possibly have meant that the old lady would still have ended up in her old people's home. Leaving the old lady to her fate by walking off and doing nothing, on the other hand, would most likely have meant that the lady would have died of hunger or cold. All things considered, I think the narrator did the right thing when he called the police. In this way he chose to pursue his sense of responsibility and compassion instead of simply looking away and moving on with his life as if nothing had happened.

b) I felt just awful. Obviously, the old lady was no longer in the house. There was only one plausible explanation for this. The police had taken the lady back to the old people's home that she had run away from. I stopped in exactly the same spot on the pavement where I had stopped the day before. My eyes filled with tears as I recalled every single word the lady had said to me the previous day. When I thought of the very last sentence she had said –'This is my home' – I started to cry bitterly.
Then the image of my own grandmother sprang to my mind. I remembered granny sitting in her favourite armchair in her old-fashioned living-room, telling me how happy she was that she could still stay in her own home rather than have to vegetate in some impersonal retirement home with hopelessly overworked and underpaid carers as well as loads of senile strangers who did not even remember their own names. Was it this kind of terrifying scenario that the old lady had been sent back to? This thought made my feelings of disgust, guilt and regret even more unbearable.
Not being able to stand this emotional stress any longer, I forced myself to think logically as best I could. My first thought was once again whether or not I had really had any other options apart from calling the police. Just walking off without taking any action at all would probably have meant that the old lady would have starved or frozen to death. In what way could I have helped the old lady myself? Providing the old lady with food, drink and a heater would theoretically have been possible, but how long would I have been able to continue this? Maybe I could have tried to find members of the old lady's family to ask them for help. However, the fact that the lady was staying in an old people's home, perhaps even against her will, indicated that whatever family members the lady may still have, they were probably unwilling to take her into their homes. Instead, they would probably have sent her back to the old people's home anyway.
As I could not think of any other options as to what I could have done, I felt at least a little relieved, which is why I finally started walking again, towards my school, towards my daily routine. However, there was a question that I just could not get out of my mind. Would my life ever be the same again after what had happened the day before?

Task 3

Text 3: Life in the Slow Lane

1. The narrow boat named "Golden Valley" is much longer than it is wide. In fact, it is about 20 metres long, but only 2.1 metres wide. Inside it almost looks like a normal flat with a living and dining area, a kitchen with the necessary appliances, a bathroom as well as a double bedroom and a single bedroom. Moreover, the boat offers heating, hot water and a TV set.

Before you actually get on a rented narrow boat, the boss of the rental company gives you instructions about how to steer and control the boat without putting you or other people in danger. Even after these instructions another person working for the boat rental company accompanies you as far as the first lock in order to make sure you know what to do there. Once you have started guiding the narrow boat on your own, a number of different things need to be done. For instance, you have to guide the boat around the bends and locks of the river or canal. Moreover, you need to get on and off the boat several times to move heavy gates, to open and close locks or to lift small bridges. In fact, guiding a narrow boat requires much more physical activity than most people think.

2. The expression 'slow lane' is commonly used for cars driving in a special lane on a motorway. The 'slow lane' is usually reserved for slow vehicles and for drivers who cannot, or just do not want to, drive as fast as most of the other motorway users. This article deals with a trip in a narrow boat. As a matter of fact, just like the vehicles in the 'slow lane' narrow boats are also very slow boats compared with motorboats, yachts or jet skis. So taking a narrow boat trip will literally slow your life down because you move more slowly than even people walking next to you on the bank of the river or canal. In fact, being passed in the narrow boat by people walking their dog is also described in the first paragraph of the article. And this first example from the article shows just how much taking a narrow boat trip is like 'living in the slow lane'.

Another passage in the second paragraph of the article which illustrates the meaning of the title relates to the three friends on the boat who have decided not to switch on the TV because during this trip they just want to 'switch off'. What they mean here is that they want to relax as well as to forget their hectic everyday life. They are probably under some pressure in their jobs and/or their family life, which is why the narrow boat trip is now supposed to help them do things more slowly or at a speed that is determined by them rather than by their jobs or family duties.

The third example from the article refers to what Linda Foster Weinreb says about taking a narrow boat trip in the third paragraph. She argues that you slow down to the 'heartbeat' of the water when you are in a narrow boat. In other words, the speed of the water, which is quite slow in most of Britain's inland waterways, somehow influences the people taking the trip in a certain way. In the end, they may even start to enjoy just observing animals or simply watching the world go by.

3. a) M: Mother F: Father A: Amanda

F: Now, Amanda, the reason why we asked you to sit down with us tonight is that your mum and I have finally decided where the three of us are going to spend our summer holidays. At first, we had thought about going to the same beach in Italy again that we went to last summer. But then mum had a brilliant idea. The other day she found a leaflet about narrow boat trips here in England on some of our historic canals. I was thrilled about that kind of holiday immediately, which is why I have already booked a boat for 2 weeks in August. What do you think about that, Amanda?

A: You must be kidding me. Do you really expect me to stay in a boat with you for two weeks? It would be fine with me if we went sailing or yachting in the Mediterranean Sea or something. But here in England? In a narrow boat? Come on, you cannot be serious. What am I going to do there all day for two whole weeks? Watch birds? Catch fish? I will be bored to death for two weeks.

M: Amanda, why are you always against what Dad and I like to do? You have never been in a narrow boat, and you have never seen our beautiful English canals either. How can you be so sure that it will be that boring? After all, you can have a swim in the canals, you can help us move gates, open and close locks or lift small bridges. That can be a lot of fun, too.

A: Mum, I am 14 years old. A narrow boat trip is a holiday for an old age pensioner. I want to have fun on a beach and with other young people. I want to go out in the evening, to a disco or a party. Why can't we go to Italy again like last year? That was great. The weather and the beach were fantastic, and I met a lot of cool people there.

F: Amanda, you know perfectly well that we would not allow you to go to discos or parties on your own anyway. So even in Italy you would be together with us most of the time.

A: But last year I was only 13! Now I am 14, and most of my friends are allowed to do a lot more things than me. You only want to stay in a boat for two weeks because you can control my every move then. All this talk about a great nature trip in beautiful countryside is just that, talk. You cannot tell me that you would really like to take a two-week trip in a boat that is as slow as a snail, in a country that has a 50% chance of rain in August, and in an area that is so far away from bigger towns or cities that you hardly meet any other people.

M: Believe it or not, Amanda, but Dad and I are really looking forward to this trip. It will definitely be a very relaxing holiday. And it will give us a lot of time and opportunities as a family to talk or play games together.

A: Since I am not allowed to go on holiday alone or with my friends anyway, what choice do I have? I need to join you, no matter what. So why did you take the trouble to talk this over with me in the first place? You know what, you just go on planning your superduper boat trip, but leave me alone. I am going to bed now! Good night!

b) There are some people who are quite convinced that a narrow boat trip is the best holiday in the world. In the comment at hand I will try to examine this opinion from various points of view in order to finally make a summarizing statement of my personal opinion.
A narrow boat trip is probably a suitable kind of holiday for people who enjoy observing wildlife. During a trip like this you can certainly see different species of birds, fish and plants. Moreover, people who are in need of relaxation may also be quite thrilled about such a trip. If you have a stressful job or family life, taking a narrow boat trip can help you to slow down, relax and recharge your batteries. The slow movement of the water and the boat will surely have a very calming effect on these people. But even for people who want to be active during their holidays a narrow boat trip may also be recommendable. After all, you need to get on and off the boat several times a day to move heavy gates, to open and close locks or to lift small bridges. Obviously, to a certain extent a holiday like this can also be interesting to adventure-loving people.
However, for many other people a narrow boat trip may be quite the opposite of a 'dream holiday'. For example, most teenagers would probably find this kind of holiday terribly boring. They are not usually interested in observing birds, catching fish or just watching the world go by. They want to go out with friends, have fun in discos or at parties. They are keen on meeting new people and on exploring the world. This is why they prefer to go abroad to warm countries like Spain, Italy or Greece to have fun in the sun on nice sandy beaches. A narrow boat trip is almost the very opposite of what they want. Furthermore, even many adults would not call this the best holidays in the world. For example, people who are interested in cultural activities and things such as art, architecture or music are very likely to prefer undertaking sightseeing trips to big cities in Europe or elsewhere. In addition, people who like to see different countries and/or stay in luxurious hotels during their holidays would possibly have the feeling of being locked up in that small narrow boat. Last but not least, people who prefer being in the mountains during their holidays would certainly not go on a narrow boat trip either.
To sum up, a narrow boat trip can be both: the best holidays in the world for some people and entirely unsuitable for other people. Obviously, this depends largely on what people prefer to see and do during their holidays. For me such a trip would be an interesting experience for a short holiday of no more than three to four days. However, for any holidays longer than that I would probably get bored too much on a narrow boat because I am quite an active holidaymaker who likes physical activities such as cycling or hiking.

D. Sprache

I. Wortschatz

1. a) argument b) numerous c) angry d) decision e) behaviour
f) succeed g) excited h) explanation i) necessary j) entrance

2. a) decision b) improvement c) sale d) flight e) beginning

3. a) trees b) centuries c) feet
d) glasses e) knives f) sheep

4. a) member b) bank c) actor/actress
d) passport e) state f) desert

5. a) border b) prize/cup c) reservation
d) hospital e) kitchen f) break/pause

6.

same meaning	opposite meaning
near – close	modern – old-fashioned
answer – reply	clean – dirty
choose – elect	cheap – expensive

7. a) freedom b) hope c) actor/actress/act d) poverty e) heat

8. 1. therefore 2. First of all 3. should 4. public
5. Many 6. types 7. will be 8. landlord

9. 1. found 2. within 3. these 4. had known
5. round 6. whole 7. branch 8. on

10. a) astonishment b) importance c) success d) fury e) obsession

11. a) expensive b) war c) answer d) difficult e) terrible

12. a) importance b) production c) electric
d) limit e) pollution f) difficulties

13. a) our – hour b) eye – I c) flour – flower d) meat – meet e) blue – blew

14. a) act**or** b) burgl**ar** c) li**ar** d) visit**or**

15. a) industries b) halves c) heroes d) lives e) buses/busses
f) proofs g) radios h) dresses i) women j) toys

II. Grammatik

16. a) Lisa and Tina are not good friends.
b) Mike will not go to New York next week.
c) My parents did not go to Paris last weekend.
d) Tom does not play football on Fridays.
e) Our cat doesn't sleep on the kitchen floor.
f) Mr Burns has not lived in Scotland for 25 years.

17. a) preferred b) don't want c) are – go – want
d) don't expect – will be e) needed – became

18. a) never spoke b) said c) give
d) could not – talk e) have you never said f) was

19. a) won't be able b) had to c) would be d) would have driven e) used

20. Mrs Jenkins said her kids had to write test papers once a month.
Mr Brown said his wife had more patience than he did so she taught their kids.

21. a) He had b) We had to train c) had to get up
d) were not allowed to have e) We had run f) there was

22. a) The doctor said, "I have proved that many kids are too lazy."
b) A trainer said, "Children had more exercise 20 years ago."
c) A friend promised, "I will ride my bike more often."
d) A health expert said, "Schools are starting sport programmes for kids."

23. a) keeping b) running c) playing d) saying
e) to make f) walking – jogging g) visiting

24. correctly – crashed – well-known – driving – high – driving – owner – extremely – deeply – hardly – himself – faster

25. a) were b) racial c) decided d) different e) religious
f) lives g) ourselves h) trained i) completely j) friendlier

26. a) beginning b) itself c) men d) origin e) led f) entrance
g) was h) directly i) for j) connecting k) naturally l) became

27. a) They always eat at Hogwart's School at 9 pm.
b) Why does Harry go to Hogwart's School?
c) Have you ever seen a wizard in real life?
d) Let's go to the cinema and watch the new Harry Potter movie!
e) Hermione is one of Harry's best friends.

28. a) dangerous b) fast c) carefully d) brave
e) unselfishly f) desperate g) well h) tragically

29. good – worse – much – many – oldest/older – easiest – late – more

30. a) which b) who c) which d) who e) which f) Who

31. your – mine – hers – her – ours – his – theirs – our

Erster Prüfungsteil: Hörverstehen – Leseverstehen

1. Hörverstehen Teil 1 (Conversation between Tom and Mary)

1. c)
2. b)
3. b)
4. a)
5. Mary's father says that paragliding is not dangerous because beginners never fly on their own but always together with an instructor.
6. a) It did not take place on Saturday because it was too windy, which is why the company cancelled the flight for safety reasons.
b) It did take place on Sunday because it was less windy than on Saturday.
7. a)
8. c)
9. b)

2. Hörverstehen Teil 2 (Wildlife Safari in Africa)

1. b) **2.** a) **3.** c)
4. a) On the first day of the safari he took pictures of giraffes, rhinos and exotic birds.
b) The next few days he took pictures of hippos, zebras, buffalos and elephants.
5. a)
6. c)
7. Peter was able to fix the car after the lion family had walked off into the bushes. The other participants of the safari had to stay in the car while Peter was fixing it.
8. c)

3. Leseverstehen (New, Multiracial Beginning in Story of "Madam & Eve")

1. a) … She's protesting by not doing her job. She's on a go-slow. / … refuses to answer it.
2. false … Based on a popular comic strip …
3. true … there are few places like television to understand how South Africans see themselves or would like to see themselves.
4. b) … television producers are turning to multiracial sitcoms as an entertaining way to deal with the country's uncomfortable past and perhaps to show a path to the future.
5. true … allowed to play with cultural stereotypes … to explore the contradictions and complexities of South Africa today.
6. true … by law, all shows must include as many of the country's eleven official languages as possible.
7. c) … Fearing that it would be dangerous, perhaps revolutionary technology, …
8. b) … Native African languages were rarely heard.
9. false … still prefer anything made in South Africa, because the shows reflect their own experiences.

Zweiter Prüfungsteil: Wortschatz – Schreiben

4. Wortschatz (The Gun: "A South African experience")

1. home / house / …
2. a)
3. were changed / transferred / moved
4. served / accepted / catered for / welcomed / accommodated
5. refused / did not want / …
6. b)
7. bulldozed / destroyed / ruined / knocked down / …
8. c)
9. a)
10. treat / take care of / help / …
11. language / tongue / …
12. c)
13. a)

5. Schreiben

1. Williams' behaviour towards Esi and his parents is characterised by aggressive intimidation, outright racism and an enormous lack of respect. As a matter of fact, Williams keeps bossing Esi and his parents around in an extremely impolite manner, treating them like machines or tools whose only function is to obediently follow their master's every instruction. Williams' behaviour is particularly humiliating for Esi's parents because he treats and addresses them like small children despite the fact that they are a lot older than he is and therefore deserve at least a minimum degree of respect as grown-ups and responsible parents.
Williams' behaviour contrasts strongly with Boss Mackay's behaviour towards Esi's family. Although Esi and his parents are employees on Mackay's farm and hence have to follow his instructions and orders, Mackay values and trusts them as hard-working and faithful employees, always calls them by their proper names and treats them with the respect they deserve as human beings.

2. Williams' aggressive, racist and disrespectful behaviour is reflected in the language he uses. To begin with, his instructions are all worded as short and curt imperatives (l. 8; l. 21; l. 22; l. 23; l. 24; l. 25). Second, his questions are not worded in a neutral way but have very aggressive and intimidating overtones (l. 8; l. 12; l. 13. l. 24). Third, his language is completely lacking in any polite forms of address, which reveals that he considers Esi and his parents to be "things" or "tools" rather than human beings. Last but not least, Williams' choice of words generally reveals his racist and depreciatory attitude. He makes a point of calling himself "Boss" and makes use of insulting and humiliating words and expressions like "boss-boy" (l. 8), "jong" (l. 8; l. 23), „Hey" (l. 21), "donder" (l. 24) or "the girl" (l. 25).
Williams' behaviour and use of language cause particular reactions in Esi. Even before Williams has started talking to Esi, he dislikes Williams' manner, comparing him to the "sneering officer in the Mapoteng attack" (l. 7). Once Williams starts talking to Esi, the impolite and bossy tone of Williams' instructions as well as the fact that he is called "jong" by Williams make Esi quite angry. However, Esi does not show his anger openly at this point; instead, he just follows Williams' instructions. As Williams' behaviour becomes even worse and involves Esi's father, too, Esi's anger grows and finally culminates in a feeling of humiliation and dehumanisation (ll. 17 – 18). But even at this point Esi still does not complain openly about Williams' behaviour. When Williams calls his mother "the girl", however, he runs to his mother and there his anger spills out immediately. He tells his mother about his anger at Williams' intolerable behaviour and about his disappointment with his father, who does not resist Williams' bossy behaviour at all. In fact, he makes it clear to his mother that he, unlike his obedient and passive father, does not want to be pushed around by anyone.

3. a) When Esi complains to his mother about his father letting Williams push him around, his mother says "What else can you do?". This statement may seem hard to understand or accept for a German teenager like me living in the 21st century. However, it needs to be seen in light of the former South African Apartheid regime, during which the story is set. This regime turned the majority of the black population into passive, obedient people resigning themselves to their white oppressors. This is certainly one of the reasons why Esi's mother believes that there is nothing to be done or changed about Williams' behaviour or her family's situation.
There are a number of factors that contributed to this kind of obedience and resignation among the black population in South Africa during the Apartheid regime. Systematic segregation in everyday life, including public services like education, health, police and justice, led to a feeling of powerlessness, inferiority and hopelessness among black people. They were afraid that any kind of resistance or opposition would result in punishment and repression by their white "masters". This is probably the very reason for the statement by Esi's mother. She feels so powerless and frightened that she does not see any chance of her family's situation changing for the better. On the contrary, she believes that any opposition might make their situation even worse.
On the one hand, I believe that the resignation and hopelessness that Esi's mother expresses in her statement are quite understandable because white dominance was so enormous during the Apartheid regime that black people must have felt extremely powerless. On the other hand, without any collective protest movements and/or courageous individuals resisting the regime there is no chance whatsoever that the regime will ever change. In fact, there were some examples of successful protest movements in South Africa, for example those led by Nelson Mandela or Steve Biko, who were not prepared to accept the unjust Apartheid regime with its systematic violation of human rights. In fact, their brave and continuous activities served as encouraging examples to a great many other black people who identified with and actively supported their aims of freedom, justice and equality.
In conclusion, against the background of the Apartheid regime, I can understand quite well why Esi's mother says "What else can you do?" to her son. The Apartheid regime had resulted in resignation, fear and hopelessness on the part of many black people. That is why they, just like Esi's mother, continued obeying white people instead of resisting or opposing them. However, to change an unjust system like the Apartheid regime courageous individuals and protest movements are needed. With regard to Esi's family, it would have been very important for Esi to see that his father and/or his mother show some kind of response to, or resistance against, Williams' behaviour. This might have encouraged Esi himself to try and change his situation, too. In my view, it usually takes some courageous individuals and/or movements that others can look up to and take as role models in the fight against discrimination and oppression.

or

b) Together with his mother, Esi walked back toward the camp. He was very angry, not only at Williams' behaviour, but also at his parents' resigned and passive attitude. He promised himself that he would no longer tolerate Williams' humiliating behaviour.

When they arrived at the camp, Williams was still sitting on the veranda, drinking the fourth can of beer by now. Seeing Esi, he shouted, "Go and get me another can of beer from the fridge. Make sure it's cold. And be quick, jong!" Now Esi could not control himself any longer. Beside himself with anger, he walked to the veranda, took the three steps up to get onto it and went straight to Williams. Pointing his finger at Williams, he shouted, "Stop bossing me and my parents around. We're not your personal servants. We are workers on your father-in-law's farm, and we are hard-working people. Your father-in-law knows that and respects us for that, too. And he has never ever treated us the way you are treating us. Go and get your beer yourself!" Esi's mother could not believe what was going on and just stared at Esi and Williams open-mouthed. Esi's father, just as shocked and surprised as his wife, started running towards the veranda.

"What did you just say, jong? Bloody nigger, are you out of your mind? How dare you speak to me like that?", said Williams angrily, slowly getting up from his chair and moving closer to Esi. Esi's mother shouted, "Boss Williams, please, I'm sorry! Don't blame the boy! He does not know what he's doing!" Esi turned to his mother, saying, "Mum, I do know what I'm doing and what I'm saying. And I mean it, too." At this moment Esi's father had reached the veranda, screaming, "Esi, stop this right away! We have no right to talk to Boss Williams like that! He is our master." Williams relaxed a little bit, smiled sneeringly and said to Esi, "You see, jong? That's the way to talk to your master. Your parents know their place. And now I will teach you to know yours." He raised his gun and smacked Esi across the face with it. Esi's nose started bleeding right away. The blood was streaming down his face.

For a couple of seconds everyone froze, not doing or saying anything, but then Esi screamed at the top of his voice, "You are a mean and bad person! Your father-in-law would be ashamed of you! You can hit me as much as you want to, but I will no longer be bossed around by you." Now Williams was getting very angry. He took his gun and pointed it at Esi's head. Both his mother and his father hurried up the three steps to get onto the veranda, ran to their son and placed themselves in front of the boy, protecting him but looking right into the barrel of the gun. "If you want to shoot him, you will have to shoot all three of us," Esi's mother said. She was surprised at her own courage and determination, but it felt good to stand up for her son.

Williams was taken by surprise, pointing his gun at three people at the same time. He nervously looked from mother to father to son several times, not really knowing what to do. Finally he lowered the gun and ran off to his Land Rover. However, before jumping into the driver's seat, he shouted, "You will pay dearly for this. I am going to come back with my father-in-law. And then all three of you, girl, boss-boy and jong, you will receive the punishment you deserve." He drove off at high speed. Esi and his parents hugged each other wildly, but they did so not only because they were happy to be still alive. There was something else they felt. It was a very unfamiliar feeling for all three of them, which is why they were not able to put it in words at the time. It was only many years later – when the Apartheid regime had been overcome and they remembered this situation – that they were able to give a name to this feeling. It had been a combination of pride, dignity and power.

Erster Prüfungsteil: Hörverstehen

Hörverstehen Teil 1 (Graduation Speech)

1. b)
2. a)
3. c)
4. a)
5. Nelson Mandela was a black freedom fighter. In the 1990s, Nelson Mandela was released from prison after 27 years behind bars. Nelson Mandela became the first black president of South Africa.
6. c)
7. They should never ever lose their respect for their neighbours, their fellow citizens, or for any human being, for that matter.
8. c)

Hörverstehen Teil 2 (Conversation between Rachel and her siblings)

1. c)
2. b)
3. b)
4. a)
5. a)
6. Because they are unhappy about Scotland having to leave the EU after Brexit and want to give Scotland a chance to stay in the EU.
7. a)
8. c)

Zweiter Prüfungsteil: Leseverstehen – Wortschatz – Schreiben

Leseverstehen

1. b); evidence from the text: "... there were at least five such incidents in Alaska alone ..." (ll. 3 – 4)
2. a); evidence from the text: "But their tradition ... is being challenged by rapid climate change." (ll. 8 – 10)
3. true; evidence from the text: "... was developed with support from the Arctic Eider Society." (ll. 24 – 25)
4. a); evidence from the text: "The multimedia platform combines ancient Inuit know-how, GPS data, and modern weather forecasting ..." (ll. 25 – 26)
5. false; evidence from the text: "... the Inuit community, whose ancestors have lived and worked in the region for thousands of years." (ll. 5 – 6)
6. true; evidence from the text: "... to give users up-to-the-minute information about ice safety." (ll. 26 – 27)
7. c); evidence from the text: "One traditional aspect of Inuit culture is making a comeback ...: the dog sled." (ll. 47 – 48)
8. A – 3; B – 5; C – 7; D – 1; E – 4; F – no match; G – 2

Wortschatz

1. b)
2. unfairly
3. a)
4. duty / responsibility / obligation
5. d)
6. offends / insults / discriminates against
7. c)
8. allowed / given a chance / given an opportunity
9. b)
10. opinion(s) / view(s)
11. violence / coercion
12. d)
13. learn / be informed / be told

Schreiben

1. 12-year-old Sipho is a black South African boy who has run away from home and now lives as a homeless teenager in a poor part of Johannesburg. He has found some other teenage friends who live on the streets, too. Together with his friends he hangs out near a supermarket, begging for money or helping shoppers to push and/or unload trolleys in order to earn some money. One day his new friend Jabu shows Sipho how to approach shoppers at the supermarket tills in order that they let the boys push the trolleys and then pay the boys for this "job". Sipho is unsure of himself at first, but he finally follows Jabu's example by offering his help to a woman who needs to run after her small son at the supermarket tills. He pushes the mother's trolley all the way to her car and later helps her to unload her shopping. The woman thankfully gives Sipho a twenty-cent coin. Immediately after this Sipho goes back to the supermarket to try and find another shopper he can help with the trolley in order to get paid for it.

2. At the beginning of this situation, Sipho is not yet familiar at all with his new life as a homeless teenager. He is "led" by his friend Jabu into the supermarket and merely observes what Jabu does to be allowed to push shoppers' trolleys. Jabu is a kind of "mentor" to Sipho, teaching him how to go about approaching shoppers in order that they let him push their trolleys (ll. 5 – 9). This lack of Sipho's experience as a "trolley pusher" is also reflected in the fact that Sipho wrongfully assumes Jabu will be sent away by the man at the till, just like he was sent away by a woman a couple of minutes earlier (ll. 10 – 11). Pushing the man's trolley out of the supermarket, Jabu winks at Sipho, thus encouraging him to start approaching shoppers. Instead of becoming active in this way, however, Sipho stands back thinking for a minute (ll. 11 – 14). Obviously, Sipho still feels uncomfortable in his new role as a homeless boy having to push trolleys for a living. After Jabu returns from his "job" of pushing the man's trolley, however, Siphos behaviour begins to change for the first time. Urged by Jabu to move quickly to get a "job", Sipho gives himself a shake, thus preparing for his first approach to the woman with her little son (ll. 17 – 19). When the lady needs to run after her son at the tills, Sipho decides to take hold of her trolley and is subsequently allowed to push the trolley to her car. He even carefully helps the woman's little boy to push the trolley and later helps the woman unload her shopping. Sipho's particular helpfulness pleases his "customer" so much that she gratefully gives him a 20-cent coin for his services. Obviously, Sipho has begun to learn his new "trade" as a "trolley pusher" (ll. 25 – 28). Although he is still shy when the woman hands him the coin, he is also a little proud of having earned his first money in his new life as a homeless teenager. Encouraged by his first successful "job", he does not even wait for the woman's car to drive off but quickly pushes the trolley back to find a new customer. This clearly indicates that he starts to accept his homelessness and that he is becoming more confident and proactive to make a living on his own (ll. 29 – 31).

3. a) In my opinion the passage from the *UN Convention on the Rights of the Child*, which says that "all children have the right to care and protection, no matter who they are and where they live", deserves and requires unconditional support as well as urgent implementation throughout the world.

Young children are usually unable to survive if they do not receive any care or protection from adults. They require both economic and emotional support in order to be able to live a decent life, including basic resources like housing, food and drink, adequate infrastructure and education as well as psychological well-being. For the most part this is also true for older children (teenagers), but it is especially true for all children living in poorer parts of the world, no matter how old they are, because basic resources are often very scarce there. Sipho's experience as a homeless 12-year-old black boy living on the streets in South Africa illustrates this problem quite clearly. Obviously he has no one to turn to for help, which is why he is forced to beg for money or to push shopping trolleys for just a few coins. Of course, these "earnings" are not enough to lead a decent life, let alone receive a good education. As a result, he will probably never find a way out of this poor life unless he is given some kind of help from adults. In other words: Sipho's lack of care and protection (including an adequate education) as a child is bound to leave him no chance to get out of this poverty as an adult. This is the vicious circle that affects so many children who do not get any kind of care or protection.

Another important aspect of the passage from the UN Convention is that all children must be given adequate care and protection, no matter who they are. Adequate care and protection should be provided irrespective of the colour of the children's skin, of their gender as well as of their physical and/or mental handicaps.

What is valid in "normal" circumstances applies even more in any sort of economic, political or family crisis because children are particularly vulnerable and susceptible to those crises. If they are not protected or cared for in such crises, they often suffer even more than adults because they are more dependent on external help and goodwill on the part of parents, guardians, government services or charitable organisations.

In conclusion, the passage from the *UN Convention on the Rights of the Child* is undoubtedly true and indeed highly important. Since the age of Enlightenment most societies on this planet have, at least officially, endorsed the idea that human beings have some basic rights. In view of the particular vulnerability of children, these rights should include care and protection for every child on our planet.

or

b) What a day this has been! But looking back on it, I think that, by and large, it has been quite a successful day after all. I have earned my first money for a job. Well, admittedly, pushing trolleys cannot be called a real job and 175 cents can hardly be called great earnings for an entire afternoon spent pushing and unloading trolleys. Nevertheless, since I ran away from home two weeks ago, today is the very first day that I've felt some sort of pride, hope and confidence that I will somehow be able to get by in the future.
I still remember the first days after running away from my parents. How awful it felt to be all alone with no money, no roof over my head, no food, no drink. I really thought about returning to my parents. However, how could I go back after seeing my father, totally drunk, fighting with my mother almost every day? No, going back was not an option, and it still isn't!
And then, about a week ago, I met Jabu, who is now really my best friend. He has already lived on the streets for two years. It seems funny now, but at first I was a bit scared of him. He seemed so unfeeling, grown-up and cheeky. But then he started to teach me how to survive on the streets. The first things he showed me were how to find shelter, food and drink without stealing. And we sort of protected each other at night from other homeless people or thugs who tried to rob or attack us.
And today Jabu actually taught me how to earn money! How I admired the clever and courageous way he approached the shoppers in the supermarket to offer his help by pushing the shoppers' trolleys to their cars! I was very hesitant at first about approaching the shoppers, but Jabu did such a good job and really encouraged me to do the same. That is why I was finally able to take hold of that woman's trolley. I was really surprised that she allowed me to push her trolley together with her son. And later, when I had finished unloading the trolley, she gave me that 20-cent coin ... wow, I can't believe how happy and proud that made me feel! That's why I was so keen on getting as many customers as possible after that.
I'd better go to sleep now because I want to be at the supermarket when it opens again tomorrow morning. Now that I know how to approach the shoppers I might earn a lot more than the 175 cents I received today. That would be fantastic.

Erster Prüfungsteil: Hörverstehen

Hörverstehen Teil 1 (The Presentation)

1. b)
2. a)
3. b)
4. old castles or monasteries; secret passageways; mysterious chambers; hidden trapdoors; mysterious events; supernatural beings; scary characters
5. c)
6. a)
7. world of wizards and witches; an old castle with secret chambers, hidden passageways and a wide range of magical powers; a forest called *The Forbidden Forest*, which is populated by all kinds of creepy, mysterious or dangerous beings
8. b)

Hörverstehen Teil 2 (Interview in Cape Town)

1. c)
2. b)
3. a)
4. sea life: penguins, seals, dolphins, sharks and whales
   landscapes: rugged mountains, lush forests, dry deserts, deep canyons/gorges
5. c)
6. a)
7. There are quite a number of different black tribes or communities in South Africa with their own social structures, traditions and cultures.
8. b)

Zweiter Prüfungsteil: Leseverstehen – Wortschatz – Schreiben

Leseverstehen

Please, Sir – sit! The story of a learning support dog

1. true; evidence from the text: "... staff managed to solve the problem pretty much overnight – not by replacing detentions with collecting rubbish, but by employing their newest, cuddliest colleague: Rolo, the school dog" (ll. 2 – 5)
2. c); evidence from the text: "'The effect was incredible,' says the headteacher, John Tomsett. Within a week of 'Operation Rolo Says No', the school grounds were spotless ..." (ll. 14 – 16)
3. true; evidence from the text: "... as the 1,500 students had worked together to clean it up." (ll. 16 – 17)
4. a) evidence from the text: "... a sign on top of one of the bookshelves in the school library shows when the puppy is at school" (ll. 19 – 20)
5. false; evidence from the text: "He has his own name tag, 'Mr Rolo', just like any other member of the staff" (ll. 24 – 25)
6. a); evidence from the text: "'In the last two or three years the number of dogs in schools has exploded in a really big way ...'" (ll. 29 – 31)
7. a); evidence from the text: "... but she is worried that too many dogs are unprepared for classroom life and have no proper training. 'It is not right for all dogs ...'" (ll. 34 – 39)
8. false; evidence from the text: "The *Department for Education* has no idea how many dogs are currently working in classrooms and does not require schools to register or train their animals." (ll. 42 – 44)
9. true; evidence from the text: "Sometimes Rolo follows Tomsett to small classes, and Tomsett settles him in a corner on his blanket. 'He's fabulous. He just goes to sleep and the children don't want to wake him so they are really quiet ...'" (ll. 47 – 51)
10. c); evidence from the text: "Rolo is learning how to become a 'listening dog' who will help children read aloud more confidently." (ll. 52 – 53)

Wortschatz

The British school system

1. b)
2. attend / go to
3. d)
4. a)
5. c)
6. examination / exam / test
7. take / do
8. a)
9. rules / requirements
10. a)
11. need / require / are in need of / are given
12. (extracurricular) activities
13. d)
14. mandatory / obligatory / compulsory

Schreiben

1. 15-year-old Jessica used to live in Cape Town, South Africa, until she was sent to live with her grandmother in London in the early 1990s. At that time there was a lot of political unrest and violent clashes between opponents and supporters of the apartheid regime in South Africa. Anti-apartheid activists were often beaten, arrested and sent to prison by the police. Some of the activists were even kept in solitary confinement or had to be in permanent hiding from the police. Most of the apartheid opponents were not criminals in the usual sense of the word, but they were political activists protesting against a regime that discriminated against black people and segregated them in all areas of everyday life.
In South Africa Jessica and her boyfriend Ben, who are both white, lived in a wealthy all-white neighbourhood, whereas most black people, including Jessica's best friend Daisy, had to live in so-called townships, often without electricity and running water. This is why black people in South Africa started asking as many people as possible in other countries to boycott South African goods so as to put pressure on the South African government. Jessica's new life in London, however, is very different. She now lives in a peaceful, democratic country where black and white children are taught in the same class.

2. Jessica seems to be a friendly, well-behaved and shy girl. When she enters the principal's office, for example, she asks very politely and cautiously why Mr Herbert wanted to see her. According to Mr Herbert, Jessica has a scared look on her face when she meets him, which indicates that she is a shy and reserved teenager. Her modesty and shyness are also reflected in the fact that she is very surprised when a well-respected adult like Mr Herbert asks her to do him a favour, namely to give a report about what happened to her friends in South Africa, at the next school assembly. Her first impulse is to refuse because she has never spoken in front of a large crowd of people, which is why she is quite frightened to do so now. However, at the same moment she is hit by a thought of her best friend Daisy as well as of her boyfriend Ben, who would both want her to give that account of the situation in South Africa. This is why she immediately changes her mind and agrees to give the speech.
This decision highlights another trait of Jessica's character, namely her uncompromising loyalty and reliability towards her friends. She feels that she owes this assembly speech to her friends because it may help them in their fight against apartheid. As a result, she is able to overcome her uneasiness in connection with the speech. During the speech itself, she is extremely nervous, but still she does not stop or give up. In other words, her sense of responsibility for her friends ultimately prevails over her fear and nervousness. When the speech is over and Jessica returns to her seat, she is proud of herself for having stood by her friends instead of giving in to her personal fears.

3. a) In my opinion there are a number of reasons why the title of the book fits very well. The word "separation" plays a meaningful role on several levels in this story, which is probably the very reason why the author has chosen this title in the first place.
To begin with, the apartheid regime in South Africa is a political system that separates people in South Africa solely on the basis of the colour of their skin. Jessica describes this systematic way of segregating black and white people in everyday life very concretely. She mentions a wide range of services and facilities (cinemas, theatres, pubs, restaurants, cafes, parks, buses, trams, trains, housing) that were open either only to blacks or only to whites, respectively. What is more, the services and facilities for blacks were invariably much worse in terms of quantity and quality, which means that this practice of systematically separating blacks and whites was part of an openly racist, fundamentally undemocratic and entirely unjust political regime.
Another level on which the word "separation" plays a role in this story is the fact that both Daisy, Jessica's best friend, and Ben, Jessica's boyfriend, are separated not only from their families and friends, but also from society as a whole. While Ben is in solitary confinement – the most horrible form of imprisonment one can imagine – Daisy is on the run from the police and has to hide all the time to avoid being arrested.

Last but not least, there is another level of "separation" in this story. Jessica is not only separated from her home country South Africa as a result of the political unrest and increasing violence in South Africa, but also from her best friend Daisy and from her boyfriend Ben, whom she calls "the love of her life".

In conclusion, in my view the author of the book "Separation", Babette Brown, has chosen a very suitable title. The word "separation" can even be regarded as a key word in the entire story because it is significant on many different levels in the story. The word characterises the apartheid regime as a whole, but, on a more personal level, it also reflects the relationship between Daisy, Ben and Jessica in a number of sad and tragic ways.

or

b) I was really surprised – everybody in my class was very excited when we came back to our classroom after my speech. Our Geography teacher, Mrs Greenwood, had quite some difficulty in getting everyone quiet. Mrs Greenwood had also been present during my assembly speech, and now she saw the pupils' emotional reaction to it. This is why she agreed to abandon her Geography lesson in order to give our class a chance to discuss my speech, adding that she was both shocked and deeply moved by my account of the situation in South Africa. Almost all my classmates were raising their hands now because they were anxious to say something.

The first pupil Mrs Greenwood picked was Martin, who said, "Oh Jessica, I'm so sorry for you. It must be terrible to be so far away from your home country and your family, with your best friend in hiding and your boyfriend in prison. How can you bear all that?" I felt tears welling up in my eyes, and in a shaky voice I answered, "Believe me, it is incredibly hard, and sometimes I fear it may break my heart." Then Mrs Greenwood called on Olivia, who said, "Jessica, what you just told us has left me almost speechless with horror. I've seen reports about South Africa on TV, of course, but when you listen to somebody talking about their own personal experiences like you did, it suddenly becomes so real, so cruel and so unbelievably horrific. I don't know about the rest of you, classmates, but in my opinion we need to do something to raise people's awareness of what apartheid means to people living in South Africa, no matter if they are black or white." At this point Mrs Greenwood picked Jake, our class clown, who can never be serious about anything and who usually behaves in a very disruptive way in class. Everyone looked at him, hoping he would not be his usual self with what he was about to say. But Jake stood up and shouted, "There are not many things I would not make fun of. But Jessica's speech is definitely one of those things. Jessica, what happened to you and your friends and, for that matter, what is happening in South Africa in general, is absolutely unbearable and intolerable. Blacks are discriminated against, people are separated from each other, be it friends, families or lovers. I say: enough is enough. As of today, I am going to start an anti-apartheid campaign at our school. Whoever would like to join me is most welcome to do so. We are going to collect signatures, we are going to design posters, we are going to create video clips and post them on various social media platforms. And in case you have any other ideas for further activities, please let me know. We need to act now to prevent the suffering, discrimination and violence that South Africa is currently experiencing." All my classmates were baffled because they had never seen this kind of sincere commitment and seriousness on Jake's part. Then their bafflement quickly turned into enthusiasm for Jake's campaign. The next moment there were shouts coming from everywhere in the classroom: "I'll join you, Jake." "So will I." "Me too." "What a great idea, Jake." "Let's start right now, Jake." I was sitting on my chair, overwhelmed by the unanimous solidarity of my classmates, which is why I could not help crying.

Erster Prüfungsteil: Hörverstehen

Hörverstehen Teil 1 (Radio Podcast "Pros and cons of living in Dublin")

1. b)
2. lonesome beaches; small towns; cattle or sheep farms
3. a)
4. b)
5. a number of big music locations; a large number of pubs and clubs offering live music several days a week; street musicians performing at weekends
6. a)
7. c)
8. b)

Hörverstehen Teil 2 (Martha's Audio File)

1. a)
2. c)
3. b)
4. b)
5. In the morning they drink strong and dark tea, whereas in the afternoon it has to be mild and light.
6. c)
7. a)
8. (morning) fog; rain(fall); (stretches of) sunshine; (strong) winds with clouds rushing by

Zweiter Prüfungsteil: Leseverstehen – Wortschatz – Schreiben

Leseverstehen

The family that is enough

1. false; evidence from the text: "... Colfer, the second of five boys ..." (l. 3)
2. a); evidence from the text: "His relationship with his brothers, he believes, explains the quick, dry humour in his books." (ll. 5 – 6)
3. c); evidence from the text: "To keep us from fighting, my dad would tell us all stories about fairies and dragons." (ll. 12 – 14)
4. false; evidence from the text: "... invented his own characters and drew and wrote his own comics when he was young." (ll. 16 – 17)
5. true; evidence from the text: "... when Eoin started to write books, his brothers became the characters. All five boys are part of the story." (ll. 22 – 24)
6. b); evidence from the text: "Eoin had written three other children's books while teaching at the local primary school in Wexford." (ll. 27 – 28)
7. false; evidence from the text: "The money was not as big as has been reported, but fame came fast and bigger money followed later." (ll. 34 – 35)
8. c); evidence from the text: "... people in Wexford aren't interested in wealth and fame: 'They've known me for decades, so they don't care'". (ll. 34 – 39)
9. true; evidence from the text: "The brothers keep his feet on the ground, too, Eoin adds." (ll. 39 – 40)
10. true; evidence from the text: "When Finn argues in the back of the car, Eoin doesn't tell stories to stop him. Instead, he tries to remember it for his books." (ll. 44 – 46)
11. a); evidence from the text: "'... Now there are struggles but not much actual violence.'" (ll. 50 – 51) Oder: "Over the next four books *Artemis* develops a feeling for right and wrong." (ll. 52 – 53)
12. b); evidence from the text: "'Once he turns completely good, that's it.'" (ll. 55 – 56)

Wortschatz

Welcome to "Thinkuknow"

1. put / post
2. b)
3. (a) secret / to ourselves
4. d)
5. send (on) / pass (on) / forward
6. a)
7. fake / false
8. a)
9. talk / respond
10. dangerous / scary / frightening
11. c)
12. b)
13. message / text / text message / email

Schreiben

1. Allie's product is a game that can be played with the help of a smartphone app. The original idea for this app came to her mind at the beginning of the "Code Girls Camp". As she did not know any of the other girls participating in the camp, she thought that it would be great if she could find out about their favourite music, their favourite books and their family situation. In this way she could quickly make new friends. That is why Allie has created an app called "Click'd", which can help you to identify those people in large groups whose interests, hobbies and preferences are similar, or indeed equal, to yours and thus make new friends.
   The game works as follows: Large numbers of participants can use Allie's app by clicking on suitable answers to multiple-choice questions about their likes and dislikes, preferences and favourite activities. The gamemaster's app quickly processes all the information entered by the participants and identifies those whose entries show the highest scores in terms of similarity. Based on the information entered, the smartphones of the participants with the highest matching scores then produce particular sounds, lights or clues which help those 'soulmates' to find each other.

2. At the beginning of her presentation Allie is obviously quite nervous. This is reflected in the fact that she takes a deep breath before she starts to speak. (l. 3) Even a couple of minutes after the beginning of her presentation her shaky legs (l. 10) reveal that she has not yet lost her nervousness. However, somewhat later she starts to become a little more self-confident and courageous. She waves her phone in the air (l. 14), starts making jokes (l. 15 – 16) and leans forward to emphasize a key point in her presentation. (l. 18) Nevertheless, just a couple of seconds later she takes a deep breath again before another key moment in her presentation (l. 21), which shows that she still has not completely managed to shake off her uneasiness. Moments later, however, she winks at her audience and notices that her legs are no longer shaking. (ll. 29 – 31) Obviously, she already feels much more relaxed at this point. At the end of her presentation everyone in the auditorium is applauding. By this time Allie is overwhelmed by feelings of pride and joy. (l. 39)

3. a) In my opinion, Allie's app "Click'd" involves both chances and risks when it comes to the desire to make new friends or find romantic partners.
   To begin with, for social gatherings like private parties, company parties or graduation ceremonies, for example, Allie's app can help some people, especially those who are shy or overcautious by nature, to find 'soulmates' with similar interests, hobbies or attitudes. This is true also for the chance of finding and getting to know potential romantic partners. After all, it is either extremely time-consuming or even entirely impossible to try and chat with every single participant of a social gathering in order to find the one 'soulmate' that fits you best.
   However, Allie's product also implies a number of risks. First, the questions which need to be answered by the participants may be too personal for some of them. They could feel forced to reveal things about themselves that they would usually prefer to be kept secret from people they meet for the very first time. This is one of the reasons why I am quite cautious about how to use social media in general. Those media do play an important role in my life, but I usually make a point of not giving away too many personal details.
   Another risk of Allie's product is that a high matching score between two participants is no guarantee whatsoever that they are a perfect match in real life. After all, the complex interplay of factors that result in two people liking or disliking each other cannot be reduced to a set of multiple-choice questions, no matter how detailed those questions are. Undoubtedly, the 'chemistry' between two people cannot be measured or predicted solely on the basis of common interests or attitudes. There are certainly various other, hardly measurable factors which are involved in this process as well.
   Last but not least, there is the risk that the person the app picks out as your most suitable participant may nevertheless turn out to be somebody you find boring, unattractive or even downright repulsive. This could lead to highly embarrassing situations when you meet your 'soulmate'. To sum up, in my view there are too many risks involved in Allie's product, which is why I would not use it personally.

or

b) **Have you been "Click'd" yet?**

16-year-old Allie Navarro is the winner of this year's Code Girls Camp. She has demonstrated her product in a convincing presentation to an audience that consisted of the other camp participants, their parents, and this year's jury. It is quite amazing what a creative and useful app a teenage girl like Allie can produce in as short a time as a summer camp. Her product is called "Click'd", and she could not have come up with a more suitable name for it because 'click' is what the users of this app need to do, not once or twice but dozens of times. In a nutshell, "Click'd" works as follows: When you are at a social gathering, the app helps you to quickly single out the most suitable 'soulmate' from all the participants of that gathering without having to chat with any of them.

First, the app presents a set of multiple-choice questions to all participants. The questions relate to the preferences the participants have about all kinds of things or activities in everyday life. With the help of Allie's app every participant then clicks on the most suitable answers. After that the app quickly processes all the information entered by the participants and identifies those whose entries show the highest scores in terms of similar or even identical answers. To increase the fun factor of this game, the smartphones of the participants with the highest matching scores produce particular sounds, lights or clues which can help the 'soulmates' to find each other.

Allie played the "Click'd" game with the audience in the auditorium, which was great fun. In other words, the audience did not merely listen to Allie's presentation passively, but they were involved in the actual game. At the end of Allie's presentation, everyone clapped their hands enthusiastically because Allie had singled out a woman and a man from the audience as two possible soulmates. And she did it by making their smartphones let out a particular sound. It was this very moment in Allie's presentation that was later talked and laughed about extensively among members of the audience and the jury. Presumably, it was also the moment that made the jury decide to award this year's prize to Allie.

Have you ever asked yourself if computer summer camps for teenagers are any good or even worth the money? Well, Allie's stunning accomplishment in this year's camp is your answer. Of course, these camps are fantastic. After all, they are about teenagers coming up with creative ideas, turning those ideas into actual products and even presenting their products in front of a large audience! That is certainly more than any parent of a teenager could ask for.

or

c) Hi everyone,

I'm happy to be back here at Code Girls Camp. I can't believe it's already been a year. So much has happened since I won last year's camp.

First of all, let me tell you about what happened right after my presentation last year. You see, when I had finished, I stepped down from the stage to head for my parents. But before I was able to do so, a woman I had never seen before approached me, took my hand and congratulated me on both my presentation and my "Click'd" app. I felt a bit embarrassed and wanted to turn away from her, but she handed me a business card and asked me if she could talk to me later in the afternoon, adding that this conversation might change my life forever. Feeling kind of annoyed by the woman's slightly aggressive approach, I put the business card in the pocket of my jeans and walked straight to my parents without saying another word to her.

It was not until after the lunch break that I happened to take the business card out of my pocket again. I was about to throw it in the trash bin, but then my attention was attracted by the company name printed on the card. It read "Do Digital Dating". I looked at the card more closely, and in the next line it said: "Jodie Gallagher, Marketing Director". Wow, I thought, why on earth does a successful businesswoman like that want to talk to me, a 16-year-old teenager? Well, I wanted to find out and called the number on the card. Girls, believe me, this phone call has really changed my life.

Well, I won't bore you with all the details. In a nutshell, Mrs Gallagher said that her company, which is one of biggest online dating services in the U.S., might be interested in developing my app further and offered me an internship. Today, only 12 months later, I even have a consulting contract with Do Digital Dating. The company has already started to integrate the basic idea of my app into their online services. And, believe it or not, in accordance with my contract the company will pay for my "Information and Data Sciences" studies at Caltech from next year.

Let me finish my speech by encouraging each and every one of you girls here in the auditorium. Let your imagination run free and believe in yourself. Then you have the same chance that I had a year ago to create something new, something extraordinary, something unique. It is summer camps like this one which are exceedingly important when it comes to giving girls a chance to boost their self-confidence and their belief that they can be as good as boys or men when it comes to using and advancing modern technologies. Go for it, girls!

Erster Prüfungsteil: Hörverstehen

Hörverstehen Teil 1 (British TV Game Show "How well do I really know the UK?")

1. b)
2. Geography; hard; Edinburgh
3. a)
4. a)
5. b)
6. c)
7. c)
8. is a member of the Labour Party; has supported the Labour campaigns in the last two general elections; has told his wife which constituency is the smallest in the UK

Hörverstehen Teil 2 (Podcast "Dublin and Belfast: travel account")

1. a)
2. c)
3. b)
4. b)
5. Her British accent may have caused the customers to look at her; her hotel was located in a part of Belfast where more than 90 % of the population were Catholics.
6. c)
7. very famous sights: Belfast Castle, Belfast City Hall, Queen's University, Botanic Gardens, 'Belfast Titanic' museum; lesser-known sights: Cuban Sandwich Factory, Belfast Gin School & Distillery, music venue "Voodoo"
8. a)

Zweiter Prüfungsteil: Leseverstehen – Wortschatz – Schreiben

Leseverstehen

The power of traditional beliefs

1. b); evidence from the text: "... that traditionally an itchy nose is a sign of an upcoming fight ..." (ll. 5 – 6)
2. true; evidence from the text: "Itching on the inner side of your hands – a sign of money to come." (ll. 11 – 12)
3. b); evidence from the text: "Many Irish parents who want their children to tell the truth, tell them 'Stick your tongue out so I can see if you're lying'." (ll. 16 – 18)
4. c); evidence from the text: "If it's the right ear that feels extremely warm, people talk about you positively, but if it's the left ear, the talk is negative." (ll. 19 – 21)
5. false; evidence from the text: "In old stories everything connected with magic is believed to be a *piseog*." (ll. 24 – 25)
6. c); evidence from the text: "An unkind person ... If you didn't find these things, your luck would turn bad." (ll. 28 – 33)
7. true; evidence from the text: "And they show how we as humans have thought, felt, and interacted with the world around us and with each other." (ll. 39 – 41)
8. c); evidence from the text: "... they survived because of repetition, not because they made sense." (ll. 43 – 44)
9. true; evidence from the text: "Based on them, each new family creates their own rituals." (ll. 47 – 48)
10. a); evidence from the text: "... so it's up to you to decide what to believe in." (l. 51)

Wortschatz

Food as a cultural experience

1. b)
2. c)
3. smell / taste
4. unwell / bad / sick / ill / under the weather
5. immigrants / expats / migrants
6. d)
7. culture / traditions / cultural background / customs / cultural heritage
8. c)
9. shops / (grocery) stores / supermarkets
10. a)
11. sold / available / offered
12. tasty / delicious / yummy / great / fantastic
13. b)

Schreiben

1. In front of the school canteen, Jaz and her classmates crowd around a new student, called Nadima, who is a refugee from Syria. Kara is the first to try and talk to Nadima, asking her where she is from and whether she speaks English. However, Nadima does not understand those questions even though Kara repeats them more slowly and more loudly. Subsequently, Nadima is bombarded with more questions by other classmates of Jaz'. As Nadima only smiles and nods without answering any of the questions, Jaz asks her classmates to leave Nadima alone. Then some of Jaz' classmates try to use Google Translate on their mobiles, but they fail because they do not know Nadima's home country or mother tongue. Bored by the fruitless attempts to talk to Nadima, Jaz's classmates walk off. Jaz, however, stays with Nadima and makes an unsuccessful attempt to speak French or German with her. Finally, Jaz offers some chocolate to Nadima, who happily accepts it and, in turn, gives Jaz a type of sweet that looks like Turkish Delight.

2. At the beginning of the scene Jaz and her classmates are quite anxious to talk with Nadima, the new student from Syria. However, Jaz senses from the very beginning that her classmates' motivation to talk to Nadima is based on curiosity and peer pressure about as much as on a sincere wish to bid the new student welcome. (ll. 2 – 3) Arguably, Jaz has a better sense of compassion and empathy than her classmates. This trait of Jaz' character is mirrored throughout the extract. For example, when her classmates bombard Nadima with questions she does not understand, Jaz starts to protect Nadima. (ll. 15 – 17) Secondly, unlike her classmates, Jaz feels embarrassed when she speaks about Nadima rather than with her. (ll. 18 – 19) Thirdly, when her classmates make an unsuccessful attempt to use Google Translate, Jaz finds a different way to communicate with Nadima by smiling and giving a comedy shrug to her. (ll. 27 – 28) In fact, this intuitive decision to switch from unsuccessfully trying to communicate by means of language to making gestures reveals another characteristic of Jaz'. She has a good deal of imagination and resourcefulness when it comes to finding alternative communication channels to get through to Nadima. Last but not least, this ability of Jaz' is highlighted in the final part of the extract. When Jaz offers Nadima some chocolate, she finally manages to break the ice with Nadima.

3. a) Jaz' decision to offer some chocolate to Nadima is an imaginative and deeply moving action. By offering Nadima some chocolate, Jaz gives Nadima a feeling of being welcome and respected, maybe even of being liked. Irrespective of the cultural setting or background, giving sweets to another person is generally considered to be a sign of welcome, friendship or gratitude, especially, however not exclusively, among children. Obviously, despite the cultural gap between the two girls, Nadima understands this gesture, which is reflected in the fact that she, in turn, also gives some sweets to Jaz. By exchanging sweets, the two girls manage to bridge the language barrier which has made any communication between the girls next to impossible up to that point. They have finally found some way of communicating with one another beyond the most common tool of communication, namely language. However, it is not only the mere exchange of sweets which plays an important role in the text. The fact that Jaz offers Nadima some chocolate whereas Nadima offers Jaz Turkish Delight in return is also quite significant. To some extent, chocolate here represents British, or rather Western, culture in general because it is arguably one of the most common types of sweets in Western countries. On the other hand, Turkish Delight in a way symbolizes Muslim or Middle Eastern countries because it is quite a popular and widespread sweet in those regions. It can therefore be argued that the exchange of these particular sweets by Jaz and Nadima at the end of the extract mirrors ways in which cultural differences can be brigded and some common ground can be reached even without the tool of language.

   In my opinion, Jaz' gesture at the end of the extract is a deeply empathetic move. It gives both girls an opportunity to find some way of communicating with one another and can therefore pave the way for a closer relationship between them in the future. Despite the fact that they do not speak each other's language, they find some mutual understanding on another level. Last but not least, Jaz' gesture shows that while language barriers can make any linguistic kind of communication impossible, other cultural elements (e.g. food, dance, music) can be alternative cross-cultural channels of communication and understanding.

or

b) Mum was already busy setting the table. Nadima just stood in the doorway to our kitchen. I saw Nadima taking a deep breath. 'Nadima, why don't you come in and say hi to my Mum and Dad?' I said. But Nadima looked at me in embarrassment and made a big comedy shrug. After just 6 weeks in Britain her English was, of course, still too poor to understand what I had just said. So I made a gesture of apology to Nadima, holding both my hands up and bowing my head in shame. Then I waved my right hand to indicate to Nadima that she could come in. When she had entered the kitchen, she still looked very shy and helpless. I took her hand and led her to my Dad, who was cooking dinner.
Seeing Nadima, Dad said, 'You must be Nadima, right? Jaz has told us so much about you already.' 'Pleased to meet you, Mr Carson,' Nadima said in a whisper. 'You can call me Ron, okay?' Dad said. 'Okay, Mr Carson,' Nadima replied. Dad and I smiled, which immediately made Nadima blush. I realised that I had to help her, so I pointed my finger at Dad and said to her, 'Dad – Ron. Dad – Ron. Okay?'. Nadima just nodded, pointed her finger at Dad shyly and said, 'Ronnie.' Dad and I laughed out loud, but this time Nadima was not embarrassed and started to laugh, too. During dinner, Mum, Dad and I tried as best we could to communicate with Nadima by means of body language such as gestures, grimaces or particular body motions. It almost felt like playing charades and eventually turned out to be so much fun that Dad, Mum and I also started to use body language when communicating among ourselves. It was obvious that Nadima was beginning to feel more and more comfortable.
When we were about to finish dinner, Nadima pulled a present out of her bag and gave it to my parents. Mum opened it. It looked like a box in which there were several other smaller boxes. Mum and Dad looked at Nadima and shrugged their shoulders because they did not know what it was. Nadima grabbed one of the smaller boxes, opened it and put a few of the red flakes from inside the box onto her plate. Then she pretended to eat the red flakes and immediately started breathing heavily in and out with her mouth wide open. Dad, Mum and I just burst out laughing at Nadima's natural comedy talent. Mum said, 'I know what this is. It is a set of hot Asian spices.' 'Thank you very much, Nadima,' Dad said, 'in fact these boxes are for me because I'm the cook in this house.' Mum and Dad both stood up, went to Nadima and hugged her.

or

c) **Bringing cultures together through food**

When I first met Nadima, the new girl from Syria at our school, we had trouble communicating with words, but "talked" to each other through food. This made me think that it might be a great idea to organise a food bazaar at our school. After all, there are students from more than 20 nationalities at our school, ranging from European countries like Italy, Sweden, Portugal, Germany, France and Spain to South American countries like Brazil, Chile and Argentina, to Middle and Far Eastern countries such as Syria, Afghanistan, Vietnam and Japan. Just imagine the incredible variety of food these students, or their parents for that matter, could offer at a food bazaar.
Just like Nadima and I "spoke" to one another through food, a food bazaar would give all our students a chance to get to know each other's cultural backgrounds a lot better. Moreover, it would give all our parents a unique opportunity to get talking to each other while tasting each other's typical or traditional food. Could there be any better way of bringing cultures together, of making the world a little more peaceful and open-minded? Music is often called the universal human language because it is "understood" and appreciated anywhere in the world. That is undoubtedly true, but in my view food can also serve as a universal means of communication because it plays an important role in any human community or culture and can therefore connect people with very different ethnic backgrounds.
As far as the organisation of a food bazaar is concerned, I have a few ideas as to how we could go about doing this. First of all, students of the same nationality should try to get together to discuss what they regard as the most typical and / or most interesting national dish or dishes. Then they can ask their parents if they are willing to prepare those dishes for the bazaar. As soon as the parents have agreed to do so, please email (jaz.carson@online.co.uk). After consultation with our head teacher, Mrs Walker, I will then set a date for the bazaar and will post it on our website. As for drinks, I will ask Mrs Walker if those can be paid for from the school budget. Last but not least, I will ask our caretakers to help me to lay out the tables, cutlery, napkins, glasses etc. on the day of the bazaar.
I hope you like my idea. If you do, I would be grateful for anyone offering to help me organise the bazaar.

Notizen

Notizen

www.pauker.de

Auf der Suche nach mehr Übungsmaterial?

- ✔ Arbeitsheft mit 17 Texten und Audiotracks
- ✔ inklusive Lösungen
- ✔ alle Hördateien zum Download oder per QR-Code abrufbar
- ✔ zum selbstständigen Training des Hörverstehens
- ✔ vielfältige Aufgabenformate und alltagsnahe Themen

Hier geht es direkt zum Buch auf unserer Website.

9 783889 978721

hutt lernhilfen

Assessment-Center (AC)

Ein weiterer gängiger Test für die Auswahl von Azubis ist das sogenannte Assessment-Center (AC). Der Begriff kommt aus dem Englischen („to assess" = bewerten, beurteilen). Grundidee ist es, die Kandidaten und Kandidatinnen in vorgegebenen Situationen zu beobachten, welche den künftigen Aufgaben entsprechen. Hierbei zählt eher die persönliche Eignung als die fachliche Qualifikation.

Bestandteile eines Assessment-Centers sind in der Regel Rollenspiele, Planspiele, Gruppendiskussionen, Einzelvorträge, Fallstudien und psychologische Testverfahren. Üblich sind diese AC mittlerweile bei Großunternehmen wie Banken und Versicherungen, aber auch bei der Polizei oder im öffentlichen Dienst.

Tipps für ein AC-Auswahlverfahren

- ▶ freundlich und offen sein
- ▶ Blickkontakt mit den Gesprächspartnern halten
- ▶ Interesse zeigen und Fragen stellen
- ▶ seine eigene Meinung selbstbewusst vertreten
- ▶ die Meinung anderer respektieren
- ▶ sich aktiv an Diskussionen beteiligen
- ▶ ehrlich sein, kein falsches Wissen vorgeben
- ▶ kühlen Kopf und Ruhe bewahren

Onlinetipps

Es gibt im Internet viele Möglichkeiten, Eignungstests zu machen und so noch intensiver zu üben. Auch zum Thema Bewerbung kann man im Internet hilfreiche Tipps finden. Hier einige Links:

- ▶ www.planet-beruf.de
- ▶ www.azubiworld.com
- ▶ www.ausbildung.info
- ▶ www.ausbildungspark.com
- ▶ www.bewerbung.de
- ▶ www.bewerbungsdschungel.com
- ▶ www.berufswahl-tipps.de
- ▶ www.azubi-azubine.de
- ▶ www.jobinspektor.com
- ▶ www.azubot.de
- ▶ www.stuzubi.de
- ▶ www.azubiyo.de

Für die Inhalte der aufgeführten Websites übernehmen wir keine Haftung. Das gilt auch für alle auf diesen Websites angebrachten Links.

Anmerkungen:

Schematisierte Darstellung des Bildungswesens. Die Verteilung der Schülerzahlen in der Jahrgangsstufe 8 für das Jahr 2016 stellt sich im Bundesdurchschnitt wie folgt dar: Hauptschule 10,8 %, Realschule 18,9 %, Gymnasium 36,2 %, integrierte Gesamtschule 16,8 %, Schularten mit mehreren Bildungsgängen 12,2 %, sonderpädagogische Bildungseinrichtungen 4,2 %.

Die Durchlässigkeit zwischen den Schularten und die Anerkennung der Schulabschlüsse sind bei Erfüllung der zwischen den Ländern vereinbarten Voraussetzungen gewährleistet. Die Dauer der Vollzeitschulpflicht (allgemeine Schulpflicht) beträgt neun Jahre, in fünf Ländern zehn Jahre, und die anschließende Teilzeitschulpflicht (Berufsschulpflicht) drei Jahre.

1 In einigen Ländern bestehen besondere Formen des Übergangs von der Kindertagesstätte oder der Kindertagespflege in die Grundschule (Vorklassen, Schulkindergärten). In Berlin und Brandenburg umfasst die Grundschule sechs Jahrgangsstufen.

2 Beschulung von Schülerinnen und Schülern mit sonderpädagogischem Förderbedarf in inklusivem Unterricht an allgemeinen Schulen oder an sonderpädagogischen Bildungseinrichtungen mit entsprechenden Förderschwerpunkten. Schulbezeichnung nach Landesrecht unterschiedlich. Sonderpädagogische Bildungseinrichtungen mit dem Förderschwerpunkt „Lernen" und sonderpädagogische Bildungseinrichtungen mit dem Förderschwerpunkt „Geistige Entwicklung" haben schulspezifische Abschlüsse.

3 Die Jahrgangsstufen 5 und 6 bilden eine Phase besonderer Förderung, Beobachtung und Orientierung über den weiteren Bildungsgang mit seinen fachlichen Schwerpunkten.

4 Haupt- und Realschulen existieren in nennenswerter Zahl nur noch in fünf Ländern (Baden-Württemberg, Bayern, Hessen, Niedersachsen, Nordrhein-Westfalen). In Bayern trägt die mit der Hauptschule vergleichbare Schulart die Bezeichnung Mittelschule. Die Bildungsgänge der Hauptschule und der Realschule werden auch an Schularten mit mehreren Bildungsgängen mit nach Ländern unterschiedlichen Bezeichnungen angeboten.

5 Die folgenden Schularten mit zwei Bildungsgängen fassen die Bildungsgänge der Haupt- und der Realschule pädagogisch und organisatorisch zusammen: Regelschule (Thüringen), Sekundarschule (Bremen, Sachsen-Anhalt), Verbundene Haupt- und Realschule (Hessen), Regionale Schule (Mecklenburg-Vorpommern), Realschule plus (Rheinland-Pfalz), Regionalschule (Schleswig-Holstein), Oberschule (Brandenburg, Sachsen), Mittelstufenschule (Hessen). Der Bildungsgang des Gymnasiums wird auch an Schularten mit drei Bildungsgängen angeboten. Die folgenden Schularten umfassen die drei Bildungsgänge der Hauptschule, der Realschule und des Gymnasiums: Integrierte Gesamtschule, Kooperative Gesamtschule, Integrierte Sekundarschule (Berlin), Oberschule (Bremen, Niedersachsen), Stadtteilschule (Hamburg), Gemeinschaftsschule (Baden-Württemberg, Saarland, Sachsen-Anhalt, Schleswig-Holstein, Thüringen), Sekundarschule (Nordrhein-Westfalen).

6 Die allgemeinbildenden Schulabschlüsse nach Jahrgangsstufe 9 und 10 tragen in einzelnen Ländern besondere Bezeichnungen. Der nachträgliche Erwerb dieser Abschlüsse an Schulen des zweiten Bildungsweges und beruflichen Schulen oder durch eine Externenprüfung ist möglich.

7 Zugangsvoraussetzung ist die formelle Berechtigung zum Besuch der gymnasialen Oberstufe, die nach Jahrgangsstufe 9 oder 10 erworben wird. Der Erwerb der Allgemeinen Hochschulreife erfolgt seit 2012 in der Mehrzahl der Länder nach Jahrgangsstufe 12 (achtjähriges Gymnasium). An Schularten mit drei Bildungsgängen wird der gymnasiale Bildungsgang in der Regel nicht auf acht Jahre verkürzt.

8 Die Berufsoberschule besteht bisher nur in einigen Ländern und bietet Absolventen mit Mittlerem Schulabschluss und abgeschlossener Berufsausbildung bzw. fünfjähriger Berufstätigkeit die Möglichkeit zum Erwerb der Fachgebundenen Hochschulreife. Bei Nachweis von Kenntnissen in einer zweiten Fremdsprache ist der Erwerb der Allgemeinen Hochschulreife möglich.

9 Die Fachoberschule ist eine zweijährige Schulart, die aufbauend auf dem Mittleren Schulabschluss mit Jahrgangsstufe 11 und 12 zur Fachhochschulreife führt. Für Absolventen mit Mittlerem Schulabschluss und einer beruflichen Erstausbildung ist in den meisten Ländern der unmittelbare Eintritt in Jahrgangsstufe 12 der Fachoberschule möglich. Die Länder können auch eine Jahrgangsstufe 13 einrichten. Der Besuch der Jahrgangsstufe 13 führt zur Fachgebundenen Hochschulreife und unter bestimmten Voraussetzungen zur Allgemeinen Hochschulreife.

10 Berufsfachschulen sind berufliche Vollzeitschulen verschiedener Ausprägung im Hinblick auf Zugangsvoraussetzungen, Dauer und Abschlüsse. In ein- oder zweijährigen Bildungsgängen wird eine berufliche Grundausbildung, in zwei- oder dreijährigen Bildungsgängen eine Berufsausbildung vermittelt. In Verbindung mit dem Abschluss eines mindestens zweijährigen Bildungsgangs kann unter bestimmten Voraussetzungen die Fachhochschulreife erworben werden.

11 Zusätzlich zum berufsqualifizierenden Abschluss ggf. Erwerb des Hauptschulabschlusses oder des Mittleren Schulabschlusses. Unter bestimmten Voraussetzungen ist zusätzlich der Erwerb der Fachhochschulreife möglich.

12 Fachschulen dienen der beruflichen Weiterbildung (Dauer 1–3 Jahre) und setzen grundsätzlich den Abschluss einer einschlägigen Berufsausbildung in einem anerkannten Ausbildungsberuf und eine entsprechende Berufstätigkeit voraus. Unter bestimmten Voraussetzungen ist zusätzlich der Erwerb der Fachhochschulreife möglich.

13 Einschließlich Hochschulen mit einzelnen universitären Studiengängen (z. B. Theologie, Philosophie, Medizin, Verwaltungswissenschaften, Sport).

14 An Pädagogischen Hochschulen (nur in Baden Württemberg) wird für verschiedene Lehrämter ausgebildet. Im Einzelfall ist auch ein Studium für Berufe im außerschulischen Bildungs- und Erziehungsbereich möglich.

15 Die Berufsakademie ist eine Einrichtung des tertiären Bereichs in einigen Ländern, die eine wissenschaftsbezogene und zugleich praxisorientierte berufliche Bildung durch die Ausbildung an einer Studienakademie und in einem Betrieb im Sinne des dualen Systems vermittelt.

16 Die Studienstrukturreform mit der Umstellung auf Bachelor- und Masterabschlüsse an deutschen Hochschulen ist weitgehend abgeschlossen. Nur eine geringe Zahl von Studiengängen führt zu einem Diplomabschluss.

Stand: Juni 2018

Grundstruktur des Bildungswesens in der Bundesrepublik Deutschland

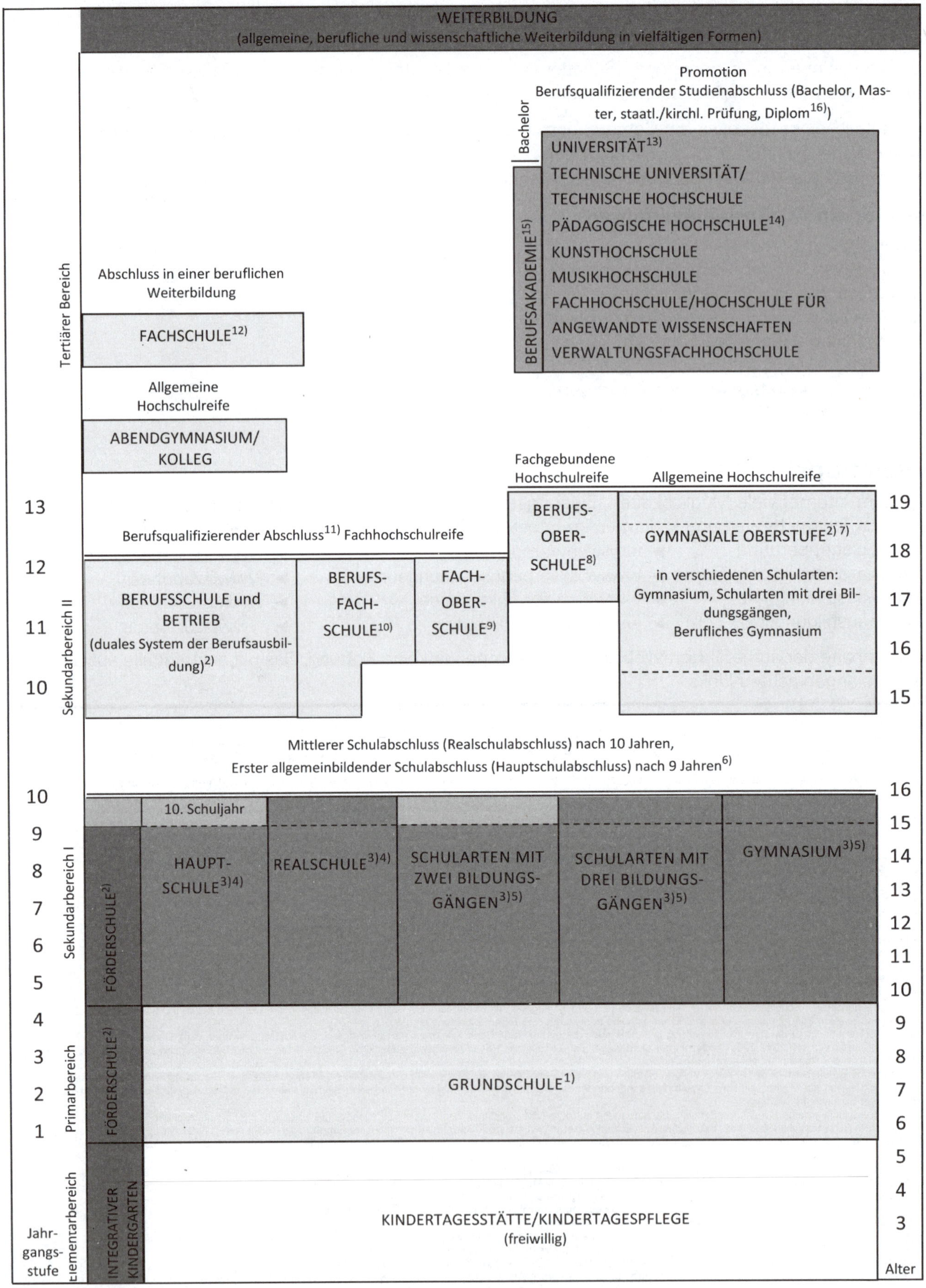

Herausgeber: Sekretariat der Ständigen Konferenz der Kultusminister der Länder in der Bundesrepublik Deutschland,
Deutsche EURYDICE-Informationsstelle der Länder, Taubenstr. 10, 10117 Berlin, Tel. 030 25418-499.